Freddie the Weaver

Mark Frankland

FREDDIE
THE WEAVER

SINCLAIR-STEVENSON

First published in Great Britain in 1995
by Sinclair-Stevenson
an imprint of Reed Consumer Books Ltd
Michelin House, 81 Fulham Road, London sw3 6rb
and Auckland, Melbourne, Singapore and Toronto

A CIP catalogue record for this book
is available at the British Library
isbn 1 85619 246 6

Typeset by Deltatype, Ellesmere Port, South Wirral
Printed and bound in Great Britain
by Clays Ltd, St Ives plc

For the carers

What defence have I against nothingness but this ark in which I have tried to gather everything that was dear to me, people, birds, animals, and plants, everything that I carry in my eye and in my heart, in the triple-decked ark of my body and soul. Like the pharaohs in the majestic peace of their tombs, I wanted to have all those things with me in death, I wanted everything to be as it was before; I wanted the birds to sing for me forever, I wanted to exchange Charon's bark for another, less desolate and less empty . . .

Danilo Kiš, *Hourglass*

CONTENTS

I

The Child

The earliest photograph of Freddie that I have was taken when he was almost one. Wearing an embroidered smock, he has his head back and to one side and is laughing. The eyes, though, are turned away from the photographer, as they are in many later photographs too. It is as if something is attracting him to one or other side of the person holding the camera. In this first photograph the eyes, whatever has caught their attention, are playful and bright – he was, everyone agreed, an unusually beautiful child – but they are different on those few occasions when they have been caught looking at the lens. Then they are serious, and sometimes ill at ease. Naked in a pool in the garden in summer, his head now covered with curls that are almost white, he looks up as though he does not understand and is on the verge of panic. Another snap shows him soon after he had begun to walk. Exquisitely dressed in white shirt and socks, check-patterned knickers, and shoes with straps and buckles, he moves frowning towards the camera as though he were puzzled by the person he sees behind it. The first surviving photograph of him and my stepmother Olivia together was taken at about this time. They are on a lawn, she in trousers and sweater, he in dungarees. She looks at him as she holds him in her arms but his head swivels away from her. From his expression it is clear he has found something else, a person or an object, of greater interest than the woman who had adopted him with the intention of loving him more than anything else in her life.

It is now well known that autistic children often avoid looking into the eyes of others. Olivia herself once noticed it in her son for on the back of a snapshot of Freddie sitting by a sandpit she wrote 'the camera seems to have made him a bit cross-eyed'. But these photographs were taken in the late 1940s when even the word autistic was barely known in Britain; and though Freddie was from the start a difficult child, most parents at that time would have rejected any suggestion that he might be unusual. As his stepbrother I think I always found him odd, though I could not have explained why. My father married Olivia in 1947 shortly after she had begun proceedings to adopt Freddie. I was twelve when I first met her at a parents' day cricket match at my prep school in which my father and I were playing. She was nervous about the encounter and brought along Kim, her Border collie that could be relied on to win over any young boy. The stratagem was successful, but scarcely necessary. Olivia enchanted me quite as much as her dog. I suppose I thought her beautiful, but I may also have sensed she was a natural conspirator with the young; with the unhappy and the aggrieved; and with the mischievous and anyone who played truant from life's stern classes. She was, I felt, on my side.

It did not affect our relationship that I was mostly indifferent to Freddie. Dividing my holidays from boarding school between my divorced parents, I was never with Father, Olivia and Freddie for more than two or three weeks at a time, and even then, because they lived in a large house in the country, I was able to pursue my own interests. But I have a clear memory of watching Freddie one summer day as he played on a lawn outside some French windows, and finding him alien in a way that I did not understand, and would never have dreamed of remarking on to Olivia. My most constant feeling about him was annoyance at the trouble he caused with his unpredictable, inexplicable behaviour. He was persistently naughty and had frequent tantrums. Almost from the start he had to be kept away from the two Siamese cats, for left alone with them he would try to get his hands round their necks and squeeze. I have a photograph taken of us having tea on the verandah. Olivia has Freddie on her knee and is smiling at him while he gazes intently at a teaspoon that he holds in front of him with both hands. My elder brother and I are in deckchairs. Both of us have turned our heads to look at the little boy. There is amusement in our faces, but mostly there is boredom with his antics.

My father's mother was one of the first people to sound the alarm over the child's strangeness. Bobbie Raiker, Freddie's first and only governess, often took him to stay at her house on the edge of Windsor Park where the aeroplanes coming in to land at Heathrow airport sometimes made a dreadful row. A pack of highly strung dogs added to the din, for they reacted to each low-flying plane as though it were the first they had heard and would scramble barking into the garden through doors that in summer were always open. My grandmother followed close behind waving an old walking cane and adding to the noise by the shouts and curses she hurled at her incorrigible animals. One day, after this scene had been repeated several times, my grandmother realised that Freddie was the only person who remained silent, lying undisturbed in his pram under a large chestnut tree. The child must be deaf, she thought, and told Bobbie, who told Olivia. It was, though, a puzzling sort of deafness, for while on occasions he did indeed seem not to hear, at other times he responded quite normally to both sounds and voices. Today a well-informed doctor should be able to recognise this as a symptom of autism. At that time it was just another piece in the puzzle of his behaviour. It was only when Bobbie began to worry that the child was making no attempt to talk apart from the occasional grunt and piercing scream, that she managed to persuade Olivia to take Freddie to a doctor.

That was the beginning of Olivia's journey round her private Stations of the Cross, a journey that would not end until she died. Its trajectory, though, was determined long before Freddie appeared in her life. Many children are born without thought or by mistake, against their parents' plans or wishes, but every adopted child represents an act of will. In Olivia's case the adopted son was supposed to replace loves she had lost, though not, I think, in a purely selfish sense. Freddie was to be a continuation of the two men she had loved most in her life. Of course he would comfort her, but he would also do honour to their memory, bringing back to the world something their deaths had taken from it. Without their memory to sustain her she would scarcely have found energy for the fight to give her child a decent life. It is with them that Freddie's story properly begins.

Their presence remains vivid for me, too, because now that Olivia and my father are dead I have become Freddie's guardian, and in a sense also guardian of the hope these two men inspired in her. Not the least of Olivia's anxieties as she grew older was what would happen to Freddie when she was dead. It is a fear all parents of handicapped children are familiar with, and which they can never banish, for what is more unpredictable, more full of possible horrors, than the life of those we love after our death? Parents know it is easy enough these days to raise sympathy for a handicapped young child. No one any more will dismiss it as mad and only worth locking away. A severely handicapped adult, unable to look after him or her self, is quite another matter. Only parents still see in the grown-up man or woman whose appearance or habits may be unattractive the child that enchanted in spite of its twisted body or impossible behaviour. The agony is all the worse because most parents will have moments of clarity when they know that, however careful their plans for what happens after their death, the future will likely make a mockery of them.

I do not know when Olivia first had the idea to appoint me as Freddie's protector in and from the world. For many years I saw little of him because I worked mainly abroad. Sometimes when I was home on holiday I went with her to visit him wherever he happened to be. Gradually I became curious about him, but I chiefly went because I loved her and enjoyed being with her. Except in the darkest years when Freddie was in mental hospitals we had a good deal of fun, for she kept the gaiety that had always attracted people to her. She asked me to be Freddie's guardian in 1980, when she was seventy-five, Freddie thirty-four and I was forty-six. That year she wrote a letter to be given to me on her death in which she outlined some financial and other arrangements she had made and worried that her foresight in making me guardian might prove inadequate.

Do hope this makes sense [she ended the letter] but I'm feeling rather old. Dad & I might both go in a motor smash! I don't know what I'd have done without you all those years & realise what a great thing you are doing by being Fred's guardian & am so grateful – Who you can leave him to if you die first God knows – Anna [my cousin, whom Olivia was very fond of] would be wonderful if she lives in England by then but she is older than you.

Olivia had a strong, uncomplicated faith that made the next world seem as accessible as Calais or Dieppe. Does it, I wonder, provide a vantage point from which she can observe the house on the Devon coast where I now go alone to visit her son? Sometimes he opens the door, for he is always told that I am coming. He puts out his arm but when I take his hand there is little response from his fingers that he holds straight and pressed together. If I have interrupted him in some activity, drinking a cup of tea in the kitchen perhaps, he will hurry back to finish it without another look at me. At other times he is impatient to be off. 'Ker,' he says, 'ker', which means car. He climbs laboriously into the back seat, bending his six-foot body carefully so as not to hit his head. He likes the car. He may look out of the window but I never know what he is seeing. If I give him a packet of crisps, an old favourite, he folds up the empty bag neatly and taps it thoughtfully with his long fingers. Sometimes he rocks a little. I talk to him as though he can understand what I am saying, or I play classical music on the cassette recorder. He likes classical music, and sometimes rocks in time to it. We go for walks, he often taking the lead, shoulders sloping, big hipped, arms away from his side and slightly bent at the elbows. His feet point out a little, but he can walk fast when he wants to.

Sitting opposite him when we eat our lunch in a pub I may look up to find his eyes fixed on mine. He peers at me – I write 'peers' because it is as though he were trying to see something in my face but cannot quite. He looks at me, but he does not see me, hence the slight frown, like the frown on the face of the prettily dressed little boy as he stepped towards the camera all those years ago. He is still handsome, but in repose his face is sad. He wears a moustache now. I was shocked by it at first because it signalled so clearly that he was no longer the child Olivia used to talk about. It was natural for her to see him as a child regardless of his age. I was told a story about Dutch parents who brought buckets and spades when they went to share their handicapped children's seaside holiday, even though these 'children' were grown-up women and men. I am having to learn to treat Freddie as an adult, and the moustache helps. It also reminds me of Sam, similarly moustached, and one of the two men who unknowingly impelled Olivia to adopt the child to whom she gave their names.

2

Freddie and Sam

Olivia Campbell was born on 10th January 1905, the second child of a younger son of the Earl of Cawdor. Impecunious, erratic but capable of great charm, her father had chosen the traditional younger son's profession of the Church. He never disguised that he would have preferred to do nothing, and indeed tried to do just that whenever he thought he could get away with it. To his wife's dismay he would stay in bed even after the bells had begun calling his parishioners to worship, and when an early attack of arthritis temporarily confined him to his chair, he remarked he would like to lose the use of his legs entirely 'so I could stay here and read and read and read'. He got his wish, for that is how he had to spend the last years of his life. His children came to accept his laziness as incurable, and Olivia's relationship with him was stormy. 'I meant to kill you,' she confessed after one china-throwing session in the vicarage. 'And I meant to kill you,' he answered, and laughed. While her father could not be bothered to write his own sermons, her mother nourished a strong Christian faith and worried about the daughter who had inherited her striking looks (especially the large eyes with provocatively heavy lids that photographs show Olivia had even as a little girl) and a good deal of her husband's contrariness.

Olivia loved the mother whose advice and warnings she usually ignored, but she adored her brother, Freddie, whose Christian name she would later give to her adopted son. Freddie was two years older, and though there was a second, younger sister, she scarcely won acceptance into their world. Jean, as often as not called 'poor Jean', was judged too timid and sickly to go on all the holidays with her wild brother and sister and their cousins at Cawdor castle in Scotland, or at one of two other large family establishments near the Welsh coast. Freddie decided, and Olivia obeyed. When they played weddings she was allowed to act groom to a three-year-old male cousin's bride; the best man, another cousin, wore a kilt (there are lots of kilts, sporrans and tam-o'-shanters in the photographs that have survived); but Freddie played the leading part of the clergyman – he had at least learned from his inadequate father how to do that. Freddie returned Olivia's devotion sufficiently to write letters to her when he went away to prep school. They were peremptory and short: sweep out the stable every week; turn over the pony's straw daily; remind Mother and Father when they next come to bring the butterfly net and 'stinkpot'. Olivia did as she was told, and if Freddie gave her a pair of boots he had outgrown she would insist on stomping around in them at home. By the time he got to Marlborough the Great War was on and he was starting his letters to her 'Dear Old Bean' and signing off, with new-found style, 'Yours to a cinder, Bertie'. There were blasé references to the war – 'You haven't been having any air raids have you by any chance?' – and the usual use of Olivia as a go-between with their parents. 'Tell Mother from

me I am 7th in maths.' Tell her which weekend he wanted her
to come visiting.

For all his boasts of success in maths Freddie did not turn out
a scholar, and Olivia's education was limited to governesses
and a spell during the war in London at Miss Birtwhistle's
fashionable Sloane Street school. They did, though, grow up
to make a handsome pair. Freddie, with something of his
mother's large, effective eyes, wore his dark hair brushed back
and parted high on the right side. There is a drawing of the
teenage Olivia, her head resting on arms propped on a
cushion, that accentuates the semi-circle of her heavy, closed
eyelids and suggests a child asleep, unaware it must soon
awake into adulthood. At about the same time a smart
photographer made a portrait of the girl who was about to be
launched into society. She has had her hair cut short above the
neck, and he makes her sit with head turned to one side and
eyes so cast down they might be shut, as though trying to
reproduce the innocent pose of the drawing, but the effect is
the opposite. It is the picture of a young woman coming
awake: head and eyes are slow to lift, as if already knowing
childhood has been left behind.

The brother's and sister's social position, like their looks,
could scarcely have been bettered; what they lacked was
money. In one way this did not matter. The British aristocracy
still took itself seriously enough to give protection to its
relatively impoverished members, at least for a generation or
two. Not to have done so would have been to acknowledge
that its eminence was based on wealth, an admission hurtful to
its self-esteem. Olivia could look forward both to the London
season and the regular gatherings of the Scottish aristocracy,
to long visits to the country houses of relatives and friends,

and eventually, arising out of these carefully managed events, to a 'good' marriage. It was harder for a young man who expected little help from a feckless father. He had to make money. In 1922, aged nineteen, Freddie went to Australia to work on a cattle station in Queensland. He was soon sending home photographs of himself in a wide-brimmed bush hat, hands self-confidently in britches' pockets, or mounted, with equal certainty of the effect he was making, on 'Grey Moari', 'Sailor' and 'Rose' – he always wrote the horse's name on the back of the picture. A keen photographer, he also sent his own pictures of the station buildings, the cattle, the other hands and the Aboriginal 'men'. His new life delighted him, and he wrote at length about it to Olivia, the one person to whom he confided his thoughts. They dissected their father's character, Freddie declaring he had 'given him up as a bad job long ago'. He encouraged her to get away from home and enjoy herself. 'Never think for a moment old dear, that I feel hurt or jealous or any rot like that, because I'm working while you're having a good time. We are each getting our experience in different ways – that is all. And I reckon the way you're getting yours is the best for you and the way I'm getting mine is the best for me.'

That serious, rather naive, tone continued through all his letters. Olivia's to him bucked him up, for she early acquired the habit of opening her heart when writing to those she loved. Making money, the brother and sister decided, was not the 'point', though Freddie 'would love to make tons of it, chiefly for Mother's sake to save her the awful worry she must have sometimes'. The 'point' for him of the Australian life he had chosen was that 'of all the work I've tried and seen and heard of this is *the* one for a man who wants to be a man'. Later they

discussed the first great crisis of her life when, to the horror of
the family, she and a cousin fell in love. Parents manoeuvred
to separate them and the regiment of uncles and aunts who
were always present in the Scottish and Welsh background
while the younger generation played joined in sounding the
alarm. The couple gave in and broke off the relationship but
Freddie, while praising Olivia for her courage, warned her not
to let herself be pressured further. 'For God's sake don't let
talking relatives drive you into marrying someone you don't
care for, as if you do, and he doesn't give you a fair spin and
makes you miserable, as sure as hell I'll come home and break
his neck if he's twice my size.' The family's high-minded
bullying encouraged both brother and sister in their distaste
for religion. Their mother's faith was 'wonderful' and probably a 'wonderful help' to her, Freddie thought, but 'I've no
time for it for myself, at present at least, and am not a bit
surprised that you haven't either.' He signed that letter with
his usual seven Xs. Seventeen months later, when his family
were expecting a telegram announcing his return home, the
news came of his death in a riding accident.

   At the memorial service for Frederick Charles Campbell at
St Martin-in-the-Fields in London, where his father was vicar,
the closing hymn was

> O love that wilt not let me go,
> I rest my weary soul in thee.

Olivia left a note among her papers asking for the same hymn
to be sung at her funeral. Perhaps she understood the religious
significance of the words, but I am sure she loved it most for
the private meaning she gave it. Freddie's death shattered her,

and her longing for him never let her go, at least until his name was transferred to the adopted child. But there was to be another love that she would lose and yet be trapped by, a love that was an even more powerful influence on the fate of her yet unborn son.

Mourning her brother, bruised by her first, frustrated love affair and at war with her father, Olivia set up on her own in London, eventually working as a *vendeuse* in the Bond Street shop of a fashionable dress maker of the day called Victor Stiebel. She lived in furnished bed-sitting rooms in and around the King's Road, and even at the end of her life (usually after an argument with my father) insisted she would still happily return to a bed-sit in Chelsea. She relished her new independence and, to her mother's dismay and her father's faint amusement, led an unashamedly wild life. 'Society' of the 1920s and '30s, and the *demi-monde* that inhabited its fringes, knew all about drink, drugs and sex. People behaved as if they knew they were living in the interim. The Great War had shaken this world that mixed the traditional pleasures of a landed aristocracy with the vices of a modern metropolis; 1939 would pretty well bring it to the ground. Olivia was poor, but she had gaiety as well as glamour, and she broke a lot of hearts. One admirer assured her she was 'more attractive . . . than almost anyone (i.e. Marlene Dietrich and possibly Carole Lombard)'. Others despaired of even attracting her attention. 'Just a line to apologise for being such a damned fool as to fall in love with you, and to thank you for being so very sweet to me,' one young man wrote, to be echoed by another whose emotion got the better of his punctuation. 'So my sweet you mus'nt bother too much if you do'nt love me like I love you. Its not your fault and perhaps it is'nt mine.' A would-be boyfriend felt the impulse to write to her as he sat alone one evening in the Café Royal in London before 'snooping off to bed, also alone, which is depressing'. A more resourceful one admitted from Paris that he had considered arousing her sympathy with a telegram announcing his death – 'Regret to inform you X's passenger plane Heracles crashed this morning – forwarding body immediately' – but thought better of it because 'you might easily be awfully bored with the body and not react in the required manner'.

Suitable suitors bored her. She preferred, without seriously losing her heart to any of them, more dangerous types, the sort of young men society mothers ruled out as escorts for debutante daughters. Many years later Olivia shocked even the worldly-wise Bobbie Raiker by remarking that, when broke, she had been ready to sleep with almost anyone who would give her a good dinner. When she was older she could play trusted confidante to the children of friends and relatives who got into scrapes because she never denied the pleasures and problems of her own youth. If the unsuccessful boyfriends apologised for their attentions, those she accepted sounded a quite different note, one of them (Ian Fleming) explaining he had not sent her postcards while she was away 'as what I wanted to say was unprintable. Hurry up and come back, gorgeous.' Friends and family worried she was exhausting herself by a life notoriously short of sleep, and she had to go into hospital for major stomach surgery. The problem, though, was neither poor health nor insufficient sleep but an inability to discover a point of rest. She found no one to replace the dead brother; or the tiresome father who was alive, but in every other way absent; or the cousin she had begun to love only to be separated from. Just as the unsettled world she lived in was tempted to find security in a strong man like Oswald Mosley, she flirted with her own risqué boyfriends, by chance among them a young Mosley lieutenant, though typically it was his looks and uniform that attracted her rather than his politics.

The upshot of a series of affairs was a disastrous marriage in 1934, its nature unwittingly revealed by the wedding photographer. On the surface all was proper: two pages, five bridesmaids, one of them 'poor Jean', and a squad of nannies in pudding-bowl hats to keep the children in order. The well-to-do groom was handsome in immaculate morning coat; Olivia ravishing in a wedding dress demurely high around the neck and suggestively tight around her very small waist. But bags under the groom's eyes suggest an anxious stag night, and he looks not at the bride but ahead, with only the tightest smile. Cradling a large bouquet of arum lilies in her arm, Olivia looks away from him. She was cruel to marry him, and would happily have left him at the church gate had decency not demanded she stay a token year. She was reckless, too, for in those days obtaining a divorce was not a simple matter. When the couple went away on a skiing holiday she sent a friend a photograph of three skiers, herself, her husband, and a tanned, dark-haired young man. 'The other man,' she wrote, 'is the sweetest instructor who picks me up when I fall down.' She was not expert on skis, and I imagine she fell down often.

When the war began Olivia was thirty-four, separated, and living in London. Later, after the fighting was over, her friends would talk of so-and-so having had a 'good war', meaning he had distinguished himself, or at least returned with honour intact. It also implied there had been moments of pleasure to snatch. A sailing-mad friend, finding himself captain of a minesweeper off the Scottish coast, admitted to Olivia that 'this war has had all the elements of an ordinary if rather crude yachting holiday and I am very nearly enjoying it'. He was about to spend Christmas at sea and expected it to be good fun, for his ship had been provided with plenty of food 'by the benevolent citizens of Dundee who I think suffer under the delusion that if I wasn't here they would have been savagely attacked by brother Bosche long ago'. Olivia, too, had her adventures, volunteering to chauffeur an ambulance for SSAFA, even though her driving habits were as un-nerving as those of Mrs Stitch in Evelyn Waugh's *Scoop* who drove along pavements when it suited her. But 'good war' had a further sub-text: the war liberated many husbands and wives – particularly husbands – from unsatisfactory marriages. In this unforeseen period of sexual freedom a woman like Olivia, alone and no longer very young, was not so much of an oddity. Images from *Brief Encounter* of heart-breaking self-denial in an austere and grubby Britain are misleading. Self-denial was not much in evidence in smart wartime London.

Sam Bucknill was married, though not happily, when he and Olivia fell in love in the third year of the war. He was two years her senior, and they both thought of themselves as almost old even though they were still extremely attractive. A friend, a young girl at the time, remembered first seeing Olivia towards the end of the war. She was getting off a train at a country station wearing a white and brown herring-bone pattern dress, and she recognised at once that this woman was 'unforgettably glamorous'. Sam certainly thought so. 'It is such fun taking you around,' he wrote in an early letter, 'I am so conceited [and] I get even more so when I see every head turn to have another look at you.'

Olivia did not hesitate to woo Sam away from his wife. 'She took what she wanted,' Bobbie Raiker would say both of the marriage with Sam and of Olivia's life in general (Bobbie 'loved Olivia to pieces', but her affection did not get the better of the judgement proper to the daughter of a Bishop of Bath and Wells). Sam was by all accounts as attractive to, as he was attracted by, women. He came from the same world as Olivia. They already had friends in common and he seems to have been struck by her at their first meeting when they were a good deal younger. But their romance only began in the war, and it is as a soldier, an almost mythical figure, that I think of him. All her life Olivia would keep in her bedroom a photograph of Sam in his uniform as a major in the Irish Guards. He wears a moustache and has the same long face, strong nose and sensuous mouth that marked some of Olivia's earlier flames. There is pathos in any picture taken in wartime, but this one reveals a strikingly thoughtful mood, a melancholy as though he were watching something or someone he fears may soon disappear.

He was normally a man who enjoyed life and infected others with his enjoyment, which showed in the scrapbook he began to keep when a schoolboy at Eton during the First World War. It recorded successes, social and athletic rather than academic, and, when he went up to Christ Church, Oxford, a young man's pleasures typical of his time and class. He stuck in menus, covered with pencil-scrawled, tipsy comments of friends, that recorded seven- and eight-course dinners held at different clubs and colleges. A passion for horses and riding took him into racing circles which, when they celebrated, sat down to put away Eggs on the Flat, *Poulet Reclamé de la Fosse Ouverte*, and Bangup Brandy. He kept cards from Commemoration Balls, the names of his partners written in against each foxtrot, one-step and waltz, the only dances officially on offer in the Oxford of the early 1920s. He also kept more questionable mementoes, like his membership to the My Cellar dance club in Leicester Square, whose professed purpose was 'to promote social intercourse as far as may be desirable and practicable, between members interested in Ball Room dancing'. When Sam went down from Oxford in 1925 the Dean of his college gave him a note of recommendation. 'Mr Bucknill,' the Dean wrote, 'has always seemed to me to present the best type of an English Public School and University man; absolutely straight in manners and in life, quiet and unassuming, but probably much more capable than he would say he was; and one of the staunchest friends and finest gentlemen anyone would wish to know.' The words sound comic to modern ears but Olivia, who kept the paper with the letters Sam wrote her, believed them to be the obvious truth.

The year after leaving Oxford Sam helped out on the Great Western Railway during the General Strike, then took up an 'honorary post' in a well-known City company so that he might acquire, as the letter accepting him put it, 'a general knowledge of business'. He toyed with the law, his father's profession, and under parental pressure did two years in the Colonial service in northern Nigeria, but resigned at the end of his first long leave home. He was comfortably off, had inherited from his father a good farm in Gloucestershire, and had the means to hunt, shoot and fish. He got married, but had no children. From the perspective of the end of the twentieth century, a life such as Sam's in the 1920s and '30s seems either charmed and miraculously protected, or selfish and wilfully blind. Like Olivia, he was carried along by the inertia of an old social system until war broke the pattern of their life. I cannot judge them. I do not want to. I tell their story and explore its ironies because the life of the future Freddie, into whose destiny I too am now woven, was so powerfully affected by what happened to this seemingly so favoured couple.

A wartime love affair meant separation. Sam was a company commander with his regiment in Scotland, Olivia in London where she had changed jobs to become a receptionist at the American Red Cross Club in Hans Crescent. He was unhappy he could do nothing to protect her from air raids, a real threat unlike those lightly mentioned by her brother in the earlier war. 'One feels so helpless stuck here,' Sam wrote, 'just when one would so love to put one's arms around you and love you all through the noises.' When he had leave she went up to stay with him in Glasgow or Edinburgh, but he was soon thinking of marriage for 'it would make me feel . . . less on edge . . . All my present life is on an edge and if I felt I could have you as my recognised (dreadful word) wife I would not be half so fussed.' Arrangements for the wedding were complicated but he still found time in his letters to exult over a military boxing tournament he had staged in which his 'Micks' wiped the floor with the Grenadier and Scots Guards. They were married in the St Giles district registry office in Edinburgh on 21st January 1943, Sam describing himself in the register as a farmer 'now engaged in war service'. The witnesses were 'poor Jean', who was in Edinburgh taking care of the troublesome father after his wife's death, and one of Olivia's Scottish cousins. A short honeymoon was snatched at the Caledonian Hotel.

At last both had a marriage to delight in. In his letters Sam
talks again and again of her beauty. 'If only someone would
leave me a legacy,' he wrote, 'I would have you painted, but at
present I honestly don't think I can afford it' (his divorce had
been as expensive as it was difficult). They had a few final days
together in Glasgow in the middle of February 1943. They
stayed at the Central Hotel and she kept their room card – *No.
330, 35 shillings a night for bed and breakfast* – and would later
scribble on it, at God knows what moment of despair, 'where
Sam and I spent our last night together'. She touched him by
pressing some chocolate into his hand when they said goodbye
at the railway station, but he felt 'flat, miserable and lonely' as
he walked away. Earlier she had taken him to a church (her
mother's death and the war had kindled her own faith) so they
could stand side by side and be blessed. He thanked her for
that, calling it, perhaps with a hint of condescension, 'a dear
sweet thought for a little word to keep us safe and happy
together'.

His letters to her in the few days before his regiment sailed
for North Africa reached extremes of delight and despair
which, apologising for his clumsiness, he struggled to express
as best he could. He had never liked telephoning her because it
frustrated him to be able to hear, but not see, her. Now he
could bear it no more, so acute did it make his sense of
separation. 'You must think me a softy but I have never been
in such a state before.' He railed against the unfairness of
finding 'the one person in the world that tears the heart out of
me', only to have to part from her. Dreams of the future made
up for the frustrating present. When the war was over they
would travel slowly through Scotland and Wales together
before going abroad – 'you know darling we still have the hell

of a lot to do before we go back to our farming.' As is the nature of goodbyes, practical matters got mixed in with the passion. At one moment he was telling her that his love for her inspired him; time and again he promises to be worthy of her. In the next paragraph he assures her she will have enough money, and warns her against staying at his mother's house in the country 'except in the warmest weather' because the old woman loved 'the spartan life and, if possible, discomfort'. He was overcome by loneliness. In Glasgow, waiting for his ship, he found himself at the Central Hotel and 'your ghost, such a wonderful one, was haunting every yard . . . I could almost touch your elbow as I walked beside you.' He ate a miserable dinner alone, trying to read Rebecca West's *Black Lamb and Grey Falcon* that she had given him, 'but I could not see properly. I wanted to talk with you and just sit listening to your lovely voice.'

During their honeymoon and on her other visits they had gone when they could into the countryside, taking Olivia's terrier Susie with them. Both would wear the same sort of corduroy trousers and tweed jackets, and he a cap, she a scarf round her head. In spite of the confusion of their lives, and the frown that war had turned on their fortunes, they looked so self-assured and handsome that anyone who saw them might have assumed they were unassailable by fate. Both had been brought up to expect they would have their way; even during a war they could be angry when they did not get it. Sam exploded when his batman said he was leaving him just as they had to get ready for the boat trip. A new servant would be bound to muddle his things, he complained to Olivia, even if the old one did not pinch some of them when he left. 'These bloody Irishmen,' he exploded, 'they really are sods to let one

down at the last minute in this way.' The same contempt
sounded in his description of the commander of the troop ship
as 'a tiresome little man trying to justify his own importance'.
The belief of those born to privilege that life should be
enjoyable came across in his account of the voyage. He
described a close torpedo attack by German bombers as
though it were a game, and summed up the officer friends
with whom he shared a table as 'all very gay and well fed'. But
by mid-March they were in a muddy tented camp in Tunisia,
where he was having to 'walk off each morning some six
hundred yards armed with an entrenching tool and normally
return better tempered'.

The three last letters, written within the space of four days,
were in pencil and on whatever scraps of paper he could find. It
rained most of the time and when he got out of his camp bed he
stepped into four inches of mud. Luxury was the first hot
water in four days which allowed him to wash himself, bit by
bit, in a basin. The nights were cold and he was now sleeping
in the corduroy trousers he had worn in Scotland, a Jaeger
jacket, and thick stockings, but he was getting used to the diet
of bully beef, biscuit and tea, and even the daily 'agonies with
the entrenching tool'. A part of him remained in Britain,
among gossip of friends. He imagined Olivia coming back to
her flat in Halkin Place after taking Susie for a walk in Hyde
Park, and changing before going out to lunch at the 500 or
some other favourite place of theirs, 'maybe with some lucky
chap whom I envy'. He had asked a close friend to send her
flowers regularly, and he hoped she was getting them.

He wrote with growing anxiety about the task ahead.
Though a keen member of the Officers' Training Corps at
Eton he was not a professional soldier, and he soon would

have to lead his company into attack for the first time. 'I have a comparatively heavy responsibility,' he wrote by torchlight from the back of a truck during a thunderstorm, 'bigger than any in my life . . . and I must not fail.' He compared his feeling to the nerves he used to have before playing a game of football or riding a race in a point-to-point. Failure would be doubly unbearable now because he believed it would also 'embarrass' Olivia.

'There is the most astonishing party in this shelter,' he began the final letter written during the night of 29th March. 'We are all waiting for a biggish party tonight. I hope to God I don't make a mess of it. I hope I will be worthy of my lovely wife.' He had time only for a short message, not even filling all the space on the precious airletter he had managed to get hold of. He told her he had that day received three of her letters; that he had called in a chaplain to conduct a short service for his men. 'All my love my angel child the time is nearly one and we must be off. God I love you so desperately. May God bless you. Sam.'

On 6th April Olivia got a telegram from the Under-Secretary of State for War marked with a red sticker that said GOVERNMENT ABSOLUTE. 'Regret to inform you of notification dated 2nd April 1943 received from North Africa that Major SJR Bucknill Irish Guards has been reported missing.' It was followed eight days later by another cable adding that Sam was believed to be a prisoner-of-war. The information was supposed to come from one of his platoon commanders who, wounded in the attack, had ended up a prisoner of the Italians. Desperate to hope in something, Olivia began writing Sam letters c/o the Italian Red Cross. The 'ghastly' telegram saying he was missing had been too much to bear.

'I've been *so* unbrave rushed about crying in the park & in churches & going *mad*, but I can't bear it for you my dear love. I know I'll never be the same after this.' Writing to him made the waiting more tolerable, even though she did not know if her letters would reach him. She had got the letter he wrote on the eve of the attack. 'I cry whenever I read it. You said you were trying to live up to me. Don't you know yet that it's *you* I want not what you do. I *know* what you are like and by their wonderful letters so do other people.' By mid-May the Allies were advancing in North Africa but the news of victories left Olivia untouched. 'There is *no* joy in it for me unless you are allright.' She felt a hundred years old, had lost a lot of weight 'and hardly turn the light on in the lift now' for fear of what she would see in the mirror. She went each day to St Paul's, Knightsbridge. Before the telegram she had 'crept' into the church to ask for Sam's protection; now 'alone I pray that you may not be unhappy & that I will hear soon & that you will come back to me'.

The torture ended only in July when Sam's death was at last confirmed. In the early hours of 30th March he had led his company to attack German positions on so-called Recce Ridge near Medjez-el-Bab. They reached the base of the ridge by 5 a.m. without being spotted, but as the advance platoon began to climb up it ran into a German post and Sam had to order the rest of the company to make a flanking movement. All three platoons reached the top, but there came under heavy mortar fire. When they tried to drive out the German soldiers dug in on the reverse slope they were silhouetted against the sky and easily picked off. Sam was hit by a shell. The company sergeant major, a great friend, was wounded by a fragment of it that lodged in his ration box. He ran over to Sam but found him already dead. One Guardsman, one of those 'bloody Irishmen', fought with exceptional bravery, advancing with a Bren gun at his hip until he was cut down, but when their ammunition ran out and the Germans started firing on any wounded who moved, the forty survivors surrendered. Sam and some twenty men who died with him were buried with all proper decency by the German troops. Such heavy losses suggest an ill-planned adventure but the official record preferred to strike a positive note. 'The whole attack,' it concluded, 'was performed with great courage and complete disregard of enemy fire.'

If I have read through these last sad documents, unpacking even the brown Post Office envelope containing the letters stamped RETURNED FROM CONTINENT IN UNDELIVERED MAILS that Olivia wrote to her already dead husband, it is because her suffering at this time explains so much of the story that follows. Without this piece of the thread it would lose its pattern altogether, for Olivia was right when she wrote she would never be the same again. She found some consolation in Sam's closest friend whom he had appointed to manage his business affairs while he was away. She gave him Sam's guns, his fox masks, and his suits of that indestructible tweed so loved by English country gentlemen of that period. They confided their grief to each other in long letters, though time and again he told her she must try to enjoy life again, because that was what Sam would have wanted. He imagined Sam speaking to them both in the way one encourages a small boy who is being sent away to school. ' "We'll be together again at the end of the term meanwhile keep your chin up. School isn't half a bad place if you work hard and keep smiling – I enjoyed it when I was there." I'm *sure* Sam's thinking that at this very moment & we've got to do the best we can for his sake till the end of the term.' If those were not words she would have picked she understood the message and knew it was right, but it did not help. Her ghost had haunted him on his last lonely night in Glasgow. Now his ghost seemed as close to her as the regimental badge of the Irish Guards she would wear almost every day for the rest of her life. The image of Sam that remained with her was perfect. He had saved her from a life that was losing its purpose. They had known brief, intense happiness dramatically framed by wartime separation imposed and the bitter-sweet pleasure of anticipated reunion. Whether either of them could have lived up to so perfect-seeming a love is not the point. This was the reality Olivia had known and lost. It would never change for her, or be forgotten.

A small rectangle of yellowing paper gives some hint of how she felt when the wound of Sam's loss was still raw. Using a pencil she copied down some verses, jumbling the lines and not bothering to note the author's name.

When a storm comes up at night and the wind is crying,
When the trees are moaning like masts on labouring ships,
I put out my hand to find you with your name on my lips.

No pain that the heart can hold is like to this one, –
To call, forgetting, into aching space,
To reach out confident hands and find beside you
      only an empty space.

This should atone for the hours when I forgot you.
Take then my offering, clean and sharp and sweet.
An agony brighter than years of dull remembrance
I lay at your feet.

Time never healed the wound. Olivia did not naturally write down her thoughts except in letters to those she loved, but almost thirty years after Sam had died, after reading a novel about a couple reunited after the husband's long absence in a prisoner-of-war camp, she took a piece of the blue writing paper she used for her letters and wrote:

If Sam came back now . . . I know we'd be just the same. How do I know this so certainly? Because you see in a way for me nothing has happened since then . . . All the time it has been an effort to go on because all the time inside I've been dead too & longing to go home to Sam. That is how I know that if he came back I'd come alive again at once & it would be the same – nothing else can bring me back & now till I die I'll be on the outside of the crowd, alone . . . I had to write this down. For weeks I scarcely think of Sam, and then I hear or read something like this morning & the tears pour out of my eyes & I realise all this & shake for the rest of the day. Somehow I've failed because he would not want me to feel this way.

3
Olivia and Freddie (1)

S am had suggested to Olivia that, if she had no child by him, she might want to adopt one, and before leaving for Africa he altered his will to make sure she had the money for it. On the eve of the first anniversary of his death his best friend with whom she shared her grief sent her flowers (as Sam had asked him to) and also a letter in which he, too, mentioned adoption. Sam, he reminded her, had adored children and 'I do wish you had a son of Sam's that one could scheme things for but if that cannot be, an adopted child would perhaps be the next best thing. Wouldn't it be fun to see him liking the things Sam liked . . .'

Other friends thought only a baby would be able to heal her loneliness, and make her feel she still belonged to life. 'I won't be surprised if you think I'm a bossy bitch,' wrote a woman friend who had known Sam well and was herself the mother of two young sons, 'but if I had my way I'd settle you down with a fine bouncing baby as soon as could be, because Olivia, I don't think that you'll ever be . . . settled and peaceful without something in your life to love a bit.' She added, shrewdly, that even 'fifty adoring children would never make up a tiny bit' for the loss of Sam, but argued that 'if once you got a baby to

be fond of, and bring up, and had it loving you like mad
and depending on you you would at least feel peaceful and you
can't feel quite alone. The thing about a child is that they do
really think you are perfection – poor misguided little buggers!
– and that is a good start to kill what you've often described as
feeling like a "mad, lonely ghost" isn't it?'

My father also supported the idea, though he had a different
reason for doing so. 'Adopt 50 children,' he wrote one
lunchtime from his office in the City where at the end of the
war he had resumed a reluctant career as a stockbroker, 'and
I'll still love you quite outrageously.' The war had killed off
his already shaky marriage with my mother. He was in RAF
fighter control, and to be near the bases where he served my
mother had moved my brother, me and our nanny from house
to house, like shadows that were becoming detached from
their object. Eventually he left for Malta, then under siege,
where he pursued his version of a 'good war', released from a
marriage he had never had his heart in. Like Sam, he came
from the same world as Olivia. They had known each other
before the war and had many friends in common. The
difference was that Olivia never fell in love with him. She was
honest about that from the start, and he accepted it, or said he
did, writing in the letter where he mentioned adoption that 'it
seems to me still to be a complete dream that you even
contemplate thinking of marrying me'. She imposed her
terms, which were those of an emotionally unequal relationship. 'I honestly feel proud that you even care for me just the
littlest bit,' my father replied one evening from his club. 'I've
got enough love for you to do for the two of us don't you
worry.' He 'quite understood about Sam' and 'from my angle
am *quite* happy about it, so you can put that out of your mind –

I don't want you to forget him or put his photos away'. He accepted, too, the key, unchanging point of her private theology – that she would belong to Sam when she died. 'The way I look at it is this,' he wrote. 'Sam I'm sure would like to think of you on this earth as being happy and well looked after for the rest of your life and honestly darling that's what I want to do for you. What happens when we die neither you or I know but I don't mind the thought of you going to Sam because if I make you happy for the rest of your life, I'll get *my* reward in heaven somehow, that's a certainty.'

Olivia's friends were advising her to remarry, not least because it made sense if she was going to adopt a child. Sam's best friend certainly thought so. He knew she would never be as happy with anyone else as she was with Sam, he said in one letter, but she ought to be 'far happier than many married folk because you don't expect too much'. At the beginning of 1947 Olivia received a nine-month-old baby boy on trial from the National Children Adoption Association. She toyed with the idea of calling him Sam but thought better of it, and gave him instead the scarcely less loved name of her dead brother. The adoption of Frederick Peter James Bucknill (the middle two names were those chosen by his natural mother) was formally completed on 22nd March 1948, by which time she was married to my father. She took the baby almost at once to the doctor who had looked after Sam and her in London and he pronounced it perfect.

It is not clear to me they understood what they were doing when they set out to re-create the life she had planned to live with Sam and, if they did, how dreadfully they were tempting fate. Olivia and Sam had imagined settling down to raise a family on his farm in the Cotswolds. My father had no experience of farming but he had never cared for the City, whereas a farm offered the life of a landed gentleman his upbringing had prepared him for but his means never allowed. They did not move to Sam's old farm – Olivia could not have borne that – settling instead, in 1949, in Hampshire.

Doiley Hill was a small but handsome establishment of some three hundred acres, with old flint and brick farm buildings, an agreeable house of pink-washed stucco and a large garden bordered by a post and rails fence beyond which grazed, in park-like fields, my father's herd of pedigree Red Polls – handsome, hornless cattle the colour of old claret. There was a cowman called Baldock; Basil the farm boy; and a gardener-handyman, Bailey, with Mrs Bailey, Berkshire folk who had worked for Olivia's mother. Inside, the house was run by Oliva and Pio, an Italian couple, though Pio, in theory engaged as cook, left the work to his less than handsome wife Oliva who was ready to put up with anything as long as she could keep her eye on her unreliable husband. My father's mistake was to suppose this trim new world was intended for his benefit when Olivia only countenanced its creation for the new child's sake. Here Freddie would be able to grow up in the sort of surroundings Sam knew and loved. My father, in this at least a surrogate Sam, would teach him to shoot and fish, and though, unlike Sam, he was not a horseman, later there could be horses too. And one day, if Freddie wanted it, the farm would be his.

From the start the child, his nursery, and the nursery's mistress, Bobbie Raiker, were the heart of Doiley's life. Bobbie's husband, a navy commander, had been killed sailing a yacht to bring back British troops from the retreat at Dunkirk. She had spent the rest of the war looking after

Winston, the son of Randolph Churchill, revealing an unusual skill at the governess's art. 'Love and attention bring out the best in children' was one of her common-sense maxims; 'at all times keep cool, calm and collected' another. She did not look the least bit like Mary Poppins or any other ideal governess most people have known. A diminutive figure, she favoured large dark glasses – an exotic accessory in those days – and, on occasions, wigs. She was also addicted to bright colours which, she said, expressed her natural cheerfulness (it was also expressed, to my father's horror, by occasional outbursts of whistling and song at breakfast). This original and hardy spirit hit it off with Olivia at their first meeting, which was just as well, for when Bobbie was preparing to set off for her new post she got a telephone call from the nanny she was to replace. The woman warned her not to take the job. Mrs Frankland, she said, 'was an enchanting lady, but not good with children', and she (the nanny) had not been able to do anything right. Bobbie did not dismiss this warning as nonsense – to her mind parents were seldom worthy of their children – but thought 'Fiddle-de-dee, that little baby's got to have someone,' and went on with her packing.

Freddie was three when Bobbie arrived, and already proving extremely difficult. He would not drink milk, not even the milk from the farm's own prize cows. Bobbie devised a nourishing alternative, a daily tumbler of freshly squeezed orange juice. He also would not touch meat, but had a passion for jam tarts which he liked to cover with mayonnaise. He was disobedient, flew into rages and once, when a friend came to stay with her baby, tried to tip it out of its pram. He was restless and, when thwarted, aggressive. Several times he escaped from the garden, managing to run a good distance before being brought back. He was slow to control his bladder even during the day. He had puzzling interests: mechanical things like light switches fascinated him, and he showed skill at manipulating them. When he played, it was on his own, never with anyone else. He liked arranging objects in pairs and groups but did not seem to play imaginative games with them by pretending, as small children usually do, that they were something else. He liked routines, and reacted badly when familiar patterns were broken. He was detached and strangely unaffectionate, never kissing of his own accord either Olivia or Bobbie, though he sometimes held his arms up to Bobbie when she was putting him to bed at night. He screeched and made other noises, but would not talk. Bobbie showed him picture books of animals and he learned to say 'moo' at the sight of a cow, and grunt when shown a pig, but got no further than that. Each evening at six o'clock Bobbie gave him a bath, and would hum him her favourite tunes from Italian opera while she wrapped him in a large towel and held him on her knee to dry him. One night after she had put him to bed she passed the nursery and heard him half humming, half singing that evening's melody. She rushed downstairs to Olivia and they stood together outside the door and listened. It seemed some kind of triumph, but what it meant they did not know.

Bobbie soon came to understand her predecessor's warning. At times Olivia proved almost as difficult as her son, for her natural impatience was magnified by the weight of hope she had put on this increasingly strange child. She wanted Freddie to be a happy, healthy child and her disappointment at his difficult behaviour easily took the form of anger. Unlike her predecessor, Bobbie stood her ground, and thought nothing of ticking Olivia off if, at a frequent moment of frustration, she slapped or spanked Freddie for some misdeed. At first Olivia would not listen to suggestions offered by Bobbie or anyone else that something might be wrong with the boy but eventually, towards the end of 1949, she gave in. London doctors carried out a physical examination that revealed a glandular deficiency for which they prescribed medicine, and within a short time the balance of the glands was restored. Freddie's behaviour, though, remained unchanged and in the New Year Olivia set off on an exploration of London's child specialists. This was the beginning of her torture. Life became a nightmare in which she was always running down a corridor, opening door after door, to find only empty rooms. The specialists willingly talked to her, but could never tell her what she wanted to hear, which was that they could cure Freddie, and so she rushed on to the next room where the same disappointment, but worse for being repeated, awaited her. Dr Mildred Creak of the Great Ormond Street Hospital for Children, perhaps the greatest authority of her kind in London at that time, was one of those who examined Freddie. She decided he was very likely both mentally backward and schizoid – that is, he suffered from a defective development of the brain and also a disorder of the mind. She thought it probable he would improve, but only up to a point.

It was, for Olivia, an intolerable diagnosis, not least because, if she accepted it, she would be left with nothing to do. She had known a good many doctors in her life and was accustomed to treating those she liked as courtiers and getting from them what she wanted. So she continued her search for cures, bombarding Dr Creak and the other experts she had consulted with suggestions picked up from friends or even casual acquaintances. They should have Freddie's brain X-rayed; he should be given insulin treatment; they should try electric shock therapy. Foolishly impatient she may have been, but at that time there was little public knowledge about mental handicap and the general ignorance was compounded, and particularly in Freddie's case, by the specialists' inability to identify the nature of his disability. The battles she had begun to fight on her son's behalf exhausted her and exasperated the doctors who found themselves the target of her verbal assaults. It was the start of a lifelong obsession.

For all her anguish about her son Olivia was never embarrassed to talk about his problems, and she had nothing but contempt for anyone who looked askance at him. Dilsey, the black cook to the Compson family in William Faulkner's *The Sound and the Fury*, defended the mad Benjamin Compson by reference to God: '. . . de good Lawd dont keer whether he smart er not. Dont nobody but white trash keer dat.' Olivia would have agreed entirely, but she reinforced the sentiment with the attitudes of a woman brought up in a socially impregnable world to which, as far as she was concerned, Freddie also belonged. She had no patience with people who questioned the energy and money she invested in the search to cure what she was now beginning to think of as her 'mad child'. In this she was unusual, for in those years mental illness was not only little talked about but often considered a shameful secret a family was wise to keep to itself. Olivia was soon reminded of this in the most painful way possible by Sam's closest friend, the man who had urged her both to adopt a child and to remarry. She had made him Freddie's godfather, but what she did not know was that his younger brother was a mongol. Today parents of children with Down's syndrome learn without too great difficulty to love and value them, but before the war such children were more likely to be considered both frightening and shaming. In this case the parents, to their credit, tried to treat the child like any other, making Sam's friend and his sister take their handicapped brother to dances and parties as if he were normal. Given the attitudes of the time it is not hard to imagine how humiliating a young boy found this experience, and once grown up he did not care to be reminded of it. He never told his own daughter about his brother, and it was only by chance she found out that she had an uncle. This friend of Sam's had invested so much hope in Freddie, imagining how he would watch him learning to love all the things Sam had taken such vivid delight in, only to discover he was at least as handicapped as the brother he wanted to forget. The pain was too great, and he disengaged himself from any further interest in his godchild.

My father, a genial if seldom present parent to my brother and myself, would also have enjoyed helping bring up Freddie in the way Sam's best friend had imagined. His inclination, though, was to ignore the unpleasant, and he was ill-prepared to be a parent for Freddie as he turned out to be. His evasions regularly caused arguments with Olivia. One Sunday morning, when Freddie had reduced Doiley to chaos, he came down the stairs dressed in a suit and carrying an umbrella. He was off to church, he said, as though the tumult around him did not exist. Olivia exploded, and his convenient appointment with God had to be postponed. Like his father before him, he kept a diary the chief feature of which was a critical record of each day's weather, as though these brief notes let them feel they had a purchase on life. Like a latter-day Psalmist seeking the Lord's attention with his complaints over the bad days and celebration of the good, my father never failed to note rain and sunshine. His diaries are nevertheless poignant documents, for beneath a surface that so determinedly supposes drought and downpour to be the worst life can bring lie hints at very different storms. In 1950, a momentous year in his life with Olivia and Freddie, he was using a large *Farmer and Stockbreeder*'s Diary that Bobbie had given him for Christmas. He records each day's work on the farm. Excitements are few apart from rumbles about his difficult relationship with the cowman. 'B. [Baldock the cowman] p.b. [pretty bloody],' reads an entry for February, 'R.N.F. [my father] had to show great restraint.' He gives much more space to the illness of Winifred and Rosemary, two of his Red Polls, than to the troubles of his adopted son, referring to the latter only obliquely, as in the entry for 16th February: 'Olivia to London with F. and B. [Freddie and Bobbie] to neurologist.' On 24th April he mentions the lease of a flat in Sloane Avenue; the next day, that Olivia was in London 'stocking it'. And on 28th April he wrote 'O.F. took Bobbie and Freddie and installed them in flat.' Olivia was back in Doiley the following day and he records that the two of them went that afternoon to the cinema. This entry ends with a rare exclamation mark, for him the equivalent of a purple passage, and surely a signal of relief that the problem of Freddie was, for the time being, out of the way.

Out of the way because Olivia had decided, on the advice of Mildred Creak and other doctors she consulted, to have Freddie psychoanalysed. For a trial period of three months Bobbie was to take him each day by bus from the flat that had been rented in Chelsea to St John's Wood. There, at a fine

stuccoed house on Acacia Road, she would leave the child
with Gwen Evans, a protégé of the great Melanie Klein, the
inventor of child analysis. Apart from the familiar enclave of
Lord's cricket ground, St John's Wood was almost *terra
incognita* for Olivia and my father. They knew it had once been
a suitable place for gentlemen to install mistresses, and
supposed it was now given over chiefly to intellectuals and
foreigners, and for that reason was a fitting home for
psychoanalysts (indeed Miss Klein herself lived her last years
just a few minutes' walk from Acacia Road). For all Olivia's
familiarity with doctors, she had no experience of psychiatry
until her problems with Freddie began. She considered herself
sane enough, and supposed all she needed from her medical
advisers were pills, potions, and the occasional cut of the
surgeon's knife. Pressed, she might have said that analysis was
pretty good rubbish. But these short journeys across London,
from 'home' in Chelsea to what might have been 'abroad' on
the borders of Hampstead, became a metaphor for the quest
Olivia – my father dawdling slightly behind – had set out on.

  Melanie Klein, acting through Gwen Evans, was to be only
the first of several unusual foreigners who would offer to
guide them through the world of the troubled mind. Had
Olivia then understood the scope of Freddie's problems, she
might have accompanied him herself to London for this period
of novel treatment on which such store was put. But my father
was keen for her to have a rest from looking after the boy and
she, too, seemed to enjoy the chance for a break. Bobbie,
though, was not pleased to be left alone with her charge in the
city. Freddie was 'happy as a lark' and little trouble when just
with her, but he hated going shopping and was frightened of
the buses on which they made their daily journey. He looked

and moved like any other child of his age, except that he was more beautiful than most. Olivia had recently had him photographed, and though as usual he avoids the eye behind the camera the impression is of an intelligence at turns lively and grave. This child and the small, merry woman who accompanied him turned eyes on London streets, and one day a woman approached Bobbie to ask if she could paint Freddie's portrait. Bobbie explained he was unlikely to put up with that, but she did agree to the artist photographing them in her studio.

The governess appears typically unruffled in these pictures, and Freddie as near angelic as any child has a right to be, but as the sessions with Miss Evans progressed Bobbie grew alarmed that, far from improving, he seemed to be getting worse. She had no idea what went on in Miss Evans's consulting room. To her indignation, the analyst only allowed her into the entrance hall, where she had to undress Freddie and put him in overalls or a bathing costume, and then leave the house for the rest of the session. There were few cafes near Acacia Road where one could pass half an hour, and Bobbie was left to stalk the streets of St John's Wood like some restless, brightly coloured bird. But one day it poured with rain, and with her shoes full of water she took shelter in Miss Evans's porch where the housekeeper saw her and had pity on her. Allowed to wait in the hall, she overheard the analyst talking to Freddie. 'Is Freddie afraid Mummy Evans is going to throw him out of the window? Is Freddie afraid that Mummy Evans is going to lock him up in a big dark cupboard?'

Bobbie had even less time for psychiatry than Olivia. She liked to tell the story of how she was asked by a psychiatrist to recount her dreams. 'I never dream, to my knowledge,' she replied. Further enquiries brought the reply 'my mind is quite in order, thank you', a statement hard for anyone who knew her to dispute. Not surprisingly she thought what she overheard at Acacia Road was 'utter rubbish and nonsense', but that if it was making Freddie worse, it was also dangerous nonsense. She begged Olivia to break off the analysis, telling her it was 'criminal' to subject the child to such treatment, and even threatening to report her if she made Freddie go on with it. She became so upset there was doubt she would continue to work for Olivia after the holiday she took when Miss Evans made a mid-summer break in the treatment. My father's diary almost achieved eloquence when she reappeared: 'Bobbie returned. *Grâce à Dieu.*'

Olivia got proof of Freddie's troubled state when he came back to Doiley Hill in July for his holiday. Miss Evans had written to say that while she could not 'promise a cure . . . there are definite changes of a hopeful kind.' After coping with Freddie for a couple of weeks Olivia wrote back describing how hard to manage he had become, and expressing doubt that it was worth going on with the sessions. The analyst asked Olivia and my father to London to discuss the matter, adding, no doubt as the supreme encouragement, that she had spoken to Melanie Klein about the case and that 'Miss Klein was very interested in Freddie's progress in Analysis and was definitely of the opinion that he should continue.' In another letter Miss Evans said she had told Freddie he was going to come back so she could 'help him some more', and therefore she did not want to break her promise to him. She also claimed – for the first time – that at their last few meetings Freddie had 'made great efforts to speak and did achieve one word with great pleasure'. She thought his difficult behaviour during the holiday was caused by Bobbie's absence and by frustration that the analysis had been suspended at such an interesting moment. It was most undesirable 'from his point of view' for it to be abandoned.

Abandoned, nevertheless, it was, and in the years that followed Olivia spoke of the episode with nothing but anger. She was wrong to do so, for though the analysis was a waste of time and possibly even damaging to Freddie, it was certainly not a frivolous undertaking. One summer many years later when Bobbie was ninety-one, I went with her and Freddie into the little church at Powderham in Devon that looks over the estuary of the river Exe. Freddie is sensitive to the atmosphere of churches and he walked at once to a pew, sat down, and looked at the windows and roof. A still agile Bobbie dipped her knee in front of the altar and went to read a notice, written in a fine Italic hand, that was pinned to a side door.

> I said to the man who stood at the gate of the year, 'Give me a light that I may tread safely into the unknown!' And he replied, 'Go out into the darkness and put your hand in the hand of God. That shall be to you better than light and safer than a known way!'

God, if He exists, seemed hesitant to give his hand to Olivia's child in spite of her many prayers, and mortals had to step forward with what light they possessed. Bobbie made a gift of hers. Melanie Klein, through Gwen Evans, offered light of another sort. It was not surprising Mildred Creak directed Olivia towards Klein, saying if anyone could help it was she. I doubt Olivia had heard the name before, and if she took the advice it was because she did not know what else to do. She might have been intrigued had she known that Klein, born in Vienna, was the daughter of a Polish Jewish doctor, for she liked a touch of the exotic in her medical advisers. Melanie Klein had been in London for a quarter century by the time Olivia came to her for help. She had pioneered the analysis of children (something Sigmund Freud had not attempted) and become the dominant force in the British Psycho-Analytical Society, where her only possible rival was Freud's daughter Anna, with whom she conducted a considerable feud.

Some people called Klein a genius, others thought her self-willed and unscientific. But even critics such as the non-comformist British psychiatrist R. D. Laing, who found her an 'absolutely detestable person' of 'adamantine dogmatism', could not help admiring her. Difficult and controversial she may have been, but she was also brilliantly original. There were some seventy-five practising analysts in London in 1950, and it was uncharitably said that most became Kleinians because only then could they hope to have the patients they needed passed on to them by Miss Klein. Those who challenged her risked excommunication; those who remained faithful risked ridicule as adepts of a sect that required total submission. It was from this powerful, not to say over-powering, woman that Olivia received the name of Gwen Evans, who was genuinely close to Klein and would be one of only fourteen colleagues honoured to attend the great woman's seventieth birthday dinner in 1952.

The handsome, soberly dressed Miss Evans alarmed Bobbie precisely because she followed Kleinian practice in her treatment of Freddie. It was out of the question that Bobbie be allowed to disrupt the link between patient and analyst by being present even in a nearby room; hence her banishment to the streets of St John's Wood. Miss Evans had Freddie stripped to a bathing costume because she wanted to watch him play, and for that purpose she provided water, along with pencils, paper and carefully chosen toys. Play was to Melanie Klein what dreams where to Freud – the raw material of analysis. She claimed play revealed the child's unconscious just as Freud's adult patients revealed their's through their dreams. Later Olivia and her friends would scoff at the idea that an analyst could do anything for a child like Freddie who could not even talk, but the nub of Klein's approach was that the child did not need to talk; it only had to play and be observed playing. Analysis, she argued, could therefore be successfully used even on two-year-olds and the older children like Freddie who had not yet acquired language.

The technique of watching a child at play is used today for diagnosing autism, but Klein's method went further than mere observation. Even if a child could not talk the analyst – and here Klein again broke Freud's practice – had to interpret aloud the material the child was presenting through its play. Something like this seems to have been going on when a horrified Bobbie heard Miss Evans ask Freddie if he was scared she might throw him from the window or lock him up in a cupboard. It was certainly characteristic that what she overheard had to do with Freddie's supposed fears, for it has been said that when Klein looked into an infant's mind she saw a seething conflict of anxieties. By bringing anxiety to the surface the analyst would help the child distinguish between what was real and what was phantasy, and hopefully release it from the terror and guilt that might otherwise cripple it.

Whereas Freud had connected the origin of anxiety with sexual development, Klein believed it lay far earlier, above all in the infant's relation to the mother's breast. Klein concentrated on what many child psychiatrists now agree are the baby's vital earliest months. The baby that at first believes it *is* the world, that everything it sees is its own creation, must undergo the shock of realising that it and the world are two separate things. The child learns that the mother's breast it originally supposed it could bring into existence whenever it was hungry is in fact separate from it. It comes to see the mother as a 'good' breast that nourishes it and which it loves, and also as a 'bad' breast that it can destroy by eating and therefore fears retribution from. In describing this relationship Klein used language of considerable savagery, for example arguing that, for the infant, 'all depends on how it is able to find the way out of this conflict between love and uncontrollable hatred and sadism'. Here, she supposed, lay the roots of character distortions in adults, and also of schizophrenia and manic-depressive psychosis, conditions that till then were thought beyond treatment by analysis. Miss Evans, by posing her macabre-seeming questions, had been trying to help Freddie resolve his primal conflict.

Bobbie was therefore right, in a way she did not realise, when she thought something dreadful was taking place in the prim surroundings of Acacia Road. If Melanie Klein was correct, taking a child back to its early months was akin to experiencing a horror movie in which the story is one's own infantile life. Bobbie was also right to be shocked because there were other analysts at hand who disagreed strongly with

Klein, and who themselves had a far sunnier view of the first months of human life. Klein, one of her critics joked, had invented 'merely a matriarchal variant of the doctrine of Original Sin'. The description of infancy offered by the well-known British analyst Donald Winnicott was much more reassuring. With Klein in mind, he thought it useful to reassure parents that 'ordinary babies are not mad', and argued that as long as the mother was responsive and caring an infant would not become terrifying or unacceptable to itself. The infant was no sadist, said Winnicott. It might exploit the mother ruthlessly, but it was not necessarily malevolent. He suggested that Melanie Klein, by using such powerful, violent language, had made seem abnormal what was in fact only ordinary child development.

Today Winnicott is regarded by many people as one of the few original practitioners of psychoanalysis there have been. A pediatrician before he turned analyst, he possessed a magic touch with mothers and children, and was at the height of his powers when Olivia was looking for help. In him she would have found an open mind, rather than insistence on a single, if complex and brilliant theory. From him she would have got common-sense advice she could have understood – Winnicott might have been describing Bobbie Raiker when he wrote 'success in infant care depends on the fact of devotion, not on cleverness or intellectual enlightenment' ('I don't need a psychiatrist to tell me that' might have been Bobbie's response). But no one seems to have mentioned Winnicott's name to Olivia, and she had little chance of discovering it through her own resources. It was an illustration of a truth she was beginning to learn: that there is no sure path that leads to correct diagnosis and treatment. The choice of medical expertise was vast, but it was as hard for her to pick the right name as it is in a country with a dilapidated telephone system to reach the number you want. In a better-functioning world she would have got Winnicott. Instead she was put through to Klein and Evans.

Nevertheless Winnicott would have seconded Gwen Evans's request that Olivia find out as much as possible about Freddie's life before adoption. Miss Evans thought these nine months might hold a key to his later problems but Olivia knew nothing about them. Under the rules of adoption she was not even told the name of Freddie's mother, let alone what sort of a mother she had been. Pressed by Miss Evans, she wrote to the Adoption Association to ask 'at what age [Freddie] was taken from his mother and whether he was ever breast fed or not. Also whether he was much neglected or left alone by his foster mother . . . not necessarily threatened but perhaps ignored.' The Association's general secretary seemed surprised, even offended, by the request. Her view was that nothing that happened to Freddie up to his adoption could affect his later development – evidence not so much of the lady's obtuseness as of the state of public knowledge about child development at that time.

Olivia in reply told her that specialists disagreed, and indeed had said such information was vital. If Freddie could not be helped soon, she went on, 'he will get worse as he gets older and will not be able to stay with us. What that means I dare not imagine.' Had they really told her that? The correspondence with the Adoption Association became bitter on both sides. In December 1950 Olivia wrote to the general secretary that 'my hopes have very slowly died in these last months though I refuse to stop trying. You wish us a happy Christmas. I don't know if you have ever lived in a house with an abnormal child who you have grown to love. Times like Christmas are when it hurts most. He ought to be loving it all so at nearly five and as things are he can have no idea what it is all about.'

Oddly, she wrote that letter after the Association told her they had made contact with Freddie's mother. It turned out he was the child of a wartime romance, and in that sense a child such as Sam and Olivia had hoped for. The mother was a Wren, the father a young married doctor serving with the Canadian navy who went back to Canada without knowing the girl was pregnant. Her family, which was well-off, persuaded her not to tell him, fearing it might force him to abandon his wife to return to make a second marriage he might not really want. The child was given into adoption, and not long after the mother met, and then married, someone else.

Olivia no longer seemed so interested in these facts because she had taken Freddie away from Gwen Evans, the person keenest to have information about Freddie's early months. The decision to end the analysis was surely correct. Melanie Klein did record one famous success with a boy whom she at the time called schizophrenic, but who today would have been diagnosed as autistic. Dick came to her when he was four, the age Freddie went to Miss Evans, but he could speak, although he had a poor vocabulary and the intellectual level (Klein estimated) of a child of eighteen months. Dick had symptoms Melanie Klein had never seen before. He showed little emotion; did not play like a normal child, that is to say, imaginatively; and he had no attachment to people, his parents included. After watching him at play in her consulting room she interpreted what he did with a train, water and other objects as attempts to attack his mother. The boy gave signs of

increasing anxiety, as Freddie did too under treatment by
Gwen Evans, but the difference was that within six months
Dick began to make progress, in particular showing greater
affection towards his parents and learning new words. By the
time he reached his twenties he was able to do a job that did not
put too much pressure on him. He also kept fond memories of
Melanie Klein, though when he read the paper she wrote
about his analysis, with its detailed interpretation of his wishes
about his father's penis and mother's body, he remarked, 'I
think she could have cut out this claptrap really.'

Dick's autism was of the mildest type, and he managed to
overcome the barrier of language that Freddie could not cross
and never would. Dick's analysis with Melanie Klein, more-
over, lasted from 1930 to 1946, with a three-year break during
the war. He then underwent three years' final analysis with
another therapist. Not the least objection to Klein's method
was its unrealistic expectation that a large number of children
would be able to receive treatments lasting ten years or more.
In Freddie's case there was a more fundamental objection.
Dick's parents, who were colleagues of Klein, had never given
the boy affection and it was on this parent–baby link, and
above all the relationship between mother and baby, that the
analyst concentrated. It was supposed that remote, cold
parents might produce remote, cold children like Dick, or
perhaps like Freddie who never volunteered to kiss his
adopted mother or governess. Donald Winnicott himself
stressed the importance of the 'ordinary good mother', and
pointed out the damage 'maternal failure' could do. Hence
Olivia's questions to the Adoption Association, for by this
interpretation an unsatisfactory foster mother might also be
responsible for much. It was an important perception, but it

proved impossible to turn up any evidence that it was relevant to Freddie's case, and (as we shall see) experts today believe the cause of autism lies elsewhere.

It was Olivia's own qualities as a mother that were about to be questioned by an expert of a quite different kind. Her lack of patience with Freddie and her fits of bad temper bothered Bobbie Raiker from the start. The doctors she consulted remarked how she was too inclined to rush from one proposed solution to another: 'Mrs Frankland seems to me to be going off at tangents,' one of them complained. A woman of considerable nervous energy, she was inclined to chase down tangents all her life, but where Freddie was concerned the chase was becoming compulsive. She had loved her brother, then her wartime husband, and lost them both. Now she seemed to be losing the child that might have replaced them, indeed had already lost him in the sense that he could not give her what she most wanted, a reciprocal love. That summer, exhausted by Freddie's rages and destructiveness during the break in the sessions with Gwen Evans, she decided she could no longer cope with him at home. This did not surprise the specialists. Mildred Creak had warned he might have to go to a residential school; another added his opinion that Freddie could soon become unmanageable. Some months before the psychoanalysis began Olivia had taken Freddie shopping in Newbury, the local market town. She parked the car outside a toy shop and Freddie, attracted by something in its window, made her go inside with him. She bought the toy he wanted, but the moment he was outside he threw it through the grating of a drain and flew into a rage, typical behaviour for him at that time. A woman who saw the scene came up to Olivia. She had a son who did things like that, she said, and she had sent him to a school in Scotland called Camphill that seemed to understand him. Olivia mentioned Camphill to her medical men. They knew little about the place, except that it was run by a 'refugee doctor', though one of them admitted to having heard well of it at second hand.

When Freddie's analysis was broken off Olivia made contact with the school, and an appointment was made to take Freddie to see its principal, Karl König, at the Harley Street rooms he used when he came to London. König asked her to bring Bobbie and my father as well as Freddie. I do not think Olivia realised she was just as much on trial that day as Freddie. König saw them all together, then each separately. Olivia was enchanted by this little man with a large head and old-fashioned clothes, a gold watch and chain threaded through his waistcoat, and at once understood she was in the presence of someone out of the ordinary. König made that impression on many people, for he had unusual presence, and possessed great powers of persuasion as well as the knack of giving his attention utterly to the person he was talking to. He must have known the impact he made on Olivia, for he was already well established as a Pied Piper, one of those people who only have to appear for strangers to volunteer themselves as followers and disciples. 'We know we have come to the right person,' she wrote to König after the meeting. This first impression never changed and was vital, for out of it grew Olivia's confidence that he would help her son if anyone could. As always with her, it was a matter of feeling rather than intellect. She felt awe in the presence of a superior brain, and would sit thrilled through his lectures even though afterwards she might not be able to explain what they were about. Neither then nor later did she come to grips with the ideas behind König's methods, any more than she understood what Gwen Evans had been trying to do in her consulting room at Acacia Road.

I suspect König guessed much of this at that first meeting, for Freddie's interest demanded that he be Olivia's dispassionate critic. It would not be surprising if he was moved by someone so beautiful and so lively, and who had put such effort into her search for a cure for her son, but when he saw Bobbie alone he implored her to stay with the child until he decided if he could have him in his school. Mrs Frankland, he told her, had too little patience and was too nervous to be able to handle the boy. He even doubted whether she should have adopted a child in the first place (an opinion the Adoption Association shared: 'We found her very excitable and over-talkative,' they wrote to Camphill, and 'not the very best type of person to deal with a child so afflicted'). As for Olivia's decision to experiment with psychoanalysis, König thought it the worst thing she could have done.

Freddie reacted as strongly to the meeting as his mother. König was famously calm and relaxed with children: it was said that when he looked at them he seemed both to take in the whole child and also to hold nothing back of himself. As they were leaving Freddie spat at him, spraying saliva down his coat lapel. König laughed and said, 'That is his greeting. Don't chastise him.'

König could not promise Olivia he would take Freddie for Camphill had a waiting list of a hundred and after Christmas, the holiday Olivia found especially painful because Freddie did not know how to enjoy it, she sent him a reminder. His reply suggested he had all along meant to find a place for the child. Of course he had not forgotten Freddie, he wrote, and would

accept him immediately after Easter. He enclosed a list of
clothes and other articles that would be needed, and added, 'I
very much hope that his present governess will be able to stay
with him until he comes to us, and then she can take a long
holiday.' He knew Freddie would be a challenge. The boy had
made an unusual impression on him, and König described him
in the notes he wrote after the examination in Harley Street as
'perhaps the most beautiful child I ever have seen. A round
perfect head, bright, wonderful eyes . . . He is full of
intelligence.' But he also noted some of the features that would
determine his diagnosis. As a baby Freddie was detached and
'did not take to anybody'. He had always rocked a great deal,
even before going to sleep. And although he had perfect feet
his hands were 'overstretchable' and the fingers very thin and
frail.

The London specialist had diagnosed schizophrenia and
König, lacking the time to make a full examination, was at
first inclined to agree. But even then he seemed to appreciate
better than anyone else the torture inherent in the relationship
of this mother with her son. Olivia and Freddie needed each
other. Her increasingly neurotic obsession with him ensured
he would get the best care possible; his troubled existence gave
purpose to her life. Yet they were damaging each other, too.
The excitability of her concern was too great a stimulus for
him; and his adventures and difficulties were too great a strain
for her.

One result of that strain was the collapse of the world at
Doiley Hill after Freddie left for Scotland. Perhaps it would
have been different had my father made a success of the farm,
but he did not. The fields that looked so flatteringly like
parkland turned out to have soil of poor quality. The

handsome Red Polls proved a poor investment; the expensive pedigree bull chosen with such care nothing short of a disaster. Doiley had been bought with Olivia's money, and it was on her insistence that it was sold three years after Freddie went to Camphill. They did not keep the leather-bound stock book in which my father recorded the names of Winifred, Rosemary and the rest of the herd he had been so proud of, but they did take with them the visitors' book, with its last entry on 7th March 1954. There had been many guests, for they were a naturally sociable couple with many friends whom they enjoyed seeing and making comfortable. The gradual unveiling of Freddie's misfortune threw shadows over the agreeable house and its garden, but there were still times when it was illuminated by Olivia's high spirits, and my father, when sitting down to write his diary in the evening, could write 'glorious day' without afterthought or hesitation.

Olivia found a flat in London at the top of a house in Cadogan Square. From the small roof terrace at the back you could have seen, were it not for the buildings along Sloane Street, the apartment block in Halkin Place where she lived during the war and, a little further to the north, the church of St Paul's, Knightsbridge, where she had prayed for the life of her soldier husband, and was now to pray for her son.

4

Unsung Heroes

K arl König's eventual identification of Freddie as autistic was evidence of his professional skill. Neither Gwen Evans nor any of the other British doctors who examined him had so much as mentioned childhood autism as a possible cause of his difficulties, and it was from König that Olivia would first hear the word. This was not surprising. Autism, which comes from the Greek *autos*, meaning self, is not a common complaint. Modern studies suggest an incidence of 4.5 to 100,000 of the population, though twice that number if cases of mild autism (like Dick, the boy analysed by Melanie Klein) are included. The first clinical description of autism was published in a learned American journal in 1943, only seven years before König saw Freddie. Its author, Leo Kanner, was Austrian by birth but after training in Vienna he left for the United States where he eventually became head of the Johns Hopkins clinic in Baltimore. The following year a similar account of autism was published in Vienna, the work of the eminent Austrian child specialist Hans Asperger whose researches were carried out independently of Kanner's. Karl König, himself Viennese-born, had evidently read one or both of these papers. Asperger was confident that once one has

recognised an autistic individual 'one can spot such children
instantly . . . by the way they enter the consulting room on
their first visit, their behaviour in the first few moments and
the first words they utter'.

Many of the symptoms of autism noted by Kanner in his
ground-breaking paper fitted Freddie's puzzling behaviour.
Kanner might have been describing Freddie when he concluded that

> The outstanding . . . fundamental disorder is the children's
> inability to relate themselves in the ordinary way to people
> and situations from the beginning of life.
>   There is from the start an extreme autistic aloneness that,
> whenever possible, disregards, ignores, shuts out anything
> that comes to the child from the outside.
>   He has a good relation to objects; he is interested in them,
> can play with them happily for hours . . . The child's
> relation to people is altogether different . . . Profound
> aloneness dominates all behaviour.

Kanner also might have been talking about Freddie
when he described autistic children's passion for repetition and
sameness. This exhausted anyone looking after them, for each
attempt to coax them away from what their carers found
impossibly tiresome rituals invariably provoked explosions of
rage and misery.

> The child's noises and motions and all his performances
> [Kanner wrote] are as monotonously repetitious as are his
> verbal utterances. There is a marked limitation in the
> variety of his spontaneous activities. The child's behaviour
> is governed by an anxiously obsessive desire for the
> maintenance of sameness.

Asperger's description of the condition was also apt, but his account of a six-year-old boy called Fritz provided particularly vivid similarities with Freddie. Fritz had been referred to Asperger by his school, which considered him impossible to teach. The doctor noted that the boy's gaze was 'strikingly odd'. It was generally directed into the void, but was occasionally interrupted by a 'momentary malignant glimmer'. The child avoided making eye contact with anyone who tried to talk to him. Instead he darted 'peripheral looks' at them which created an 'as if he wasn't there' impression. Fritz did not know how to play with toys that were given him and either chewed them or threw them under beds. He ate 'the most impossible things', such as pencils, wood and (a particular favourite of Freddie's, too) paper. He was a mischief maker. After sitting with a vacant look in his eyes he would jump up 'and before one could do anything he would have done something mischievous'. He knocked things off tables, hit other children (most likely the smallest), turned on taps, ran away.

Fritz's and Freddie's behaviour recalled accounts of a famous problem child of the Napoleonic era who, it is now supposed, may also have been autistic. Victor, who came to be known as the Wild Boy of Aveyron, was found in a forest living wild like an animal. Jean-Marc-Gaspard Itard, the young Frenchman who took Victor under his care, one day brought his famous ward to dine with the fashionable beauty Mme Récamier. One of the guests left a description of what happened that recalled some of Freddie's own startling performances at meals in public places.

Mme Récamier seated [Victor] at her side, thinking perhaps

that the same beauty that had captivated civilised man would receive similar homage from this child of nature . . . [But] too occupied with the abundant things to eat, which he devoured with startling greed as soon as his plate was filled, the young savage hardly heeded the beautiful eyes whose attention he himself attracted. When dessert was served, and he had adroitly filled his pockets with all the delicacies he could filch, he calmly left the table . . . Suddenly a noise came from the garden, and M. Itard was led to suppose his pupil was the cause . . . [The boy was spotted] running across the lawn with the speed of a rabbit. To give himself more freedom of movement, he had stripped to his undershirt. Reaching the main avenue of the park . . . he tore his last garment in two, as if it were simply made of gauze; then, climbing the nearest tree with the ease of a squirrel, he perched in the middle of the branches.

Eventually a gardener armed with a basket of peaches tempted Victor back to earth while the other guests, among them a famous playwright and an astronomer, exchanged reflections on this 'useful comparison between the perfection of civilised life and the distressing picture of nature untamed' that Victor had presented.

Asperger might have been describing Victor and Freddie when he wrote of Fritz:

In each of these situations it was always the worst, most embarrassing, most dangerous thing that happened. The boy seemed to have a special sense for this, and yet he appeared to take hardly any notice of the world around him! No wonder the malicious behaviour of these children so often appears altogether 'calculated'.

What struck me when I read these words was the choice of the words 'malignant', 'malicious', and

'mischievous'. It brought back my memory of looking at the
very young Freddie and finding him, in a way I could not
explain, alien, and even frightening. The pretty child had
given me a 'peripheral look' that seemed nevertheless to
convey dislike. I felt guilty about thinking this, and for many
years wondered if I was jealous of the adopted child who
dominated my stepmother's attentions; but I never much
believed in this explanation and was grateful when Asperger's
paper finally killed it off. An autistic child's 'maliciousness' is
different from that of an ordinary child. A child like Freddie,
by the nature of his condition, was locked within his isolation
and had little or no awareness of other people's feelings.
Asperger identified 'impoverished emotionality' as the reason
for these children's occasional malice and cruelty, and for their
heart-breaking habit of turning nasty when someone is nice to
them. Several friends and acquaintances who came to Doiley
Hill commented, though not always to Olivia, on the pleasure
Freddie seemed to take in being naughty and destructive.

Highly strung at the best of times, Olivia had interpreted her
child's bad behaviour as a deliberate challenge and punished
him accordingly. She had no way of knowing what Asperger
had observed in Fritz, namely that whenever emotional
demands were made on such a child – and her approach to
Freddie was always emotional – he would show his incompre-
hension by reacting with some particularly gross misbe-
haviour. Asperger concluded that any teacher of an autistic
child had to act with his or her feeling 'turned off'. The teacher
should 'never become angry nor should he aim to become
loved. It will never do to appear quiet and calm on the outside
while one is boiling inside.' This, he added, was extremely
difficult 'given the negativism and seemingly calculated

naughtiness of autistic children'. It would certainly have been difficult for Olivia to curb her desire that Freddie love her, or to stop demonstrating her own love for him, something König seems to have understood at their first meeting. It explained why he was so anxious for Bobbie Raiker to stay with the boy until he could go to Camphill. Bobbie may not have achieved the extraordinary serenity and detachment that marked some of the teachers who later worked with Freddie, but she fitted Asperger's requirement that anyone caring for an autistic child had to be 'calm and collected and . . . remain in control'.

It was perhaps lucky Olivia knew nothing about autism, for the prognosis, especially if Freddie remained unable to speak, was not good. Baffled though she was by her son's behaviour she was convinced he had moments of great happiness as well as great misery. In fact the balance was most likely in misery's favour. Thomas Weihs, a skilful specialist who would work with Freddie in Camphill, commented some twenty years after the publication of Asperger's paper that the happiness of which an autistic child is capable is limited, while 'anxiety, severe despair, and profound unhappiness, for no tangible reason, are generally preponderant'. The nature of the autistic child's despair was suggested in particularly horrifying terms by Bruno Bettelheim, the well-known psychoanalyst who, like so many of the other healers who appear in this story, was born in Vienna though, like Kanner, he later moved to the United States. Bettelheim was imprisoned in Buchenwald and Dachau during the Second World War. Afterwards he founded and ran Chicago University's Orthogenic School, an original attempt to create perfect conditions for the education of mentally handicapped children. Combining the experiences he gained at his school and in the camps Bettelheim made a startling link between autistic children and the most demoralised inhabitants of Hitler's prisons.

Called 'Moslems' by the other prisoners, these wretched people behaved 'as if they were not thinking, not feeling, unable to act or respond, moved only by things outside themselves'. Unlike other prisoners who each day tried to improve their condition in some way however small, the 'Moslems' first stopped doing anything, because all action seemed pointless to them. Then they stopped feeling, 'because all feeling was painful or dangerous or both'. Like autistic children the 'Moslems' never looked anyone straight in the face, but only darted surreptitious glances, because they felt it was not safe to let others see them observing. The final stage came when it was impossible to arouse any emotion at all in them. They even gave up fighting for food 'because the food stimulus no longer reached their brain clearly enough to lead to action'. Nothing could influence them any more 'because nothing from the inside or outside was reaching them any more'. Bettelheim pointed out that the camp nickname was inaccurate, for true Moslems may choose to submit to fate of their own free will while these men and women had done something very different: they had 'given the environment total control over them'. He explained this as an attempt to blot out an experience they could not cope with. These prisoners 'internalised' the camp guards' opinion of themselves, namely that they were sub-human, despicable creatures without a will of their own. The concentration camp 'Moslems', Bettelheim concluded, had surrendered 'the last, if not the greatest, of the human freedoms: to choose [one's] own attitude in any given circumstance'.

Bettelheim thought that the link between such camp inmates and autistic children lay in the suppression of the self. While the utterly cowed among the prisoners had sought safety in dehumanising themselves, 'autistic children withdraw from the world before their humanity ever really develops'. It is hard to imagine a more powerful, more unbearable image. What can life be like for a little boy (by no means all, but a majority of autistics are male) if what he perceives of the world terrifies him as much as Dachau and Buchenwald, where the threat of death was always present, terrified the most psychologically vulnerable of their inmates? Infantile autism, Bettelheim concluded, was a 'state of mind that develops in reaction to feeling oneself in an extreme situation, entirely without hope'. The less the child existed, the safer he was from attack by an outside world that was everywhere and always hostile. Some children managed this withdrawal so successfully that they not only failed to react, like Freddie, to certain sounds and noises. They also managed to block out intense stimuli such as great heat or cold and many forms of physical pain. Bettelheim noted that one of his pupils showed no signs of discomfort even when his appendix burst.

Because autistic children have withdrawn from the world they have no chance to develop a proper understanding of causality, and as a consequence do not know either how to predict or how to behave in order to get things, or make them happen. Bettelheim concluded that 'an inner life that is not validated against outer experiences and then organised through such validation, remains chaotic'. He accordingly supposed that the children's obsession with rituals and with arranging and grouping objects, far from being an attempt to

cause events, was rather meant to stop incomprehensible
things from happening – and if he was right most events were
incomprehensible to them. He also supposed that while
autistic children have a sense of space they have none of time.
Bettelheim believed his pupils perceived something he called
'space-time'. School, for them, was both space and time. A
holiday in strange surroundings was not school, and could
therefore touch off a panicky feeling that they were lost.
Bettelheim wondered if autistics disregarded time because it
destroyed the sameness that seemed to be their protection
from chaos. Some of his pupils who were able to talk would
not use the past tense 'because to them such events are still in
the present'. If true, this handicap at least had one advantage
for Olivia and Freddie; Olivia worried he would pine for her
after she had been to visit him at school. In fact he gave the
impression of ignoring the gaps between her visits and when I
go to see him today I have the impression that I have simply
stepped into his space, and will step out of it, but not into the
past, when I leave.

Once one is aware of the fragility of the autistic child's sense
of self much that is puzzling in their behaviour begins to make
sense. Autistic children who can speak often avoid using the
personal pronoun I, and will refer to themselves by their
names or as You (a girl at the Orthogenic School told
Bettelheim she would not write a capital 'I' because she had
'too little of a personality'); or they will avoid using their own
words at all and just copy what they hear others say.

What happened to such children to make them, in
Bettelheim's words, 'withdraw from the world before their
humanity ever really develops'? Not surprisingly he looked for a
cause as powerful as the conditions in Nazi prison camps that

turned the most vulnerable inmates into zombies. He was not the only specialist to notice that the symptoms of autism are rarely spotted in early infancy, but usually appear in the child's second and third years. Perhaps inevitably given his psycho-analytical background, Bettelheim looked for the cause in the parents, and above all the mother, for he could not accept that a child might be born with an innate inability to make emotional contact. Autistic children, he decided, were not indifferent to other people: rather they were *disappointed* in them, and the first candidate for causing disappointment was naturally the mother. He observed that these children seldom cried or smiled, and suggested this was because they did not know that anyone existed who could respond to such signals with empathy. Prison camp 'Moslems', he observed, did not cry for the same reason (other prisoners did, but only when they felt they had a sympathetic audience). He concluded that chronic autism could result if the child rejected the mother because it felt she was responsible for its difficulties after birth, and if the mother, in response, herself withdrew from the child.

This takes us back to Acacia Road and Gwen Evans's Kleinian probings into Freddie's supposed anxiety about his mother. Melanie Klein had noted that Dick, the autistic boy she analysed, grew up 'in an environment unusually poor in love' and that his mother's feeling was 'from the very beginning cold'. Klein seized on this as the origin of Dick's problems. Kanner was also attracted by the idea that a 'refrigerator' mother could, as it were, freeze her child into autistic responses.

Asperger, like Kanner, also commented on the predomi-nance of well-educated people among the parents of the children he diagnosed as autistic, but drew a different conclusion, namely that the parents of autistic children were likely to show some traits of autism themselves. This certainly seemed the case with the parents of Fritz, the boy described by Hans Asperger in his paper on autism. Fritz's mother came from a well-known Austrian intellectual family, but what struck Asperger most was how similar she was to her son: both were obvious loners. He described the pair of them walking in the hospital grounds.

> The mother slouched along, hands held behind her back and apparently oblivious to the world. Beside her the boy was rushing to and fro, doing mischief. They gave the appearance of having absolutely nothing to do with each other . . . [The boy's difficulties were clearly not just internal ones but due] also to the mother's own problems in relating to the outside world, showing as she did a limited intuitive social understanding.

Fritz's father came from a farming family but rose to senior rank in the Austrian civil service. Marrying late, he was fifty-five when his son was born. Asperger noted that he, too, was distant, hating to talk about himself and 'extremely correct and pedantic' in his behaviour.

Intrigued by the similarities between parents and their autistic children, Asperger pursued this line of enquiry and found that of the two hundred boys and girls (predominantly boys) that he observed over ten years, there were 'related incipient traits in parents or relatives in *every* single case where it was possible for us to make a closer acquaintance'. Sometimes it was a matter of parents showing only certain autistic peculiarities, but there were other cases where parents themselves displayed the 'fully fledged autistic picture'. Most of the autistically tinged fathers were in intellectual professions and in the few instances where they were manual workers Asperger judged them to have very likely missed their true vocation. Many of the children had intellectual ancestors going back several generations; some were descended from celebrated artistic and academic families.

Asperger discovered what later specialists confirmed, that many mildly autistic people fit well into the rational, science-oriented modern world. He showed that intelligent or above-average intelligent autistics could attain positions of eminence and 'perform with such outstanding success that only such people are capable of certain achievements'. They seemed to develop abilities to counter their disabilities. An intellectually able autistic person's limited interest in, and contact with, the world allowed him to pursue his special talent single-mindedly, without the distractions and deviations that hinder people who are better socially and emotionally integrated into the world around them.

Was there not a large measure of autistic-like detachment in many famous feats of abstract thought? Might not some world-famous brains have been mildly autistic? What about Sherlock Holmes, whose mind could solve the most complicated crime mysteries because it was detached from the problems of everyday living? The great detective certainly had the same sort of narrow, specialised interests that are typical of reasonably well-functioning autistic adults, for example his study of the different sorts of ash produced by one hundred and forty varieties of pipe, cigar and cigarette tobacco. Asperger observed one striking non-fictional example of autistic brilliance over a period of thirty years. Extremely autistic as a child, this man grew up to have no interest in other people. He remained clumsy and gauche. He had, though, a passion for mathematics and, in spite of poor performance in other subjects, managed to pass the entrance exams to university where, while studying theoretical astronomy, he proved a mathematical mistake in the work of Newton. He went on to become in record time an assistant professor in the Department of Astronomy (the American movie *Rain Man* tells the story of a character who has even less talent for social life than this astronomer, but possesses the same kind of acute though narrow mental skill).

Did any of these perceptions have relevance for Freddie? Olivia told König that his doctor father was supposed to be very intelligent, and König underlined that in the notes he made after his first examination of Freddie. The father never saw his child, indeed was apparently unaware of his existence. Freddie's mother, whether calmly or with anguish we do not know, handed him over to foster parents soon after he was born. It seemed believable that her state of mind both before and after birth might leave their trace on the child. It was, though, an example of fate's black humour that Olivia, and by proxy Sam, should have adopted a boy whose future might have been damaged by over-intellectual, inadequately responsive parents. Sam was sharp but would have flinched at being called an intellectual. Olivia was almost uneducated in the academic sense. Ideas scarcely interested her and she seldom read anything heavier than the novels of Graham Greene. On this score, at any rate, there can have been few women seeking to adopt who less deserved to receive an autistic child.

Anyone who goes in search of experts for advice on complicated illnesses of the mind or body is likely to discover that doctors who from afar seem Olympian on closer aquaintance turn out to be far from all-knowing. The longer a malady's history the more likely that one age's brilliant perception becomes a comic delusion for the next, like the belief of those cultivated nineteenth-century Frenchmen that the Wild Boy of Aveyron was obviously 'savage' because he had not known the benefits of civilisation. Some of the past's wrong theories are regarded more severely, as though the people who advanced them are in some way guilty. The pioneers in the study and treatment of autism may have described the symptoms accurately, but their suggestions about its causes now meet with downright hostility. Their stress on the links between the autistic child and its family background and mothering have been replaced by the theory that autism has a biological cause that results in the abnormal functioning of certain organs.

That epilepsy has been found to occur in a third of autistic adolescents (Freddie is one of their number) is now taken as disproving the old theory that denied autism was an organic disorder. Not the least attraction of the new thinking is that it explodes the notion of 'refrigerator' mothers who trigger autism in their children because, from the time of breast-feeding and perhaps even from before birth, they cannot establish proper emotional links with them. This idea was bound to become unpopular in a feminist age when the woman's viewpoint is argued much more fiercely than when Asperger, Kanner and Bettelheim were active. An American mother struggling to bring up an autistic boy at home in the late 1960s remembers reading *The Empty Fortress*, Bettelheim's book on autistic children, with anger and disbelief. She was enraged by his psychoanalysis-influenced assertion that 'the precipitating factor in infantile autism is the parent's wish that his child should not exist'. Twenty years after the publication of his paper on autism Leo Kanner publicly conceded he had been wrong to suppose that mothers were in some way to 'blame' for the condition of their autistic children. A biological explanation also seems to remove the accusing finger from the too intellectual professional families that Kanner and Asperger associated with autistic children, perhaps for the obvious (with hindsight) reason that in those days working-class and other less-favoured parents were unlikely to be able, or know how, to have their children examined by such eminent specialists.

The British research scientist Uta Frith has devised a mnemonic to sum up the 'long causal chain' that contemporary researchers believe leads to autism: hazard, followed by havoc, followed by harm. The hazard can be of many kinds: family genes, chromosome abnormality, disorders of the metabolism, a virus, immune intolerance, and lack of oxygen just before and after birth. Any one of these hazards has the potential to cause havoc to the child's nervous system. The result may be 'lasting harm . . . to the development of specific brain systems concerned with higher mental processes. The harm may be mild or severe, but always involves developmental arrest of a critical system at a critical . . . time.' It is then, according to this theory, that autism occurs.

No one has identified the critical system that is supposed to be damaged. In most children the mechanism that allows the development of social and communication skills (for example, the ability to relate to people and to talk) is well protected and able to survive a good deal of harsh treatment. But autism sometimes exists in pure form, that is, without any of the other handicaps often associated with it, which suggests that this particular system can on occasions be targeted quite accurately by the hazard–havoc–harm process. In most cases, though, and that includes Freddie's, damage to one part of the nervous system most likely involves damage to other parts, too.

For anyone who has absorbed Bruno Bettelheim's comparison of autistic children with concentration camp inmates driven by fear and despair to shed their humanity, this biological explanation comes as relief. If Bettelheim's theory is 'romantic and wrong', as modern thinking asserts, then perhaps autistic children are not so 'entirely without hope' as he supposed. But if the problem is a medical one, in what way does it affect autistic people? If they are not driven to despair by faults in their parents and their background, how do they look upon the world around them? Why do they have so little normal contact with other human beings? What is it that so obviously disorients, and sometimes terrifies, them? Autistic children may not feel despair for the reasons Bettelheim supposed, but they are indisputably dogged by some kind of misery that seems hardly less acute.

Uta Frith suggests that the thread linking the various disabilities of autism 'is the inability to draw together information so as to derive coherent and meaningful ideas. There is a fault in the predisposition of the mind to make sense of the world.' Autistic people may have perfectly functioning senses; in some cases their senses are unusually highly developed. It is not uncommon to find autistic children with perfect pitch, which allows them to become first-class piano tuners. The problem lies in what they do with the information they receive from their senses. Since they lack a normal inclination or ability to look for a meaning or order in things – in other words since they lack the usual human 'drive for central coherence' – events, people and objects that make a meaningful pattern for most of us remain for them pointless bits of a puzzle they can never assemble. They do not know how to assign priority to the information they have at their disposal, and therefore often become obsessed with things most people ignore or soon become bored by. As a small boy Freddie, like many autistic children, loved to make objects spin. He would watch them intently, as though they offered entry into some fascinating world. Even now he is grown up, after drinking a can of Fanta or Coca-Cola he sometimes holds it in one hand, taps it with his long fingers, and gazes at it as a connoisseur might admire a masterpiece. This knack for deep, but extremely partial, areas of interest becomes obvious in autistic grown-ups with the power of speech. A young man who had shown traits of autism since childhood revealed an obsessive interest in collecting the addresses of juvenile courts. Asked why he was not interested in other kinds of court he answered, 'They bore me to tears.' He apparently could not grasp that there could be a general purpose behind the pursuit of a particular sort of information. The absence of a drive for coherence also affects the way the memory works. A doctor whose daughter's autism led her to study the subject described her mind as being like an audio tape that every now and then plays back a complete section. The memory stores data in its entirety, unlike the normally functioning mind which processes it, keeping the meaningful bits while discarding the rest. This may explain why some autistics are capable of extraordinary feats of memory. They may know train timetables by heart, or be able to recite the Top of the Pops going back ten or twenty years.

Although the autistic mind is flawed in such a way that it lacks the 'predisposition of the [normal] mind to make sense of the world', this flaw nevertheless coexists with, or perhaps is compensated by, a passion for repetition and routine in random areas. I met a boy in a school for autistic children who, whenever he came across shoes in a room, arranged them in a neat straight line. It is a common sort of obsession. When Freddie and I have lunch in a pub he tackles his plate item by item, first the egg (the white and the yolk separately), then the chips, then the beans. Sometimes he changes the order but there cannot be alternate mouthfuls of egg, beans and chips. The egg, if it is started on first, must be polished off before the chips may be attacked. The final moment in Faulkner's *The Sound and the Fury* conveys on a grand scale the horror Freddie has shown when precious routines are broken. The black boy who is taking the handicapped Compson son Benjamin out for a drive in a horse and carriage does not do as he is told and turns left at a monument instead of the customary right.

> For an instant Ben sat in an utter hiatus. Then he bellowed. Bellow on bellow, his voice mounted, with scarce interval for breath. There was more than astonishment in it, it was horror; shock; agony eyeless, tongueless; just sound . . .

Ben calms down when his brother seizes the reins and brings the carriage back round the monument's right side. He becomes 'serene again as cornice and facade flowed smoothly once more from left to right; post and tree, window and doorway, and signboard, each in its ordered place'. Though

Freddie is less rigid in his patterns of behaviour than he used to be, a sudden departure from the expected – for example, if a car reverses when he is expecting it to go – may still produce from him a cry of anger and alarm not far removed from 'horror; shock; agony . . .'

Autistic people possibly suffer from an even more fundamental flaw than this inability to impose coherence on what they see and hear. It is the absence of any awareness of mind, both in others and in themselves. This 'mindblindness' would explain why autistics cannot make ordinary emotional contacts; why they cannot, in Uta Frith's words, 'realise fully what it means to have a mind and to think, know, believe and feel differently from others'. It also explains their difficulty in operating in the social world, which requires an ability to guess what other people are thinking and feeling, to sense their level of knowledge and their backgrounds, and to grasp their jokes (I am not sure that I can make Freddie laugh, though he had an obviously mischievous sense of humour when he was a child. The only moments when he seems to laugh a little resemble those flashes of pleasure he showed when trouble-making as a child).

None of these social skills are possible if one has little or no awareness of what another person's mind is. This suggests another explanation for the oddity of the autistic person's gaze. An autistic child looks past people rather than at them, just as Freddie avoided the camera, and the photographer's eye, in the early photos of him. But if a child has little awareness of the existence of other people's minds, why should it look at the camera-holding person on the lawn rather than the branch of a tree or a patch of daisies? An autistic man complained that 'other people talk with their eyes'. Since this language of the eyes was incomprehensible to him, he preferred not to look into people's faces. Sometimes when I arrive to take Freddie out he puts his face close to mine and stares me in the eyes. When we are eating a meal together I may look up to find his eyes again locked on my face, the effort making him screw up his mouth which, because of his moustache, gives him the look of a cartoon cat. This gaze only lasts a few seconds, and for the rest of the day he reverts to his usual behaviour, which is to make use of me as a real cat makes use of humans, sometimes politely, at others insistently, interested in me chiefly for the things that I can do for him. In neither case do I feel he is looking at me. Is his stare the gaze of someone who does not know what he is looking for?

If Freddie cannot grasp what another mind is, what awareness can he have of his own mind? Uta Frith argues that 'the culmination of mentalising ability is self-consciousness'. If autistics cannot mentalise, they cannot be self-aware, except in the simplest sense of knowing their own body and the difference between people and things. In his cat-like way Freddie recognises me, but does he recognise himself to the extent of being self-conscious? When he looks at me I have the impression not only that he does not know what he is looking for in the person he recognises as 'Mark', but that there is only a ghost looking out from the person I call 'Freddie'. Someone lacking self-awareness, Uta Frith suggests, 'would be totally on their own but unable to keep company even with themselves. The company of other people would not be a companionship of minds, and hence not necessarily preferable to that of mindless things.' Put another way, many autistics may lack the ordinary and comforting human ability to make novels of their lives, to appreciate their progress through the years as a story.

A world that lacks cohesion, and is nothing but a collision between unrelated pieces, a world in which other minds do not properly exist and in which you yourself barely exist in a conscious way, such a world may not be like Dachau and Buchenwald, but it is scarcely less chilling. Even if autism does have biological causes, Bruno Bettelheim's words about working with autistic children may still be relevant. To help them make their 'ascent from hell', he wrote, the adult helper must be ready to make a 'descent to one's own hell, however far behind one has left it'. Bettelheim attributed certain feelings to autistics because of his own experience in the camps and his training as an analyst. While he may have been proved wrong about the cause, his description of autism as resulting in a feeling of being in permanent jeopardy, of powerlessness to protect oneself, remains valid. It has been said that Bettelheim 'would have included autistic children among the unsung heroes of our time'. The judgement still stands: consider these scenes from the Loddon school, near Basingstoke, where some twenty children, almost all with autism and severe related mental handicaps, are being coaxed towards living in the world.

Each child – there is the usual preponderance of boys over girls – is accompanied throughout the day by a helper who often, and in some cases all the time, holds it by the hand. There is certainly something of an 'ascent from hell' in the scenes repeated every day as these fragile but often stormily resisting children are led from room to room and up and down stairs by quietly encouraging adults. Their day begins slowly. Getting up is painful, for it is like birth. They are treated as though they were still babies; they get only the easiest food for their first meal – eating is often a moment of crisis for them.

The morning is gentle in order to allow the baby gradually to become a child. They do their hardest work after lunch. Life slows down again after tea, when they are treated more like old people than children. Although they spend the day in groups and small classes they scarcely acknowledge each other's existence. A class goes into a large room to dance to Ravel's *Bolero*. Each child is given black and yellow streamers to hold, but only four of the children deign to take the floor and, though led all the time by their helpers, even then remain detached both from the others and from the clumsy movements their own bodies make. One of the non-dancers is a beautiful Greek Cypriot girl. She sits to one side near a wall, hands intertwined, rocking slightly. Two boys, one of them from Ghana, are slouched by a window. The dance ends with the helpers and the four participating children sitting on the floor, each holding on to the person in front. The children do not actually resist: it is as if they were not there, *as if there were nothing in them to be there*.

Three children are taking part in a morning massage session in the hall. A tall teenage boy lies on the sofa, occasionally allowing a woman to touch his feet. Another woman lies beside a sallow-skinned boy on a huge floppy cushion. She massages him, occasionally kisses him or puffs air into his face. The boy's eyes remain distant, and he often draws back from her. There is no other response. The figure that commands most attention is a sparrow of a girl who sits hunched forward on a sofa between two carers. They massage her hands, and later manage just to stroke her head and the back of her neck. Anna is fifteen. She wears cherry-coloured stockings on legs like sticks but she is fat compared to the three and a half stone she weighed when she arrived at Loddon (a hospital that took her in was exhausted by her within a year). Anna's two helpers never leave her side. At first they carried pieces of food in their pockets and fed her whenever she was willing. It is a triumph she now eats proper, if small, meals, though never together with the rest of the children. She needs her constant pair of helpers for she is both self-destructive and violent, a head banger and a head butter, and has broken a helper's arm with one jab of the head. When she came to Loddon she would only sleep on the window ledge in her bedroom. Later she moved to a blue plastic barrel on the floor. She still sleeps in the barrel, but now allows it to be placed on the bed. She has gnawed the sides of the window sill and her bunk bed. She once destroyed five beds in one week. She is incontinent, and smears excrement on the walls and floor. Unless someone holds on to her she 'falls apart'. When she goes home her father keeps his arms around her all the time, even when she is sleeping. If Anna does not improve she may end her life in the locked ward of a mental hospital.

Since Freddie, like most of these children, cannot speak, there is no way of proving that he and other silent autistics feel the way we suppose they do. We have a hint only from the accounts of intelligent and far less handicapped autistic people who did learn to talk and have mastered their disability. Their stories and memories about how they felt as troubled children are the best hints we have of how people like Freddie felt and to some extent still feel. What they have to tell us is often frightening: Olivia was more accurate than she knew when she said she feared her adopted son lived much of the time in a nightmare world beyond the comfort of others.

Jerry, a young boy when Leo Kanner diagnosed him as autistic, talked about his childhood after he was grown up. He remembered it as a time dominated by 'confusion and terror', a world of 'painful stimuli' he could not master. 'Noises were unbearably loud, smells overpowering. Nothing seemed constant; everything was unpredictable and strange.' Dogs terrified him, as did other children because he feared they would hurt him. School was a 'total confusion' where he felt he would 'go to pieces'. He did enjoy some things, spinning objects was one of them, but could no longer remember what he felt when he did it. His life improved when, at the age of eight, he discovered multiplication tables. The psychiatrist who interviewed him noted that Jerry denied liking arithmetic because, as might have been expected, it 'helped give his world a sense of order; he said he simply liked working with numbers'. Jerry was equally unforthcoming about his need for sameness and rituals, saying simply 'that was how things should be'.

Similar feelings occur in the childhood memories of Donna Williams, a highly intelligent Australian woman who was not diagnosed as autistic until her early twenties. She, too, saw things 'bit by bit', never as a whole. She lost herself in parts of the whole, in the patterns of wallpaper and carpets or a repeated noise, 'like the repetitive hollow sound I got from tapping my chin'. Until she was almost four she got hypnotic pleasure from colours, sensations and sounds (as a child Freddie got obvious pleasure from making a hollow clicking noise with his tongue inside his mouth). Because these sensations were so vivid in spite of being partial, Donna Williams calls her childhood world a rich one, 'but like many rich people I was very alone'. She could lose herself in things but was unable to take in people because she found it hard to grasp the meaning of what they said. Although she soon learned to talk she did not answer questions, but mimicked what had been said to her. As she grew older she loved to copy and put things in order. She liked telephone books, counting the number of people with the same name or noting those names that were rare. She explains this as 'exploring the concept of consistency'. She began to bring home stray kittens and gave them the names, in alphabetical order, that she found in a street directory.

This ordering of things she could control provided relief from a world that was like a 3-D movie, where things, people and events came hurtling towards her all out of control. 'The constant change of most things never seemed to give me any chance to prepare myself for them. Because of this I found pleasure and comfort in doing things over and over again.' Even as a teenager she found it hard to generalise. When a teacher told her not to write graffiti on a wall she started scribbling on another one, not understanding it as a general command not to write on walls anywhere. Sean Barron, a young American who like Donna Williams battled his way out of autistic behaviour, also remembers repetitions and the collecting of what to others seemed quite pointless lists of numbers and names (one favourite was the call letters of local radio stations) as his way of establishing control over an otherwise incomprehensible and therefore unmanageable world.

Sean Barron's story illustrates how baffled the autistic person can be by what others say and do. He 'couldn't understand why they behaved as they did' or 'the signs people used with one another'. At the age of fourteen he astonished his mother by saying 'I need to get a sense of humour', which he tried to do by memorising passages from popular television comedies. He could not understand why no one laughed when he repeated them. Similarly baffled by meaning and emotion, Donna Williams read books but could not pick up what they meant. People became her 'enemies, and reaching out to me was their weapon . . . Gentleness, kindness and affection terrified me . . . Being hugged felt like being burned.' Fear of being emotionally touched survived into her twenties. It was something she 'always experienced . . . as the threat of death'. The fear of being touched seems to have been linked to her tenuous sense of self. She remembers that until she was almost four she, like Leo Kanner's patient Jerry, was easily hypnotised by colour, sensation and sound.

> This hypnotic fascination . . . left me with very little sensation of my own body except for the shock and repulsion of the invasion of physical closeness . . . There was something overwhelming that always seemed too powerful in giving in to physical touch. It was the sense of losing all sense of separateness between myself and the other person. Like being eaten up, or drowned by a tidal wave, fear of touch was the same as fear of death.

In her pre-teens, 'aware of how little I was able to show my true self', in fact believing that that self was an 'emotionless and empty shell', she demanded that her schoolmates call her by other names. She eventually acquired a repertoire of nicknames that she was known by. When she came home from school she

> would . . . spend hours in front of the mirror, staring into my own eyes and whispering my name over and over, sometimes trying to call myself back, at other times becoming frightened at losing my ability to feel myself.

Passages like this justify the title – *The Empty Fortress* – of Bruno Bettelheim's now controversial book about autistic children. Freddie the child and other children such as he may often present grim, turreted walls to the outside world but the greatest tragedy is the insubstantiality of the person hiding inside those walls. Hope lies in coaxing the child to accept its self, and then to venture into the world that seems so frightening to it. Luckily Olivia did not grasp the irony that the strength of her love for Freddie, and the nervousness that followed from it, were obstacles to that emergence.

König's letter saying he would take Freddie lightened her mood, though she could not have explained why Camphill might succeed where everyone else she consulted had failed. I asked a psychiatrist who worked for many years in child guidance in London what professionals thought at that time about Karl König and his school. 'Nothing,' she said. 'They didn't exist for the profession . . . We regarded them as a place of last resort. They took children no one else would.' For a woman as desperate as Olivia that was all she needed to know.

5

Letters from Scotland

A sprig of heather, kept for over forty years, slips from two small sheets of writing paper.

May 27th '51

Dearest Mummy,

 I thank you so very much for all your love, for your parcel with sweets and cars and your card. I liked the dog on it very much and I think I remember our Kimmy.

 I am so happy here with all the other children together. I do not pull my sleaves anymore and I start slowly to eat also food, which I refused always before. I know quite well, that I shall only feed myself with my right hand and with the spoon – I do so mostly but sometimes I do not want.

 In the moment I like to run off quickly in the direction to the lodge or cottage, because this people there like me too. Therefore Lucie must now always be with me, in one way I like that very much although I must laugh about her but mostly only inwardly.

 Yesterday when we where for a walk I picked this little flower for you. You know, mummy, I was happy when Lucie gave me a big kiss of your because I remember you very well.

 I start slowly to help to dress myself. I said already twice quite clearly No. Do you think I shall make a great effort and start to speak once? I will also think about that and – do it perhaps one day.

At the moment I do not need anything to dress, my things are all very nice and if there is something needed, we will tell you . . .

Lucie thanks you so much for your lovely letter and sends her kindest regards.

> I send you lots of love
> and many kisses
> your
> Freddie.

Olivia and her closest woman friend took Freddie to Dr König's Camphill school in April 1951 and within days the letters began arriving from Scotland. She cannot have been surprised by their warmth for on returning to London she had written to Alix Roth, the school matron, that she returned home with 'a heart full of gratitude & a feeling of peace that I [have] left him in hands so much more capable than mine'. Together with the annual school reports these letters were part of a routine that was to last for twelve years. Its other components were night sleepers between King's Cross and Aberdeen for the journeys Olivia made at least twice a year to see Freddie; trips south by Freddie to spend part of his summer holidays with Olivia; precariously wrapped parcels, sent as often as three or four times each month, in which Olivia would none too tidily cram Freddie's favourite sweets, an eye-catching toy or two (which he would soon break), a jersey, a pair of Wellington boots, a sun hat – whatever his nursery mother at Camphill thought was needed, though the sun hat was perhaps as much a reflection of her own Central European upbringing as of the fierceness of the Scottish sun. There were presents, too, for those who looked after him; for Lucie Sieg who wrote the letter in Freddie's name and was his first Camphill nursery mother it was a scarf from the Festival of Britain on London's South Bank that everyone that year wanted to visit. In answer to the letters from Scotland Olivia would send long messages back to the co-workers, as the Camphill staff were called. Full of questions about Freddie's health and behaviour, these letters also contained reminders of what he did and did not like doing, would and would not eat, and were permeated by the anxiety of a woman who had surrendered the person she loved most in the world into the care of others.

Lucie Sieg set the tone in the letter she wrote for Freddie. It is typical of all the ones that were to follow in its awareness that the mother needed reassurance quite as much as her child needed attention, and there was always a stress on each sign of hope (a hope also expressed by König when discussing Freddie with other doctors). Lucie's letters conveyed, too, a sense of her own delight in the Camphill world, and of her and Freddie's part in it, another characteristic of other letters sent from Camphill over the years ahead. The sometimes incorrect English set a pattern, too, for most of the men and women who worked in Camphill were not British-born. Their twists of spelling, grammar and meaning added to the impression that these were communications from a special place; the unusual use of English words seemed to mirror what Freddie felt more accurately than conventional vocabulary and syntax. Freddie's difficulties were not denied, but they were viewed from an angle that was meant to give them meaning rather than leave them as pointless suffering. The anguish so obvious in Olivia's own letters (sometimes preceded and followed by

long telephone calls), her collapses into despair and her
impatience found their reflection in her Camphill correspon-
dents' encouragement to endure.

While looking after Freddie Lucie Sieg reported that he had
come round to drinking a glass of hot milk laced with cod-
liver oil each morning and evening, something Bobbie Raiker
could never get him to do even without the cod-liver oil. He
was also 'warm with us as he never has been', she reported in
another letter a few weeks later. 'You know what he did last
night? When I said "good-night" to the kiddies, he pulled my
head down and gave me a big kiss right on my mouth, he did it
for the first time and I am very proud about it.' The Scottish
weather was stoically, and occasionally joyfully, accepted.
Freddie's first July at Camphill was cold and rainy, 'but as
soon as the sun looks out of the clouds we are outside. To-day
the children were terrible tired. Freddie enjoyed all the little
pools and water-drops everywhere. He was jumping about
and laughing and at the end sooo dirty, sooo tired – *sooo happy*.'

Freddie's nursery mothers changed quite often and
Günhilde, Lucie's successor, described his first Christmas at
Camphill. It was, she wrote, 'full of light and peace. All the
children were extremely good. And on Christmas Eve, when
we all stood round the Christmas tree and Miss Roth [the
school matron] read the Gospel of S. Luke, Freddie with his
candle in his hand really looked like an angel and he was
absolutely perfect.'

Childhood illnesses, chicken pox included, came and went.
At first it was not thought wise to let Freddie attend all the
classes of nursery school for, as one letter explained, 'we have
to find out how much in every direction he can stand'. The
signs of progress reported as the months went by at the same

time hinted at the continuing difficulty of his confrontation with life, hints that Olivia's ever-anxious eye never missed. 'He stopped to tear up his clothes but books are still not quite safe in his hands.' 'He eats well in the moment, specially he liked the bread, which is made in our own bakery and which is very nourishing' (which Olivia took to mean that he was eating poorly before). A description of his sixth birthday in April 1952 was typically touching, yet at the same time contained enough echoes of old problems of behaviour to set Olivia's mind racing.

> [Freddie] enjoyed it from the beginning to the end. At the mealtimes he had a big candle and flowers round his place. In the afternoon, as there were 3 children of mine in bed, we had the birthday-table in my nursery. He had a big cake in the middle and 6 candles, and all over the table the toys which he likes very much, and sweeties and chocolate. He was so very nice, a little bit excited, sometimes dancing round the table. And I am sure he grasped quite properly, that it was a day specially for him. He was really so charming, not sweating once and so happy!

If the birthday party conjured up familiar images of Freddie at his most manic, the Easter celebrations that followed seemed Camphill's world at its most soothing. When the children woke up, Günhilde wrote to Olivia, they found an egg under their beds 'and the surprise started'. There was a morning walk in glorious sunshine along the sandy shore of the Dee but the real excitement started in the afternoon.

> All the children from whole Camphill House gathered together in a big circle and we all sang an Easter song and then off everybody went hunting all the eggs and wonderful things. After that we rolled eggs down the slope which is

at the back of the house and the children had to catch them you can't imagine the noise, laughter, tears and broken eggs! The bigger children still carried on then with singing and playing, but I took my little ones underneath my arms and put them to bed as quick I was able.

A more disturbing picture of Freddie's first couple of years in Scotland was painted by König's right hand Thomas Weihs in a letter to Mildred Creak, the authority on children whom Olivia had consulted in London. On arrival, Weihs wrote, Freddie had been 'unapproachable if not withdrawn, very restless, often screaming or flying into violent tempers without any obvious reason'. He tore up and ate paper and clothes, and daubed his saliva everywhere. He could not dress himself, made no contact with the other children, and seemed to be frightened of them. And although he gave signs of understanding what was said to him, 'most of the time he did not want to listen'.

The earlier letters were not misleading for their chief message was one of patient caring, while Weihs's purpose was to compare the very disturbed boy who had arrived at Camphill with the far more settled child of three years later. In spite of this progress Olivia never reconciled herself to the regular changes in the people looking after Freddie, even though each new nursery mother seemed to fall in love with him. 'He is very "cheeky", just as I like little boys best,' one wrote, '. . . so awake and so full of energie.' 'We are happy – our little treasure Freddie has come back so well and happy,' wrote another after he had been on one of his first trips south for a holiday with Olivia. Some years later another nursery mother confessed to being 'so touched by his brave life and sad case-history. One has to bring to him much love and respect as he is such a noble little personality . . . And you know, it is strange how serious every adult who has to deal with him takes Freddie – somewhere as if he would be an adult person himself.' These tributes of love and admiration were not enough for Olivia. She did not doubt they were genuine, but she was convinced that each new nursery mother, however devoted, would be ignorant of some of Freddie's foibles and would fail to notice things that would never escape her own eye. On one of his first trips to London for a holiday she discovered that his shoes were too tight – she developed a sixth sense that told her if he was suffering some discomfort that he could not speak to anyone about. Never shy in such situations she let his nursery mother know about it, and got a prompt, chastened answer. 'Very sorry indead that I waited so long with his shoes to tell you that they had become too small!! . . . That will not happen again!'

Some of the letters from Scotland described tantalising signs that Freddie might be about to speak. 'He babbles a lot . . . and sometimes he comes near to one or the other word when he tries to speak it.' A love affair with a Teddy bear seemed to give him a new interest in talking. 'He started to call him "Teddy, Teddy", and he spoke it to me as soon as I entered the nursery . . . You can watch the most charming conversation he has with him. Last Wednesday the haircutter was here and when Freddie was finished, he quickly fetched his Teddy for a haircut. He even gives him something to eat from his lunch.' Freddie was twelve when he fell in love with the bear, a toy the size of a four-year-old child. It belonged to another autistic child who showed no interest in it and Freddie, having fallen for it, took it everywhere. He had it in his bed at night, and once pretended it had wet the sheets, and giggled with delight when Gerda Blok, his house mother at the time, discovered his trick.

Gerda, too, was enchanted by him, and thought him 'so lovely and orginal I wished I would have kids like this'. She did not find him unmanageable, and she was encouraged by his passion for the bear. Freddie had always broken and torn apart his other toys but he seemed able to connect with this toy animal. He did once make a hole in its stomach to see what was inside, but afterwards coloured the wound with a red crayon and took it to the school nurse to be bandaged. Gerda taught him to say new words like Fur and Paw and they are still among the few words he says today. He remained mischievous. He would pee into a bottle and then pour it into the concave porcelain lightshade in his dormitory, turn on the light and giggle as the liquid sizzled. Thanks to the Teddy bear he became less interested in eating paper and balloons, though he still sometimes hid newspaper under his mattress and at night chewed it into little balls which he flicked onto the ceiling, a habit Gerda found endearing more than anything else. 'It was so nice the things he invented, so original.'

Hard though it was for Olivia to believe, Freddie gradually became a regular schoolboy. The Central Europeans who inspired the Camphill experiment were determined to create a proper British school, so Freddie and the other boys wore grey flannel shorts, sweaters, white shirts and ties, and in winter duffle coats (König had first decreed that caps and blazers be worn but they were soon abandoned). The school was a curious marriage of infinite patience and warmth with the traditional values of *Mitteleuropa*, the birthplace of most of the teachers. An article about Camphill that appeared in *Picture Post* in 1949 and drew much attention to it was headlined 'A school where love is a cure', but König and his followers never equated love with softness. They were free of any inner uncertainty that might have prevented them imposing discipline, and Dr Spock failed to win admirers among them. The staff could be as ingenious as they liked. Friedwart Bock, Freddie's class teacher for his first few years, noticed that light had a disturbing effect on him, particularly the strong light of the northern summer when he could become 'quite weightless, like an elementary particle'. Bock hit on the idea of suggesting to Freddie that he should rest every now and then by climbing into a cupboard in the classroom (it was typical of Camphill that such advice was offered as a 'suggestion'). Freddie agreed and seemed to benefit from it. He remained fascinated by light, and when each year Bock took a picture of his class Freddie's fair head was instantly recognisable in the photograph, for it is the one turned up to the sky while the other children look towards the camera. Like any ordinary schoolboy Freddie had a nickname, the Bucket, and sometimes managed to make a special friend of the child he sat next to. One of these was the daughter of a Camphill co-worker, whose children attended the first years of school alongside the handicapped pupils. She knew him in one of his good periods and remembered him as living 'in a different landscape from the rest of us, one where the sun was always shining'.

The school never failed to cast its spell over Olivia during her visits. She found many of its ways strange, and some of them comic, but she was awed by its handling of the children. Camphill House was a grey granite mansion just outside Aberdeen in the Dee valley. It stood in park-like grounds, and looked down a grassy slope (where the eggs were rolled on Easter day) to the fast-flowing river Dee below, the sort of stern Scottish building Olivia knew well from her own childhood holidays in the north. This was the heart of the school, for it was here that König had his living quarters and his library full of medical books and journals, and where he took his meals in the kitchen that was warmed by an Aga stove. Later Freddie moved to other nearby and equally handsome estates that the school gradually acquired; first to Murtle, a white stucco classical temple designed by the most fashionable architect of nineteenth-century Aberdeen, and finally to a former hunting lodge, another grey and granite house, at Newton Dee. Less familiar were the new buildings that Camphill put up, for König was an ambitious builder. Here there were suggestions of Art Nouveau sinuousness, both in roof lines and the use of carved wood. Floors and staircases were usually of wood, too, creating *gemütlich* interiors with a distinctly Central European feel.

Sometimes when Olivia visited Freddie she would eat in his house, and she watched amazed as restless children were calmed by rituals of silence and the recital of grace so that, however disturbed, they were able to sit together at tables with their carers like any large family. A candle was lit at the beginning of the meal, and extinguished at the end. Each child had its own napkin in a bag embroidered with its name. Everyone helped wash up, and drying dishes was the first domestic skill Freddie acquired. Electric dishwashers were (and still are) spurned and so in the first years were floor polishing machines so that boys could learn the satisfaction of shining the wood floors with traditional buffers. Brought gently into the morning by the sound of a flute or a recorder that was played along the corridors, the children were soothed before going to sleep by the music of a lyre. Olivia watched children whose instinct was to throw their bodies about like fish struggling to keep quiet as they watched the puppet shows that Camphill used as a discreet path to the emotions of those like Freddie who would have shrunk from a direct approach.

By this time deeply and uncritically religious herself, Olivia was enchanted by the simple services held every Sunday for the children and by the more elaborate ceremonies celebrating the Christian and seasonal calendar that were an important part in the school's life. Even a sceptical child care professional who was unsympathetic to the school's religious side was impressed by a visit to Camphill in those years. 'They preached at these broken-down children – and it worked.' Another equally doubting observer remembered that 'the handicapped children at Camphill never looked apologetic. They were totally at home with everyone.'

Freddie's dark side, though, did not vanish. Deeply attached to Gerda – this relationship was itself a sign of his progress – he had the habit of going into her room even when she was not there and lying on her bed and gazing at the sky through the window. One day when she was away he went to her room and found it locked. Somehow he found his way to the boiler room which was meant to be out of bounds. No one knew why he burned his toy. Perhaps he opened the furnace door to watch the flames – he liked fire – and finding them low threw in the once beloved bear to bring them back to life.

In the end the bear failed to bring out Freddie's speech as did every other method that was tried. One involved putting him in a barrel of warm peat water while he did speech exercises. Freddie enjoyed this, and he made serious attempts to talk but still did not manage it. Aged ten, he had shot out single words, though at the cost of emotional strain, and now his efforts

were increasingly despairing, leading Camphill to suppose
that brain damage might have left him aphasic, able to
understand only the simplest words and gestures. In puberty
aphasic children's frustration at being unable to express their
mounting feelings may turn to violence, and so it was with
Freddie. Between the age of thirteen and fourteen he seemed
to be two people, one of them with his best qualities, the other
(in the words of his school report for that year) driven by a
'restless, destructive and aggressive and greedy passion'.

Olivia had her first inkling of this during a visit to Scotland
in April 1960. After 'two glorious days' there was a frightening scene, with Freddie 'throwing himself on the ground on
his knees & banging his head violently against the stones'.
Olivia rushed him back to the Station Hotel in Aberdeen
where she was staying and took him through a back door up to
her room. He calmed down there, but was restless for the
remainder of the day, and when they had lunch his hands
shook as he crammed food into his mouth. Later, as the crisis
deepened, he smashed glasses and window panes, and on one
occasion filled a bath to overflowing and then jumped in
wearing his clothes. Sometimes he hummed without break
and then passed into long bouts of giggling when it was
impossible to make contact with him. He would cry and howl
and urinate anywhere, and ate large quantities of wood, paper
and rubber. It became impossible for him to attend school.
The restlessness and rocking continued at night and for almost
a year he would not sleep properly, so one of the male co-
workers had to move his bed into Freddie's room to keep
constant watch over him. Olivia knew about this, and suffered
with him. It was small consolation to her that during this
period there were also days when he behaved well, and for the

first time in his life helped to serve at meals and even tried to tell stories by means of noises and gestures. He was, the report said, either a lamb or a little wolf, and it was this Jekyll and Hyde capacity for sudden change that scared her most.

Freddie spent most of this critical period living with Friedwart Bock and his wife Nora, and however disturbed his behaviour they always felt he wanted them to help him. 'He would take your hand and put his head on your shoulder as though to ask for help.' Small wonder Olivia did not lose her trust in Camphill, and her belief in the school first nourished by König was further sustained by Thomas Weihs, his much younger successor as superintendent of Camphill schools. Weihs, like König, was Vienna-born, and like him, too, a powerfully attractive figure. Photographs of him as a young man show him looking remarkably like the Austrian ski instructor who picked Olivia up whenever she fell down on her skiing honeymoon before the war, and when she got to know him better she always referred to him as 'darling Thomas'. But neither the atmosphere of Camphill nor the mesmeric, for Olivia, presence of König and Weihs could lessen her despair when during his holidays with her Freddie reverted to his bad old ways.

'Did it happen often that Freddie bit you?' asked his nursery mother in a letter written after Freddie had been on holiday with Olivia in 1953 (Freddie always pinched people he was angry with but biting was something new). 'I dont hope it,' the letter continued. 'He has never found out the possibility of biting here, that little rascal. Isn't he a wonderful little fellow?' It was easier to smile at such things in the structured world of Camphill, where life was organised to support the children and, equally important where care of the handicapped is concerned, also those who taught and looked after them. When Freddie behaved badly on holiday with Olivia she was often on her own and had no one apart from Bobbie Raiker to call on who knew how to cope with him. König had spotted at their first meeting that Olivia was part of Freddie's problem; not the cause of it, of course, but contributing to its development by the anxiety she felt for him. There was always a speck of guilt because she had sent Freddie away to school rather than look after him herself, for she could not see as clearly as others that this was the best thing she could do for him. It was not surprising that when she was with him she spoiled him to make up for the months she had not seen him. Bobbie sometimes went with Olivia to Camphill and disapproved of the way she treated Freddie during those trips. They would pick him up at the school and then drive back for lunch at the Station Hotel. Olivia always arrived at Camphill with a bag of sweets and chocolates, but at each village they passed through she would stop to buy him an ice cream or more sweets. Small wonder, thought Bobbie, that once when they sat down to lunch in the hotel dining room Freddie was sick over the table before they had begun to eat the soup.

On other occasions, when Olivia's Scottish sense of economy got the upper hand, she would stay as a paying guest in a house in a nearby village, though the cold and damp she often had to put up with were bad for the arthritis she already suffered from. She could ignore the discomfort because of the happiness of being with Freddie, particularly when he was in good form. Then she did not mind his mischievousness and sometimes conspired in it, as when she took him to lunch at the Caledonian, Aberdeen's grandest hotel, and Freddie, finding Brussels sprouts on his plate, picked them up and put them unnoticed into the pocket of a man at the next table. Olivia said nothing – the man would discover them soon enough without her help – but told the story when they got back to Camphill, where everyone laughed and said how typical of dear Freddie. Her own appreciation of his mischievous moods and princely manner was one of the strongest bonds with Freddie, and she loved Camphill more because it appreciated them too.

The summer holidays were an even greater strain. Olivia knew that she fretted too much for Freddie's good, and two years after he left for Scotland she wrote apologetically to König that she 'could never be as calm & unworried as I should like' when she was with Freddie, and 'even when I see a letter from Camphill I find my hands shaking as I open it'. It soon became obvious Freddie could not spend several weeks' holiday in the London flat which he roamed in search of amusement and, unless constantly watched, soon had washbasins overflowing and electric plugs pulled apart. Remembering the childhood holidays at her family's Gothic mansions on the Welsh coast Olivia hit on the idea of taking him to the quiet Suffolk seaside village of Walberswick. But though she equipped herself with the necessary buckets and spades and picnic baskets the result could not be the same. At first they stayed in lodgings, where both Freddie and she caught fleas and he was often uncontrollable, but she soon bought a pleasant cottage with a garden in the middle of the village. This was to be Freddie's world, a place and a way of life designed for him, but the greater space gave him more freedom of movement and made looking after him even more exhausting, and in 1956 she admitted her defeat to König. That summer had been 'more difficult than any we've had &

by the end I was really ill'. Freddie was too big and fast for her, and sometimes was very rough, knocking people off bicycles and once pushing a fisherman into a river. He was also 'inclined to attack any stranger who speaks to me . . .' It was all the harder to bear because at moments he was 'closer than he has ever been . . . [but] now he loves me he seems to want to possess me utterly. By the end I was covered in bruises & bites & so tired I could not eat or sleep.'

Walberswick had raised expectations he could enjoy the seaside life of an ordinary child, but when he remained locked in his old, disruptive patterns of behaviour his mother's disappointment was all the greater. It was even harder to bear because as he grew up he still looked like a normal, active boy. He had gone to Camphill with a child's plump, round face. By the time of the holidays on the Suffolk coast he was thinning out, but without losing his good looks. And in spite of the cautiously hopeful report from Camphill, his continuing inability to talk cast a shadow over any hope that he might one day lead a more ordinary life. Olivia had at first delighted in his efforts to say words like 'Teddy' and 'fur' but eventually it became frustrating to hear him repeat this tiny vocabulary like an animal performing tricks it does not understand.

If the early letters from Camphill supported Olivia by their loving account of Freddie's life and progress, in later years they were sometimes almost entirely directed towards con-soling a mother close to losing heart. This encouragement was most needed whenever she had seen him and gone away depressed that, though perhaps he was as happy as he could be, he was not improving in the way she so desperately wanted. 'I have often the feeling that he is very near to be normal in many ways,' his nursery mother wrote encouragingly after Olivia had been to visit Freddie one summer, but then, apologising for her 'crooked English', she went on:

> dear Mrs Frankland . . . I hope you have overcome your depression about Freddie. I think you and he belong together like a real mother and child. You had to sacrifice a tremendous amount in agreeing with the state he is in – but you *are* able to accept and still love – how many others can do that? Imagine he would be with his real mother! Which trial – when they would have seen in which way he developed. I am sure you and he are the better relatives than he with his natural mother.

Another visit to Scotland the following winter brought on a similar bout of depression, and in turn another letter of encouragement. Torn along its edges, it bears the signs of having been much read. Going beyond the usual attempt to give her heart, it urged Olivia to accept her child's destiny rather than to fight against it.

> I was so sad to hear that *you* were so sad and defeated on your return [from Camphill to London], although I can in a way understand it and feel my way into it. But I have a very strong impression about Freddie and that is that he in a way has arranged for his destiny very well. I personally am convinced of the existence of a Guardian Angel belonging to each one of us who leads and guides our destiny and the angels of the children we care for are often very tangible for us. Freddie certainly has a strong and good protection of his own and though he is very ill I always feel he is safe and will not be disposed to anything that he could not really manage. All this may sound at first somewhat strange to you but if you carry these thoughts a little around with you for a while may be you will be able to understand me, and it may also be of a help to you.

Such thoughts did help, though it was typical of Olivia that she did not leave matters to his Guardian Angel, but tried to force his hand when she saw the chance. In spite of her admiration for König and Thomas Weihs she was never overawed by them any more than by other medical specialists she knew. She might give in to temporary enthusiasm for this or that doctor and his favourite remedy – to her later regret a fashionable dentist persuaded her, soon after Freddie went to Camphill, that he could cure her sinus trouble by extracting all her teeth – but she always supposed she might find someone with better advice round the next corner. Shortly after Freddie began his schooling in Scotland Olivia heard of a London healer called Mary Austen. Olivia was never clear about what Mary Austen did for Freddie. She said Mary Austen was 'putting Freddie on the box', and though she never said she absolutely believed in the 'box' she never dismissed it as nonsense. Her attitude was that it might do good, and could do no harm.

Mrs Austen acquired a good practice in London and, being a sensible Scot, claimed never to promise anything she could not deliver. A well-off couple once asked her to cure their young son who seemed to be a congenital liar. Send him to Eton, Mary Austen advised them, and let them teach him to lie with grace. Olivia took Freddie to see her on one of his first holidays from Camphill. Mary Austen drew up astrological charts for the three of them, and told Olivia she could 'deal with his hormones and emotions'. Her apparatus was a so-called 'radionics box' which, according to Stephen Fulder's *The Handbook of Complementary Medicine*, is based on the theory that 'all life forms, including man, are submerged in and interpenetrated by a common field of energy'. The medical possibilities of radionics were first explored by an American doctor at the beginning of the century. Mary Austen used homely terms to describe her British-made box, explaining that it worked 'on the same principle as radio and TV transmissions'. Consisting of copper wiring and magnets, the relevant parts of the patient's body were fed into it as numbers through dials that did indeed look like the knobs on an old-fashioned radio. At the same time a small specimen from the patient such as a speck of blood or piece of hair was put in an envelope and inserted onto a sensitive plate in the box. The box both diagnosed and treated, but could only be used by those with the skill. What counted were the operator's hands: Mary Austen described hers as 'feeling it out'.

From then on Olivia regularly rang up the healer to ask her how Freddie was. Sometimes Mary Austen would telephone to warn Olivia of problems, for example, that Freddie's teeth needed looking at, which in one case turned out to be true. When there was a full moon, which Olivia believed disturbed Freddie, Mary Austen would put him on two boxes instead of the usual one. The beauty of it was that the box – so the theory went – could work its benign influence on Freddie wherever he was and, since it did not interfere with any other treatment, Olivia did not have to tell Camphill what she was doing. That Mary Austen was always available at the end of the telephone line for Olivia to consult and pour her heart out to became a powerful added attraction as the years went by. She made one such telephone call when Freddie was in London with her for one of his now only brief holidays. He was thirteen and going through puberty, and he exposed himself while they were in Regent's Park. Someone complained and the police were called. It was a nasty business, not because it embarrassed

Olivia (she could turn most things he did into a joke) but because it forced her to look into a future when Freddie's behaviour might become so difficult that even Camphill would no longer be able to look after him.

The sixteen-year-old boy described in Freddie's final school report was nevertheless unrecognisable from the wild creature that had been brought to Scotland ten years earlier. He had emerged from the puberty crisis and become much more composed apart from restless, giggling spells that happened about once every month. He seldom became really wild, and these spells, when they happened, did not last long. His teachers thought he had grown more appreciative of others and now understood 'a great deal when one talks to him and his consciousness is quite awake where his own deeds and misdeeds are concerned'. He was eating well, perhaps too well, for he had got the habit of pinching food from the kitchen, but he still searched waste-paper baskets for paper to eat and whenever he could took a large piece to bed with him. He had sat through school classes. Organic chemistry, Napoleon and Oliver Cromwell, the respiratory system, the steam pump and the geography of Australia and New Zealand were among his form's subjects in that final year, it being Camphill's practice to move children up through classes according to age regardless of whether they could grasp much or anything of what was taught.

Left to his own devices he liked being out of doors, 'and is often seen jumping about, balancing paper in his hands'. Indoors he tended to lie on his bed, and only took part in the activities of the other boys when encouraged to. He had become a good worker, making the 'great step' of doing jobs that combined a number of activities, such as looking after a dormitory or cleaning the dining room, but he 'still does not regard work as a matter of necessity but rather as a kind of game . . . He would not mind if he were not asked to do any.'

For a mother worried about what would happen next to her son the progress noted in the report was of course insufficient. At Camphill the story of the sixteen-year-old Freddie was seen from a different point of view, and the school's tranquil optimism permeated a description of Freddie's years there that was published in the Camphill house magazine *The Cresset*. It captured what his teachers believed to be the essence of his life at Camphill, and conveyed his charming but at time frightening complexity both as a child and a teenager. But it also contained a good deal more than mere description of Freddie: beguiling in its acceptance of his foibles, it was an expression of the most positive approach possible to the difficulties of the handicapped, and of the belief that helping them is of as much value to the helper as to the one that is helped. Above all it was infused with a conviction that many people cannot accept, namely that the life of someone like Freddie has a purpose. It was Olivia and Freddie's good fortune that Camphill did not recognise the word despair.

Freddie [in the original version his name was disguised as Jeremy] came to us twelve years ago, an unusually beautiful child of five – fair-haired, blue-eyed, intelligent, but although he absorbed everything that went on around him, he never spoke, apart from some odd sounds. Already as a baby, he had always been very detached and far away, rocking a great deal and not seeming to be interested in other children, or indeed in anyone . . .

He was very wild when he came [to Camphill], running about in any direction, easily flying into a temper; he did not

like the other children – there were too many of them and
they got in his way, so he would pinch and kick them. He
was like a drop of quicksilver, never still, running on tiptoe
over the ground, but gradually, gradually he learnt to be
still, at least when others were, in morning prayer or story-
lesson or puppet-show. This was not easy for him and it
took not only days or weeks but months and years to help
him to be at peace with himself, hours of intensive therapy,
worked out especially for such children, years of merely
living the quiet and unhurried rhythm of nursery and
dormitory life.

As he grew older, his difficulties did not decrease; at
times he was very restless and uncontrolled, he hardly slept
for nights on end . . . He thoroughly enjoyed going to
school which he started at the age of seven and although he
did not produce a great deal in his books, he followed what
his teacher said or did with real interest, especially if it had
to do with chemistry or physics; in the later years of school
he followed experiments with some measure of intelligence. He was not a very peaceful member of his class,
some days being restless, jumping up and down and
giggling constantly. But he was grateful to be able to go to
school, to be included in all that went on.

Freddie could not bear to get himself dirty; if by some
dreadful mischance, his hands became muddy, he had to fly
at once to the nearest tap. Clay-modelling . . . was
anathema to him; those who cannot stand the thought of
plunging their fingers into grease or jam can perhaps
understand this feeling of Freddie's although he had a
different reason for his repulsion. For clay is of the earth, a
cold, hard and solid substance and Freddie is a light, ethereal
being, dancing Puck-like hither and thither, a finger here,
an inquisitive look there – he would rather have nothing to
do with this earth of ours.

His speaking was for a long time a great riddle; he had a
few sounds and one could often guess what he wanted to say,
especially as he was very good at pointing to whatever he

wanted. But there was the question: could he or could he not speak, did he want to or not? When he was younger he made many more attempts than he does now and he often seemed on the brink of speech, copying sounds again and again. Growing older, however, he became more and more frustrated whenever we tried to make him speak and we then realised that he is unable to, however much he would love to and however much of a release it would be for him to express himself in words. But this will never be, although his understanding for the visual world is remarkably good.

At times Freddie is very aggressive, usually because he feels slighted by someone, or because he is unable to make himself understood, but also because he 'just feels like that'. His most difficult time was when he entered puberty, when, as it were, he simply had to come down to earth, willy-nilly and whether he wanted to or not . . . Gradually the gaps between these spells grew farther apart until they quietly slipped out of existence. Not that he is a peaceful fellow now by any means, but he is now much more balanced; if he does become over-excited one can call on him and he quite soon calms down again.

Freddie is cheeky. There is no other word to describe him – cheeky in a Puck-like way, grinning at one with wide open eyes as if to say, 'Well, what are you going to do with me now?' or giggling and looking very knowledgeable as if he wonders how far he can go this time. Being cross with him when he is in this kind of mood has no effect whatsoever, one can only learn to be patient. When he is in a good state, however, and does something wrong he knows very well that he has misbehaved and will look most contrite, taking one's hand and trying to speak . . .

In his home life, Freddie is even now no paragon; he still likes to pinch (both people and food!), he still gets angry at times but how much more he is in harmony with his surroundings, more of a citizen of this world, than the Freddie of only a few years ago! Is it not a miracle that he has learnt to weave so perfectly, and is it not completely worthwhile to have helped him through all the difficult times, to give him the satisfaction of being able to *do* something, to work for his living? How can we not be grateful to children like Freddie who teach us, perhaps in a harder way than we would like, that life is not meaningless, that there is a golden thread of destiny along which each one of us walks, but that some of us, the Freddies of this world, need more help and guidance to follow this thread . . .

6

The Carers

In the spring of 1963, when Freddie turned seventeen, Thomas Weihs wrote to assure Olivia that he would fight his hardest to get Freddie into one of Camphill's new villages. 'We are well aware and quite determined that we will have to battle for Freddie to be somewhere in our Movement . . . yet I feel we must be confident and full of trust.'

The glamorous Weihs had taken over as superintendent of Camphill schools six years earlier, though König was to remain its guardian spirit until his death in 1966. Like König, Weihs was concerned with all aspects of what Camphill called curative education (an anglicised version of the *Heilpädagogik*, the synthesis of educational and medical methods practised in Germany and Austria and which, in its more conventional form, was epitomised by Hans Asperger). Weihs particularly endeared himself to Olivia because she sensed his heightened interest in autistic children like Freddie. He saw autism as 'a special challenge', and admitted to feeling 'more involved in, more responsible for this condition' than for many others. He had his own approach – a Camphill approach – to autism. He was conventional enough in interpreting it as an inability of the child to fit into the social world around it and, more

significantly, an inability 'to develop an appropriate experience of Self'. Catholic about the possible causes of autism,
he saw the essence of the autistic child's drama in its inability to
cope with the growing awareness of the self that normal
children develop between their second and third years. The
infant's belief that the world is an extension of itself fades as it
begins to distinguish for the first time between itself and a
world it is only part of. Whatever the reason, the autistic child
cannot cope with this crucial moment in growing up; instead
there is a 'panic reaction to the overpowering and precipitate
awakening of their own ego-experience'. The result, Weihs
believed, could be

> a self-denial, an increasing resistance to the integration of
> the ego, to the extent that, for example, the child uses the
> pronoun 'I' impartially, as though it were a designation like
> any other, for any other person, or refers to himself as 'you'
> or simply by his own name as though he were someone
> else. This transposition of the personal pronoun is perhaps
> the most unique and classical demonstration of the panic-
> reaction against the dawn of one's ego-experience.

The autistic child's failure to experience itself as a person
explained why it could not form proper relationships with
other people: someone who does not acknowledge his own
existence can scarcely recognise the full existence of others. It
also explained why an autistic child is so much happier in the
world of inanimate objects like light switches that can be
switched on and off with absolutely predictable results, or
shoes that can be put into neat straight lines. 'In the inanimate
world he can display, practise and develop his faculties, skills,
manual dexterity and intelligence freely, without coming up

against his threatening developmental problem, that of encroaching self-awareness.'

Weihs believed that treating the autistic child was therefore a matter of helping it to acknowledge and develop its self. None of these ideas were controversial but in his writing on autism Weihs occasionally slipped in suggestions that moved that debate on to quite another plane, and one where most professionals would not have followed him. For example he turned to the Book of Genesis for a story that he believed mirrored the child's fright at having to recognise, for the first time, its own separate self. The modern world gave the biblical account of the temptation and fall of Adam a sexual interpretation. Weihs suggested this was because of a failure to understand that Freud's discovery of infantile sexuality meant not merely sexual activity but the 'knowing of creative power' that comes to a child when it recognises its separate self. Adam's fall, understood in terms of man's evolution, could similarly mean that 'this creative power was injected into Man prematurely'. What possible relevance, a specialist might ask, could the myths of Genesis have to the treatment of the mentally handicapped? The answer for Weihs and those who worked with him at Camphill was – everything.

In the letter to Olivia expressing his determination to keep Freddie, Weihs used the word 'Movement', an odd way of describing a school for children with learning and behaviour problems. In fact it was obvious to anyone who went there that Camphill was a great deal more than a school: it was a community and way of life that embraced both children and adults. That in itself was not new in the treatment of handicapped children. Hans Asperger and Bruno Bettelheim had both stressed the need to create an all-embracing thera-

peutic environment for autistic children. Bettelheim had gone
into Hitler's concentration camps a convinced practitioner of
psychoanalysis. He was much less sure about it when he came
out. Psychoanalysis, his camp experience suggested, under-
estimated the power of environment to bring about radical
change in personality, as in the dramatic example of the
prisoners turned by their camp existence into autistic-like
'Moslems'. He concluded that while psychoanalysis might
reveal what was hidden in man, it could not explain what
made a 'good' person or a 'good' life, and was therefore an
inadequate approach for the treatment of autistics. Putting
together his observations from the camps with his knowledge
of these children he decided that what the latter most needed
was 'an environment that offered meaningful human relations, satisfying living conditions, and significant goals, not
simply the application of psychoanalysis to the life they
already knew'. His aim was to create 'a milieu that was totally
therapeutic and still a real life setting'.

Long before the war Asperger had begun to create a
therapeutic environment for children in the University
Pediatric Clinic in Vienna. The children's remedial ward was
transformed from the usual neat lines of hospital beds into
specially built and spacious rooms with furniture and wall
paintings all designed by one architect. Asperger developed
programmes of work, education and play for his children in
which the Freudian analysis that dominated Vienna at that
time played no part at all. The atmosphere of such a place
naturally depended on the people who worked there, and
Asperger insisted that everyone employed by him be
'governed by the wish to understand and help children'.

Olivia only gradually came to appreciate the novelty of

Camphill and the reason the people who worked there thought of themselves as a Movement. Dr König, so small yet so authoritative, led a little team of mostly foreigners with strange names and still imperfect mastery of the English language. With her weakness for the out-of-the-way and the unusual she quite liked that, just as she liked the religious ceremonies that she noticed were such an important part of Camphill life. Her clergyman father had left her with little loyalty to the traditional rites of the Church of England. Her own faith was idiosyncratic and undenominational and she had no trouble in enjoying the sometimes unusual Camphill services especially as Freddie seemed to enjoy them too. She learned that the people who worked at Camphill, the co-workers, got no salaries apart from 2s. 6d. weekly pocket money, and that when they needed clothes or other essential things the community bought them. And although she never doubted their love for Freddie, she became aware of a calmness carried to the point of detachment in these men and women who spent so much of their lives with very difficult children, a calmness conveyed in the letter of the nursery mother who counselled Olivia not to worry so much because Freddie was somehow taking care of his own destiny.

Everything Olivia found strange at Camphill and some-times commented on with amusement was part of a greater whole, quite foreign not just to Olivia but also to the British experience. Everything there was linked, from the altar frames of sinuously carved wood in the Camphill chapel where Freddie went to his first service to the large hall with the contours of an Art Nouveau whale that was built next to the classic mansion at Murtle; from the graces the children heard before meals to the paintings on the walls of their houses that recalled Turner at his haziest. Without realising it, Olivia had once again found herself in a world whose origins went back to Vienna and the fertile last years of the Austrian empire. But if her brief acquaintance with Viennese psychoanalysis in the person of Gwen Evans was unhappy, her scarcely more comprehending encounter with the ideas and beliefs that inspired Camphill was to develop quite differently. It was an encounter that raised the questions of most passionate concern to any family with a handicapped member. Who could one trust to look after such a child, and was it possible to trust their good will as well as their professional competence? Was kindness alone enough motivation for taking care of people condemned to lives that could easily seem pointless? These questions were of special importance to a mother who was beginning to understand that her handicapped but beautiful little boy was growing up into a still handicapped but far less immediately attractive adult, and as such would one day no longer be able to count on the sympathy shown children, no matter how difficult.

The handicapped are vulnerable, yet they are also often exhausting and exasperating – a dangerous combination that invites neglect if not maltreatment. Care for them is seldom lightened by the dramatic successes that make the work of the conventional doctor and surgeon so rewarding. The carer may be motivated by scientific interest, by religious, or simply human, compassion. Nevertheless it is hard to remain at all times enthusiastically committed to looking after the permanently handicapped, or to avoid becoming downhearted over their apparently pointless fate. Ordinary doctors, Thomas Weihs pointed out, were so carried away by the increasing treatability of illness that they became helpless when faced with the untreatable. For this reason, when a handicapped child was taken to a specialist, 'the consultation ends on a note of finality, and this sense of impotent finality gives rise to fear in the parent' – an accurate description of some of the encounters Olivia and Freddie had in Harley Street. Weihs argued that the mistake was to look for a cure rather than looking at the child's development. This could be achieved not by changing the child, 'but by changing the understanding and attitude of persons in the environment of the child'. One of König's and Camphill's greatest contributions to the education and development of such children was to assert their positive value and the meaningfulness of their at first sight meaningless lives. The lively, unapologetic boys and girls that visitors were surprised to discover at Camphill were the result of this approach, and in Freddie's case the result was lasting. Something from Camphill would seem to stay with him during the most dangerous moments of his life; and to provide the rock on which he could build his recoveries. For that reason the origins of Camphill's unusual methods and beliefs are part of his story too.

Karl König was born in Vienna in 1902, the only child of modest Jewish shopkeepers. His feet were slightly crippled from birth and he never grew to average height, but as he became older his small stature served to accentuate his large head and strikingly eloquent eyes. He celebrated his bar mitzvah like any other Jewish teenage boy, but his parents had discovered a picture of Jesus Christ in his bedroom when he was only eleven, and he soon converted to Christianity. König studied medicine, and showed unusual talent as an embryologist, but he became interested in the treatment of children in need of special care, working in Silesia until he was forced by

Nazi hostility to return to Vienna in 1936. He quickly became popular in his home city both as a physician and a lecturer. Among those who went to hear him were Thomas Weihs and another young Viennese medical student called Peter Roth. Both came from well-off, assimilated Jewish families; both later became Freddie's guardians. König escaped from Vienna in the nick of time after Hitler's annexation of Austria in March 1938, and with his wife Tilla, Thomas Weihs, Roth and a tiny band of other followers found refuge in Britain on the eve of war. Almost no one in the group spoke more than a few words of English, and König did not even consider his new island home to be part of Europe. The British people's way of life, he wrote later, 'was not my way and their past was almost unknown to me', and he would remember the wartime Scottish north as 'a human desert'. Nevertheless he was determined to do something to oppose the Nazis who had turned his continent into 'a camp of nationalists'. He began plans to 'take a morsel of the true European destiny and make it into a seed so that some of its real task may be preserved . . . a piece of its humanity, of its inner freedom, of its longing for peace, of its dignity'.

The expulsion of this doctor who represented the best of Vienna and of *Mitteleuropa* by that other, also typical in his way, offspring of Vienna, Adolf Hitler, might have remained one of the many unrecorded ironies that give the history of twentieth-century Europe its peculiar bitterness. König, though, was too gifted not to make his mark. As a teenager he had studied with what he himself called 'primeval force', devouring the work of such different sages as Freud, Buddha, Lao Tzu and Balzac as well as his chief – and, for the schoolboy son of Orthodox Jews, unexpected – passion, the New

Testament. When König was nineteen he began reading Rudolf Steiner and everything he had learned and thought about till then fell into a coherent whole. Steiner, who died in 1926, was another Austrian phenomenon: a polymathic talent as ambitious and rich as a Mahler symphony, and as remarkable in his way as that other Viennese pioneer, Sigmund Freud, though a good deal more controversial. Typically after Thomas Weihs and Peter Roth learned about some of Steiner's ideas during that first lecture of König's they assured each other that once was enough. They had gone to listen to König because they had a niggling feeling that something was lacking in the ordinary medical training they were getting, but his message was too strange for them. They both belonged to Vienna's *jeunesse dorée*. Their well-to-do Jewish families had converted to nominal Christianity – they considered themselves patriotic Austrians until Hitler forced them to remember their Jewish origins – and Weihs had little interest in religion of any kind, let alone an exotic brand like Rudolf Steiner's. Yet the two of them did return to hear König a second time, and after that would remain loyal to both him and Steiner for the rest of their lives.

Steiner belonged to that group of turn-of-the-century explorers of religion who hoped to pass beyond mere belief to scientific knowledge of spiritual truths. This was heady stuff, and it turned the heads of several of the spiritual pioneers themselves, most famously Mme Blavatsky, the stoutly built Russian aristocrat who was one of the great adventuresses of the nineteenth century. Helena Blavatsky was co-founder of the Theosophical Society to which Steiner for a while belonged because it was the first audience ready to listen to him. She claimed to be both guru and occult voyager, and to be in touch with the Great White Brothers of the Universe, the spirits who, according to her, controlled the world.

Although Steiner made claims many dismissed as fantastic he was, unlike Blavatsky, always serious and serious-looking; indeed if a film were ever made about him the British actor Jeremy Irons should play his part for he shares his dark intensity of looks. Steiner was a learned man. In his auto-biography *The Story of My Life* he comes across as idealistic and a little ponderous, and it is not surprising he soon broke with the mercurial Blavatsky and her often raffish friends. But like them Steiner remained committed to the belief in a universal key to life, a key he claimed to have discovered by means of an occult science as ambitious as anything Blavatsky thought up, and which he called anthroposophy. It was anthroposophy that struck the young Karl König with the brightness of sun emerging from dark cloud, and it was the whole complex of anthroposophy that Thomas Weihs, Peter Roth and the other men and women who went to work at Camphill learned from König. They embraced, as Camphill today still embraces, Steinerism in its entirety, ranging from the most practical insights into curative education, architec-ture and community living to belief in *karma* or destiny, reincarnation, and a spirit world and spirit history which is to anthroposophists as real as the visible world that is the subject matter of orthodox science. It is a whole whose parts cannot be separated. Anthroposophy for a man like König included the belief that humankind's greatest enemies are the spirits Lucifer and Ahriman who embody pride and materialism, *and* the conviction that a deeply disturbed child like Freddie Bucknill, whom no one else seemed to know what to do with, could be helped to live a life that had meaning.

Small wonder the young Thomas Weihs and Peter Roth were at first unable to make the jump of faith that König demanded, a jump that meant accepting him not only as a doctor who had proved his skill as a healer of children, but also as a teacher of spiritual truths that were part of a mighty cosmic theory. If Weihs and others could make that jump and never once look back, the reason lay in part in Steiner's own character and achievements. He came from a simple background – his father was a huntsman who later worked on the Austro-Hungarian railways – but he received an excellent education in Vienna during which he developed a passion for Goethe, the greatest of German sages, and in particular for his scientific writing. His skill as a Goethe scholar won him an invitation, at the age of twenty-three, to edit Goethe's scientific works for a new collected edition under preparation in Weimar, which at the time was still ruled by the old Grand Duke who remembered seeing Goethe as a boy. In Weimar Steiner met many of the famous people of the day and was asked by the sister of Nietzsche to put in order the library of the great but already blind philosopher. He knew the Austrian socialist leader Victor Adler and would later lecture to German workers at a Berlin school founded by Karl Liebknecht, but typically he abhorred the Marxist tide that was sweeping over the left-wing movements of Europe. 'It was a personal distress to me,' he wrote in his autobiography, 'to hear men say that the material economic forces in human history carried forward man's real evolution and that the spiritual was only an ideal superstructure.' For Steiner it was 'the tragedy of the times' that social and political questions should have fallen into the hands of men and women 'wholly possessed by the materialism of contemporary history'.

Steiner's belief in the supremacy of the spiritual set him
against both the Bolshevik revolution in Russia and the early
National Socialists in Germany. The latter soon threatened his
life, forcing him to leave Germany, and both communists and
Nazis continued to do Steiner the posthumous honour of
persecuting his followers whenever they got the chance. His
belief made him an isolated figure, but he had begun to
reconcile himself to that in boyhood, when he first felt he was
able to 'see' things of a higher order of reality than anything in
the normally accessible material world. This claim of access to
a spiritual world – an access Steiner did not claim to be his
alone – is the chief barrier to the acceptance of anthroposophy,
though while Steiner was alive he could help people over that
barrier by his own powerful lectures. One admirer who
declared himself ready to cross the Atlantic to hear him talk
recalled that when Steiner described the 'spirit-world . . . he
made [it] so visible that cosmic phenomena appeared actual.
Listening to him, one could not doubt the reality of his
spiritual vision, which appeared as clear as physical sight.'

It is unlikely that König, the Jewish convert to Christianity,
would have been attracted to Steiner's ideas if they had not
assigned a central role to Christ. It is most unlikely Olivia
would have surrendered her son into the care of people who,
whatever their success with handicapped children, proclaimed
themselves Buddhists or followers of some Oriental guru.
What Olivia found at Camphill were recognisably Christian
services and a calendar of celebrations that fitted into the broad
Christian scheme of things. There was, though, much more to
the community's religious life than that. The key link between
the beliefs of König and his followers and their ability to
devote themselves totally to the handicapped was the drama of

evolution in which Steiner assigned Christ a major role. Charles Darwin is an anti-hero for anthroposophists in so far as he describes evolution exclusively in material terms. For Steiner, the evolution that counted was that of the spirit, an evolution to which he assigned a quite different time frame from the one outlined by Darwin. According to this, human-kind had begun its existence able to achieve a primitive contact with the world's spirit background, but gradually lost it as its knowledge of the material world increased. Steiner asserted that Christ was born at this low point in human evolution in order to save man from the corrupting powers of self-sufficiency and materialism. His birth allowed man to resume his proper upward path of spiritual evolution.

Since Steiner believed that the successive reincarnation of human souls was the motor of this evolution it was an easy step for his followers to make sense out of apparently senseless tragedies of untimely death, and of children born deformed in mind or body. If there was reincarnation, these shortened or limited lives were not pointless: they were necessary though hard to understand moments in the spiritual journey of a human soul. In a lecture König gave in 1959 he spoke of the handicapped child as being more than his body, emotions and words. The child's appearance is 'merely the outer shell of an infinite and eternal spiritual being'. Every human being 'has his individual existence not only here on earth between birth and death, but . . . every child was a spiritual entity before he was born, and . . . every man will continue to live after he has passed through the gate of death'. It followed that no handicap is 'acquired by chance or misfortune. It has a definite meaning for the individual and is meant to change his life.'

Olivia never accepted the idea of reincarnation, which

seemed to contradict her certainty that after death she would
be reunited for ever with Sam Bucknill. Further journeys in
the world below had no place in her plans for either of them.
Nevertheless the commitment she sensed in König at his first
meeting with Freddie followed logically from Steiner's theory
that we lead multiple lives. In König's eyes Freddie was not an
embarrassment or a burden: on the contrary, like every other
human, he had a purpose. Therapists and patients, he said in a
lecture, 'are all both examiners and examinees', first playing
one role, then the other. 'I am not "above" and the child
"below"; we are there for and with each other.' This was
entirely in the spirit of Steiner who suggested that a handicapped child might be born to parents who needed this burden
of responsibility or had the right qualities to help such a child.

König railed against the idea that the life of a handicapped
person was a wasted life, and he was particularly incensed by
an incident in 1960 in which a British army officer gassed his
three-month-old baby son after being told he was a mongol.
He remarked that no one in court objected when throughout
the trial that followed the baby was described as 'to all intents
and purposes an idiot'. The judge, while sentencing the father
to a year's imprisonment for manslaughter, commiserated
with the parents. 'No right-thinking person could feel other
than the greatest sympathy when you and your wife found
that she had the misfortune to give birth to a mongol child.'

König was an early expert on mongols, as people with
Down's syndrome were still commonly called, and for him
the tragedy revealed 'an abysmal lack of information, understanding and common sense'. He blamed modern medical
science for misleading the father into supposing such a child
could only have a miserable existence, even though there were

already many cases where Down's syndrome children had acquired a fair amount of training and education. 'We know,' wrote König in his reflection on the story published in Camphill's *The Cresset*, that such children are 'lovely human beings, full of kindness and love. We know that they enjoy life and can make the life of their family a very happy one.' Thomas Weihs described mongols as possessing 'a family feeling for the whole of mankind'. Because they were so 'loving, innocent [rarely developing sexual awareness] . . . unintellectual [and] helpless', they were to be regarded not as an illness but as 'a medicine . . . in our time'. At Camphill such children were looked on as 'invaluable healers of others', and Weihs especially valued them for their unique ability to 'overcome the isolation and withdrawal' of autistic children like Freddie.

For König, everyone in the Camphill movement was 'graced by destiny to be allowed to do this work', however hard it was. He would tell the children's parents that while their sons and daughters might not be cured medically, 'look at it differently, take it as a grace that you have such a child, because not everyone has'.

In these so-called retarded ones, [he went on] there is manifest and lives much more humanity than in us who work and are active. It is not that these children and adults live among us as a burden. In future times one will look back on our century and will say: our time had to learn that the outsiders are the ones who lead us back into the path of truthfulness and honesty. It is the ones whom we consider to be the last who will be the first. They are the ones from whose sacrifice we live and these [Camphill] villages are signs of re-awakening humanity.

König expresses the traditional Christian respect for the Beatitudes, the belief that no one is more blessed than the poor in spirit and pure in heart. The sentiment can easily tip over into sentimentality, but not with him. We need to look at the handicapped, he once said, 'with devotion and a good dose of compassion – not the kind you drown in, but the kind that can be transformed into deeds of love'. He spoke with the conviction of a man with a mission, a mission he had discovered in the ideas of Rudolf Steiner. I cannot follow him into the spirit world that Steiner claimed to be as real as the familiar one we perceive with our bodily senses. But if Karl König had not been able to, there would have been no Camphill; and without Camphill there would have been even less light in Freddie's and Olivia's troubled lives.

It began as a marriage of adventure and high seriousness. In the spring of 1939 a handful of Central European men and women, all intellectuals, and most of them used to the comfortable life of the Viennese *haute bourgeoisie*, found themselves trying to start a community for the care of the handicapped in a gloomy manse in the north Scottish country-side. The house, provided by British admirers of König, naturally had no central heating, so there were fires to be laid and lit each morning. Lamps which needed regular trimming replaced electricity. Laundry had to be washed by hand in an outside copper. Meals were cooked on a smoky paraffin stove. These daily chores were as strange to them as the communal living, but König kept them up to the mark in both. His own simple origins had prepared him for any kind of work, and his wife, who was an unusually competent and practical person, thought nothing of preparing meals for several dozen people. The Königs demanded a high standard of order and cleanliness. Every new step in the would-be community's life was first thoroughly thought through and then scrupulously carried out. 'For Dr König,' noted Thomas Weihs's wife Anke, 'there was no fumbling or skipping lightly towards an ideal way of life.' Within six weeks the first handicapped child arrived, a German-Jewish boy whose parents had escaped to America but were forced by immigration rules to leave their son behind. The boy could barely speak, was continually restless, and searched obsessively for cigarette packets. Both the Königs had established reputations as teachers of handicapped children, but the others had little experience of children of any kind, let alone handicapped ones. Anke Weihs had been a successful ballet dancer who, to her horror, was once commanded to dance for Hitler before she was swept up by König. Peter Roth's sister Alix was a successful photographer.

From the start they tried to avoid creating an institutional life for the children. König told his little band to take them into their lives and live with them as fellow human beings, advice that could only be put into practice by wrenching their own lives out of familiar channels. Neither housekeeping nor the children were considered excuses for ignoring further self-improvement. Each evening they would gather however tired to study anthroposophy under König's guidance in the library where 'the wind whistled up through the floorboards . . . causing the carpets to heave great sighs at our feet, and the heavily quilted curtains billowed in the draught as we became stiff with cold'.

They spoke German among themselves. Grace before meals

was in German, too, and for some years König's standard English responses would remain 'absolutely no' or 'absolutely yes'. The war soon broke up this precarious and very obviously foreign group. On the evening of Whitsun 1940 the Scottish police, after telephoning in advance, politely led the men away to internment on the Isle of Man as potential enemy aliens. This turned out to be an unexpected bonus, for it gave König the chance to organise an uninterrupted programme of anthroposophical studies for his young followers; many of the ideas around which their community life would be organised came out of these Isle of Man seminars. König was the first to be released, but when he returned to Scotland in the autumn of the following year the six women and the children had already moved into a far more agreeable house called Camphill close to the river Dee.

König's home-coming was not easy. Anke Weihs called it a 'stormy wedding feast between male and female components of our community'. This Camphill language hints at explosions on König's part when he found some of the groundwork laid in his absence. This was the paradox of Camphill: a community in which carers and handicapped were to be equal citizens was essentially the creation of a man whose supremacy everyone took for granted. Early visitors to this Scottish experiment who had no time for anthroposophy, and in some cases were repelled by it, usually went away impressed by König. Everyone agreed he was a striking presence. His voice was rich, his laugh deep, and he had a conspiratorial smile that won people over. Everyone commented on the rapport he established with children. A woman who worked at Camphill in the early years but left because she could not accept the beliefs that inspired it remained devoted to König: 'he commanded everyone's respect without having to say a word.' Within Camphill this respect followed from his greater age; from his immeasurably greater experience with children; and from his mastery of Rudolf Steiner's ideas (the last carrying particular weight among such eager novices). Anke Weihs first met him in Vienna in 1938 when she went to him for relief from an allergy. Friends warned her against him. They had heard that there was Something odd about this doctor newly returned from Germany, that he practised some kind of 'spiritism' and other sorts of 'abracadabra' in dark rooms. When she went into his consulting room she saw

> a very small man with a large – a lion's – head. He wore a physician's white coat. His eyes were very big and grave. When they rested on you, they did not only see <u>through</u> you they seemed to create you anew. Something dormant in yourself responded whether you wanted it or not; you seemed to become what you really were, beneath the layers of habit, inhibition and illusion.
>
> This peculiar gaze . . . was one of the unique characteristics in Dr König. I would call it a 'creative gaze'. He not only saw what you were but what you were meant to be.

Children, she noted later, responded just as powerfully to this gaze. König 'was not a bit sentimental and he expected the most, even of a disabled child', and he could become forbidding when a child played up. But his grave look, she believed, could encourage even the most disturbed child to open up like a flower.

It is no mystery why there was never a hint in Camphill of the sloppiness that affects experimental communities where the members expect their new life to be an escape from the discipline of conventional living, for König was as demanding in small matters as in great. In the first years at Camphill everyone learned German poems which then had to be recited in his study with the appropriate gestures. If the gestures were wrong, the recital was repeated as many times as was needed to get them right. Songs, too, had to be learned and sung, at appropriate times of the day, 'without reserve and inhibitions'. A highly disciplined man himself, König expected others to be no less. His own desk was always in order; he never left books lying around, and there would be a storm if during a meeting he noticed a volume out of place on a bookshelf. He could not stand unpunctuality. Meetings and lectures began on the dot and latecomers were shut out. He made the most concentrated use of his own time. Co-workers who needed to see him were given a strict fifteen minutes, though to them it could seem much longer because he listened so intently to what they said.

Some twenty years later König described the sort of environment he wanted his houses at Camphill and elsewhere to provide. 'It is an environment of loving peace and peaceful love. It is a house without noise and hurry, without restlessness and quarrel.' It was also a house that avoided the modern 'temptations' of 'television, radio, drink, chatter, gossip and the many things that make life so difficult and unbearable'. A life dominated by such trivia was, he believed, 'the greatest enemy of the handicapped child'. The radio was to be switched on only 'when special occasions make it necessary'. Television was banned completely (a ban that remains in general throughout the Camphill movement today, though it is used for watching selected videos).

Even the most loving reminiscences of König make it easy to understand why some outsiders thought him a tyrant, albeit a benevolent and perhaps miracle-working one (a woman who knew him well in the early years and remained devoted to him suggested a comparison with the father of the Iranian revolution, the Ayatollah Khomeini). He 'could be testy' says a description in his overdue entry in the Dictionary of National Biography. He expected a great deal from people and found it hard to forgive them if they disappointed him. Even his greatest admirers described him as 'imperious' and admitted that 'things mostly had to go his way'. They put up with this because they usually found his way wise and good. They were also won over because he accepted 'fair correction', though never, it seems, downright opposition. And they knew that, although he 'sought for the central, perhaps the omnipotent place' in their life and had a 'confessed love for the red carpet', at the same time he fought what in their eyes was a heroic battle to achieve humility. It helped, too, that in spite of years of exile he remained a Viennese, with a sense of humour typical of his native city.

The story is told that while still in the unwelcoming manse, before Britain had declared war on Germany, König dreamed that Noah's Ark, far from coming to rest on Mount Ararat, had landed on the peak of Bennachie, a hill that could be seen from the window of his new Scottish study. This meant, he concluded, that 'now when the floods of terror and warfare are once again covering the face of the earth, we too must build an ark to help as many souls as we can'. When a few days later a perfect double rainbow spanned the hills it was not difficult for these exiles to believe they had found a holy mountain in the Scottish countryside.

König, it seems, had not lost the Jewish visionary strain. In Camphill the age-old Jewish search after truth and the

meaning of life had simply taken on a novel form. Some of
König's young followers responded to this vision with all the
enthusiasm of those other young Jews who tried to make a
new socialist life in Europe, or a new Jewish one in Palestine.
There was also, as König intended from the start, a determination to preserve the values of old Europe that had once allowed
nationalities as different as the animals in the ark to lead a life
together. In Scotland König was to affirm those values in a
new way. Driven out of Europe because he was both a Jew and
a follower of Rudolf Steiner, he would make a community
that included on equal terms the incompetent and the crazy,
creatures who like him were the target of Nazi persecution but
who in those days were also considered frighteningly, even
dangerously, alien by many people in Britain. Few refugees
can have less deserved interning in wartime Britain than
König and the other men from Camphill for they, too, were
preparing to fight, on their own battleground, a war against
the essence of Nazism. Although scarcely anyone noticed
them at the time, their world of refugees and troubled children
represented both an attempt to preserve what Europe had
achieved, and a model of what it might again become.

Such were the vast if unspoken pretensions of the tiny, and
still little known, school that Freddie joined in the spring of
1951. He lived the next twelve years according to a rhythm
that was intended to be as meaningful as the routine of
religious life in the Middle Ages. However slow and uncertain
his progress, he could always count on an appreciative
audience. Thomas Weihs said the handicapped child was like
an artist who has to play on a faulty instrument: his carers
should therefore concentrate not on the instrument but on the
child's frustrated artistry, otherwise the child would see them

as an 'unmusical' audience. A child's lack of success, he warned, was 'no true measure of intention'. The life Freddie joined at Camphill was built around this perception. Weihs called it a community *with* handicapped children, not a community *for* them. He compared it to a marriage in which adults had continuously to adjust the relations between each other, while a special dimension was added by the presence of these troubled children. The latter taught the adults both the vulnerability and the meaning of the human condition. The carers should not say 'there but for the Grace of God go I', but '*this* child has something to teach me about the grace of God'.

While agnostic parents might regard the religious under-pinning of Camphill life as secondary to the care of their children, for König and his followers it was the foundation without which nothing else could be built. Weihs thought it natural for a community for the handicapped in a Western country to be Christian in the broadest sense because Christianity was the West's spiritual heritage. What counted for him was how the community believed, rather than what it believed. A world perceived to be without meaning was particularly dangerous for such vulnerable children, and the aim was therefore to suffuse the life at Camphill with meaning.

Each day began with a morning prayer before breakfast which was said by children and co-workers standing in a circle. This was meant to challenge 'the minds of children and adults alike to face the coming day with their best powers so that it is . . . a new opportunity, a singular event'. Grace was then said at the table, with everyone at its end adding simple words such as *May the meal be blessed*. One of the graces were German verses which, after the early years, were translated into English:

The Bread is not our Food,
That which feeds us in the Bread,
Is God's Eternal Word,
Is Spirit and is Life.

The day ended with an evening prayer because 'before sleep, there is still the need of an individual child for "dialogue" with *his* God'. Among them was a prayer, written by Steiner, that spoke of knowing God:

In my Father and Mother,
In all loving People,
In Flowers and Trees,
In Beasts and Stones,
Then no fear shall I feel,
Only Love can then fill me,
For ALL that is around me.

Olivia was given a copy of this prayer and grace, typed on a little piece of paper. It is yellow now, and grimy at the edges. At some moment, whether of despair or hope I do not know, she folded it four times and put it away with the letters she had been sent from Camphill.

At the regular Sunday service, Weihs believed, the children could achieve 'great dignity and profound awareness'. They were helped prepare for this by a religious lesson the day before in which they were told Bible stories they could identify with. These Bible evenings, devised like so much else at Camphill by König, were at first only for the carers. Wearing their best clothes they gathered round a table where a candle was lit for a token meal. A passage from the Bible was read and then discussed. From the start a focal point of the community's life, the Bible evening was eventually enlarged to include the children themselves. For Peter Roth this was like 'stepping from holy secrecy into open daylight, a step into humanity at large'. Camphill celebrated the great Christian festivals as 'pillars in the course of time' and 'points of spiritual reference', and König wrote a play for each of them.

The school took some two hundred children aged from five to eighteen with the largest possible variety of handicaps. 'The greatest variety,' Weihs believed, would 'depict the totality of human possibility,' while a concentration on just one or two kinds of disability would 'inevitably stress the handicap and not the individual'. That would lead to the carers treating afflictions rather than human beings, and leave the children 'trapped' within their handicap. Weihs thought it particularly valuable for autistic children to mix with those with other disabilities, for autistics grouped together risked exaggerating their common problem. The original aim was to have one staff member for every two children. The size of house in which children lived under young house mothers depended on what suited each child, and after experimenting it was found best to have houses mixed in sex and age as well as handicap.

Even while König was alive there was not supposed to be a hierarchy of command at Camphill. Policy was made, Weihs said somewhat vaguely, by 'those who feel responsible for the community', with decisions taken by consensus. The possibility of conflict was minimised by saying that what counted in a community's life was not so much opinions as good will. Joining a community was an act of spiritual commitment, and Weihs taught that the 'iron rule' of community living was constant reference to the 'spiritual potential of others'. In modern man there was 'a profound fear of loving the spiritual potential of our fellow men, for if we do so unreservedly, we would re-enter Paradise, and life on this stricken, precious, terrible and beloved earth would lose its purpose'.

The most obvious expression of Camphill's spiritual ambition was the absence of salaries. In the aftermath of war this idealism attracted young people from the Continent, including some from anthroposophical families who had been persecuted by the Nazis. Camphill's founders took the decision to abolish salaries in the first year, believing it followed logically from Rudolf Steiner's thinking on social matters. According to König, 'we could not do our work in the same manner if we were employees and received a salary . . . Paid service is no service; paid love is no love; paid help has nothing to do with help.' The community met people's needs as they arose, while what each co-worker received depended on the community's resources (Camphill's income was then and remains now made up of state grants for children placed there by local authorities; private donations, including in recent years fund-raising which at first was frowned on; and the profits of its workshops). The result was not equality – this was never the aim – but what they called a hierarchy of needs. Peter Roth commented cryptically that 'a good amount of talking, friendship and empathy is necessary to come to a real concept of "I need", particularly in relation to another person'. No salaries meant no national insurance payments and therefore no state pensions in old age; when co-workers were too frail to work any more, the community would look after them. Weihs denied that they had created a 'false paradise' in which co-workers lived irresponsibly, free from the discipline that earning a living imposed in the world outside. As members of a house all co-workers were account-able for the money the community assigned for that house's running costs, and this was thought scope enough for learning financial responsibility.

Thomas Weihs always said Camphill schools and villages had to have links with the outside world, and should not allow themselves to drift into a segregated life. This was not always easy because Camphill's purpose was to be different from the world in which people earned wages, watched television, and (or so König and his followers feared) had little awareness of the spiritual in their lives. It was this difference that allowed the adults and children of Camphill to form a relationship that would have been impossible in the conventional world, and in the very first years there was even a desire to keep the children permanently at the school on the grounds that only Camphill understood what they needed. Not surprisingly the school could seem not just strange but priggish to those coming from the outside. After all, this rare community existed because there was an imperfect outside world, just as poison provides a purpose for the life-saving antidote. And was there not a suspicion that the co-workers needed the damaged children of the ordinary world so they could construct this pure community for themselves, a community supposed to be a precursor of the way in which all humankind would live once it was enlightened by anthroposophy? If the world at large was indifferent to the teachings of anthroposophy, these troubled children offered a rare opportunity to put those teachings into practice.

There was nothing new in this ambiguity of a small community that tries to lead a better life than the sinful world around it. The riddle of whether monks and nuns indulge themselves by fleeing from the world, or whether by the sacrifice of prayer and example and good works they make it a

better place will never be answered to everyone's satisfaction.
In Olivia's case it was a riddle of no importance. What
mattered was the fate of her child, and here there were few
who doubted Camphill's touch. König and Weihs won over
Olivia not by their religious beliefs but by their grasp of her
son's problems.

Even today, when autism has been so much written about,
many doctors barely recognise its existence. It is still not
mentioned in the general training of British medical students.
The chief current British textbook on paediatrics has only one
sentence about it, and that is misleading for it describes autism
as an emotional disorder caused by bad parenting. Yet König
and Weihs were able to imagine the mind of their autistic
children as long as forty years ago. The young Australian
Donna Williams who has overcome her autism describes in
her autobiography states of being remarkably like those
intuitively imagined by König and Weihs. While she could
lose herself in colours, sounds, patterns and rhythm, König
described autistic children living not in their bodies, but 'in the
table, in the chair, in the daily routine, in the cup, in the milk,
and in everything else that surrounds them'. When Thomas
Weihs explained the best way to approach autistic children, he
used words that also might have been written by Donna
Williams. Speak to them indirectly, she advised, and do not
try to engage them too intently. The autistic child, wrote
Weihs, should never be confronted directly: 'we should never
look into his eyes and address him as we would another person
. . . When we address the child, we do so while looking the
other way . . . Speech should be gentle, non-committal and
vague rather than forceful and to the point.'

Although Weihs quickly became for Olivia the chief source

of Camphill's wisdom she had no way of judging the correctness of what he told her about Freddie's condition. Whom else could she turn to? The specialists in London had thrown up their hands. The National Autistic Society which today represents the interests of parents with autistic children did not begin work till 1962. Its first school opened only in 1965, and its first centre for adults nine years later. If König was sometimes described as a man convinced of his mission, Weihs appeared to be driven by compassion, and it was this that earned him Olivia's trust. He not only showed particular feeling for these autistic children who demanded a 'peculiar intensity of compassion' to live with, but above all, as Freddie approached the end of his school years, he understood and shared Olivia's anxiety about what would happen to her son next. 'We do the greatest, and possibly the most unforgiveable injury to the handicapped person,' he wrote, 'when we consider his case is closed. This is tantamount to murder.' Strong language, but it did not sound melodramatic to a mother like Olivia. Her son was now on the brink of an adulthood that might mean years in a mental hospital, where his case would indeed to all intents and purposes be closed. All her hope centred on Weihs being able to find Freddie a place in what he called, in the letter he wrote her in the spring of 1963, the 'Movement'. What she did not understand was that much depended on Freddie too, for Camphill no longer looked on him as a child, but as a young adult who had to shape his own destiny as best he could.

7

Eden

The road north from the pretty village of Hutton-le-Hole takes you onto the Yorkshire moors. At any time of year these may be enveloped in fog or low cloud, when there is little to be seen from the road apart from the sheep that graze its edge, ignoring the corpses of their brothers and sisters who have been killed by cars and lie with their legs sticking out like wooden toys. On such days the moors are not a place to linger, and the traveller is thankful to catch a glimpse, through a break in the damp grey mist, of a valley that falls away beneath the moor. It is green there, and there are trees and houses nestling together in small groups. With luck a patch of sunshine may brighten and deepen the colours in this inviting world below. Turn right down a steep road and you are in Danby dale, and among the farms that make up the Camphill community of Botton village. Even when there is sunshine on the moors and the purple heather is in flower, to reach the dale is like arriving in port after a hard sea journey. If the moors represent life that must be endured, the dale is life that can be lived.

In winter the dale itself is sometimes scarcely inviting. Wind and rain may sweep its narrow length; it can be laid siege to by snow; and what sun there is disappears quickly behind the abrupt slope down which the heather creeps like an advance party reconnoitring from the hostile moorland above. For Olivia, though, this was Freddie's Eden. It was the place she wanted him to be, the only place she felt he had a chance to be happy, but her discovery of Botton did not bring her peace of mind. While Freddie was living at the village she worried whether he was going to be able to stay; during his years of exile she would scheme tirelessly to get him back. She tortured herself and plagued my father and pestered anyone she thought she could enlist in Freddie's cause. His arrival in Botton in 1966 was an occasion for rejoicing, but it was a nervous joy, for so much effort and anxiety already lay behind it.

The photographs Olivia kept of Freddie's schooldays unwittingly recorded the mounting graph of worry that began while he was still in Scotland. When she first went to visit him at school she found the child she remembered, the pixie-like balaclava helmets his nursery mother made him wear against the Scottish winter matching his familiar not-quite-of-this-world manner. Soon, though, he was a real schoolboy and her race with time began. Her son becomes a little tough running in bare feet round the garden of the holiday cottage in Walberswick, or pausing briefly, to be snapped sharing a chair with his mother, his feet in a bowl of water, probably in preparation for having his toe nails cut, an operation he never cared for. At other times he is in a smart little boy's tweed overcoat, squinting into the sun with his mother's arm around him. On a visit to London Olivia took him to the funfair on the Battersea bank of the Thames where he fell in love with candy floss. He is long-legged by now, and approaching the crisis of puberty, and he seems far away in a world of his own as he holds the soft pink ball of sugar in the long, extended fingers of both hands.

At seventeen, he looked both young for his age and on the verge of being grown up. When she was in Scotland in the summer Olivia took him for picnics on Deeside. She packed tartan rugs to spread on the sandy ground under the pine trees, thermoses of tea, sandwiches, everything needed for a Scottish picnic, including extra coats to ward off any chill in the air. On these outings he wore what any older boarding-school boy at that time might have worn, grey flannels, a grey tweed jacket, yellow pullover, and a neatly knotted tie. His hair has lost its childhood fairness and is cut short at the sides and brushed away from the forehead. He poses with his mother like any ordinary boy, leaning against the bonnet of a car with his arm through hers and smiling towards the camera. Another picture has evidently been taken hastily, for mother and son, sitting on the ground, are to one side of the frame, and their feet have been cut off. She smiles while he leans towards her to fix the clasp of a bracelet round her wrist. Small wonder the photographer – my father, perhaps – hurried to take that snap, for it summed up how far Camphill had succeeded in helping Freddie break out of his isolation. The child who was locked in his own world when he went to Scotland for a moment seems able to attend to his mother as any son might do. But there is another photograph taken the same day that pushes him back towards the frightening years when he had little contact with anyone. He is standing among the pines, as straight as they are and almost as thin, and clapping his hands. This clapping was a gesture of defiant joy, often the sign he had done some mischief and knew it, and was expecting Olivia to call out his name, at first in amusement but then with a hint of irritation revealing the anxiety that behaviour like this always triggered in her.

He could look so normal, yet she knew he was incapable of leading what passes for a normal life. The same thought had already impelled other parents with children at Camphill to ask König to take a step beyond his school, and to set up communities where their sons and daughters, if they remained unable to move into the outside world, could continue to live and work under some supervision, if need be for the rest of their lives. The alternatives for such grown-up children were grim. Either they would go into a mental hospital where they might be safe and cared for, but where before long they would become creatures of an institution, doing nothing for themselves, not even choosing whether to make a cup of tea or coffee, and where they would be praised for being quiet, in other words content to doze their drugged lives away in a chair. Or they could have an isolated existence in their own home. Some parents who shrank from letting their child go to a hospital were tempted by this, as long as the son or daughter was not impossibly disruptive or violent. They reasoned they knew and loved the child better than anyone, and therefore could care for it better too. Yet was it right for the handicapped child to be held all its life in the time warp of parental affection? Thomas Weihs pointed out that while a normal child is dominated by its parents for the first fourteen years of its life, there then comes a shift in the family balance of power as the child increasingly assumes the upper hand. This necessary transformation does not take place in families where children are in some way disabled, which explains why so many parents of even middle-aged handicapped sons and daughters treat them, and talk of them, as though they were still little boys and girls. For Olivia, too, Freddie was always a child. It did not matter how big he grew, or how unchildlike his behaviour. She still called him Freddles, his little boy's nickname. She went on buying him the same sweets and ices he liked when he was a little boy. She saw the growing man but she did not pay attention to him. In her heart she saw and felt the child, always vulnerable, forever demanding her attention and care.

König and Camphill took a different approach. Freddie, like all children in the school in Scotland, had moved up a class each year according to age and regardless of ability and achievements. Freddie might be handicapped, their theory went, but in many vital respects he was undergoing processes common to everyone's development, and these were not to be ignored. At sixteen he was expected to behave as much as he could like a sixteen-year-old, and was also entitled to be treated as one. Once an adult he should learn as best he could the rules of the adult world. The idea of a disabled adult leading the life of an isolated child in a warm family bolt-hole went against everything Camphill believed, and it was not surprising that König, with his builder's spirit, responded to the challenge of setting up a network of villages for the adult handicapped. The first attempt at such a community was made on familiar Camphill territory when part of the school at Newton Dee was turned into a working village. Shortly afterwards the Macmillan publishing family offered König Botton Hall, a house with a surrounding estate of three farms that they owned in Danby dale, and the first co-workers and former school pupils, now called villagers, arrived there from Camphill in 1955.

In Botton, as in all the villages and adult communities that

Camphill eventually created, *work* was the key word. The question was could Freddie do a real job of work. His last school report from Camphill contained some worrying words: though Freddie had developed into a 'good worker', he still did not 'regard work as a necessity but rather as a kind of game'. For anyone who knew his skittishness that sounded like a loving understatement. There were, though, some hopeful signs. Older Camphill pupils learned crafts, and Freddie had successfully tackled rug-making and then gone on to weaving, in which he showed unusual skill, working very fast and making complicated patterns without needing to be taught. Typically Camphill regarded weaving as more than just therapy. The first operations of carding and spinning wool on a traditional wheel were certainly soothing, and helpful to the concentration, but the weaving itself, according to a Camphill primer on education for special needs, built up 'an inner fabric, an inner sense of creation, of self-worth, an inner tapestry of morality'.

It was reason for hope that Freddie seemed poised to master a craft that he could put to productive use and through which at the same time he might weave for himself a more grounded life, both an inner one, and one in the wider society of a Camphill village. Olivia could count on the support of her 'Darling Thomas' and of the Bocks who had guided Freddie through what they called his 'valiant and dramatic break-through into adolescence'. Weihs assured Olivia they would fight 'a persistent battle' to get him into a village, charac-teristically adding that he would like her to 'support us with your prayers. Every year we are faced with this problem [for other children], and somehow it does always work out.' The interim solution was for Freddie to go on living with the

Bocks for another year while working in the village that had been set up on the Newton Dee estate. It was a success. Nora Bock thought he became more mature and self-controlled. Not only did he continue to make progress at weaving but when he returned from the village workshops he went straight to the kitchen to help with the washing up. He no longer needed much supervision in the details of daily living for he liked to keep himself clean. He had better contact with people, and enjoyed watching other children play even though he seldom joined in their games himself. A concern for others that is often lacking in autistic people seemed to show in his reluctance to start his meal if another boy was missing from the table. He never refused to help when asked, and sometimes even offered to help off his own bat if there was enjoyment in it. There had, though, been one episode of a different kind: during his first days in the weavery he had 'made a thorough investigation of all the electrical appliances . . . without thought of the consequences'. Freddie had not done anything like this for several years, and for Nora Bock it showed how dependent he still was on the support and guidance of those around him.

Thomas Weihs wanted to place Freddie in the village at Newton Dee where he would be close to people he knew and liked, but the weaving master left and in the end Freddie was sent to the Grange. König acquired this thirty-four-acre estate in Gloucestershire as a place where boys who had left school could be prepared for life in one of the adult communities, and Freddie would be able to continue with his weaving there. His last report from Camphill judged him to be 'well equipped' for village life and forecast he would make progress 'once he had adjusted himself to the new surroundings and routine'.

Olivia fretted while Camphill debated whether Freddie was capable of fitting into village life. In a letter to Weihs she confessed, 'One wants a lot of physical strength for these children . . . & calm nerves. I fear I have neither.' And though she was 'quite wild with joy & relief' when she heard Freddie was to be allowed to move to a village she was apprehensive that the Grange was not the right place. When Freddie stayed in Cadogan Square on his way to Gloucestershire she found him unsettled and inclined to fly into rages, and the reason, she was sure, was that he knew he had left the routines and people he had known and loved. Once at the village he quickly quarrelled with the boy he shared a room with, and he would no longer weave properly. Within days one of the women who ran the Grange telephoned Olivia to say they might have to put him into a mental hospital.

This was Olivia's worst terror, for she had convinced herself that once in hospital he would never leave. König did his best to pacify her. He, too, 'hated the idea' of sending Freddie to a hospital but he added that 'an entirely new environment will probably make [Freddie] face life in a new way'. He might also have added that at the Grange, as throughout Camphill, they did not like to use tranquillisers and as a result knew little about them. Freddie had been very mildly sedated during puberty, but the Grange wanted to know what drugs might help him more permanently, and only a hospital had the skills to decide that.

Once König told her he agreed with the decision Olivia, too, accepted it, but not before fierce and sometimes hysterical telephone conversations and the shedding of a good many tears. She tried to explain herself to Thomas Weihs: 'Perhaps my main fault is to try to live Freddie's life for him & to be his

voice as he cannot speak.' But her faith in Camphill was jolted
again when she discovered Freddie had been put in the hospital
without her being given a chance to take him there and explain
his foibles to the staff. When she did get through on the
telephone to a nurse in Freddie's ward he asked her, 'Can he
speak, or is it just that he is afraid?' It was, she told Weihs, as
though Freddie were 'a little orphan with no parents to care for
him . . . After 12½ years of love and trust for Camphill we
would never have believed this could happen . . . I feel I've let
Freddie down dreadfully.'

Her anger passed but she had learned two lessons. Even in
the Camphill movement not everyone had the skill and
empathy needed to handle Freddie. And, as König hinted in
his letter, Freddie had set out on an adult life in which it was
neither possible, nor right, for him to remain as cocooned as
he had been at school in Scotland. It was hard for Olivia to
appreciate that even Thomas Weihs thought it might be good
for school-leaving children to have a break in the outside
world before, if they could manage it, returning to one of
Camphill's adult communities. He did not even rule out a spell
in a mental hospital with all the suffering and unpleasantness
that might involve, for this, too, Weihs could accept as part of
the widening of experience as the child became an adult.
Autistic and unable to speak and apparently incapable of
independence though Freddie was, it was argued by Weihs
that Freddie needed to gain some understanding of how the
outside world viewed him and his peculiarities. This approach
followed from König's confidence that every handicapped
person had a destiny in which 'happiness' might have only a
sporadic part to play. It is typical of many who devote their
lives to caring for others that their compassion goes hand in

hand with what, to outsiders, may sometimes look like callousness. The explanation lies in the carer's acceptance of the handicapped as a person of equal worth, an equality that brings with it the old human entitlement to experiences that are bad as well as good.

It was Thomas Weihs, Peter Roth (now in charge of Botton village) and Gerda, the nursery mother at Camphill who watched Freddie's love affair with the Teddy bear and thought him 'so lovely and so original', who rescued him from hospital. Gerda saw Freddie as a 'heavenly' person, and had never forgotten how as a child in Scotland, given a pair of very heavy boots to slow him down a little, he would still try to hop, giggling as he made this effort to reassert what she thought of as his natural lightness. A handsome woman, she radiated calmness, the quality possessed by all who have cared successfully for Freddie, though her calmness did not prevent her from loving him just as he, in his inimitable way, was attached to her. She had married another co-worker, a young Dutchman called Peter Blok, and they had moved to Botton to become house parents responsible for the little group of villagers who lived with them. Weihs had the greatest admiration for Gerda, whom he considered a born curative educator. No one was better qualified to give Freddie the support he needed to survive at Botton, and it was largely thanks to her that he had his taste of Eden. In 1964 he left the hospital with a prescription for tranquillisers and settled down with the Bloks at Hall North, the part of the old Macmillan mansion where they looked after a household of some dozen villagers.

Olivia knew it was a moment of truth. Freddie's behaviour at the Grange could be explained by the shock of change after years of stability in Scotland. At Botton he was going to live with people he knew, and he also had the additional support of drugs. His autism and lack of speech by no means ruled him out as a candidate for becoming a good villager. Thomas Weihs believed it was possible to put to productive use the obsessions that can be so marked in someone like Freddie, for he had known cases where people with comparable disabilities had become symbols of 'conscientiousness and exact workmanship'.

In addition to doing real work Freddie would also be expected to be 'socially cooperative', and to make his own contribution to village life. This was part of what might be called the social contract of these communities, for in return the co-workers were not supposed to make any distinction between themselves and the villagers. König and Weihs were most insistent on this. Weihs warned against looking on the adult villager as a patient who was undergoing treatment. Rather he was to be 'accepted as he is and his dignity as a person upheld'. At Botton all were 'adults, some more handicapped and peculiar than others, living and working in a generally therapeutically oriented community'. As at the school in Scotland co-workers received no salary yet were expected to commit themselves totally to village life, treating every problem that arose as their own. The community did not deny the right to private life – König insisted people should have as much privacy as they needed – but only the fully committed were likely to flourish under such conditions.

A major part of Botton's therapy was the rhythm of the life of the village and of each house within it. König ruled that villagers should not live in dormitories but 'in small houses in the lap of the family to which they belong and where they feel safe and secure'. Life in a Botton house began more robustly than in Scotland. Instead of a gentle waking to the sound of a recorder played in the corridors, one of the house members summoned the rest to breakfast by thumping a gong. There was most likely a cock crowing in a farmyard along the dale, and perhaps the companionable sound of ducks outside the window. All the inhabitants of the house, as many as a dozen people, came together to eat round one large table. If the house parents had their own children they, too, ate with everyone else, the belief being that both the children and the villagers benefited by the mixing. As at the school all had their napkin, kept in a ring or in a little cloth bag embroidered with their names. As in Scotland each meal was preceded by a short silence and then grace, and for lunch and the six o'clock supper a candle was lit at the beginning and ceremoniously put out when all were finished eating and the table cleared. The food was simple, with plenty of salads, fruit and brown bread made in the village bakery. There were no fulltime cooks. House parents helped by co-workers and villagers prepared the food as best they could. Other domestic duties were shared according to talents. The house's compost buckets had to be emptied and there was a good deal of washing up to be done. Dishwashers were as taboo as television sets, confirming washing-up as a communal activity even the most handicapped, Freddie among them, could share in. The houses were either remodelled or specially built to create a warm atmosphere; as in Scotland wood was the favourite material. The style evolved by the Camphill Movement's own architects stressed natural, flowing shapes; and the dale acquired buildings that were modest echoes of the Goetheanum, the vast and original hall designed and built by Rudolf Steiner at Dornach in Switzerland as an expression of his cosmology.

The result was a piquant marriage of the English and the continental in which houses and farms in dour Yorkshire stone aquired double windows sturdy enough to satisfy older co-workers who remembered the civilised ways of pre-war bourgeois Vienna.

Botton was above all a working community. Today it has a population of three hundred and with its forest and five farms covers seven hundred acres. It is one and a half miles as the crow flies from Botton farm at the settlement's north end to the cluster of houses round the farm called Honey-Bee-Nest at the southern tip of Danby dale. The bakery is next to Botton farm; also close are the workshop where farm machinery is repaired, the sawmill and the woodwork shop. The dairy producing milk, yoghurt and a hard cheese that today sells in fashionable shops in London is close to the main house of Botton Hall, with the plant that processes the produce of the Botton gardens next to it. Further south along the dale is the dollshop, the weavery and, within a minute's stroll from Honey-Bee-Nest farm, the candleshop and the Camphill press.

Villagers switch work according to need or the season. Some do two different jobs each day, perhaps household duties in the morning and garden work after lunch. This makes it impossible for all to live next door to their place of work and getting to work can involve a walk along pathways constructed by the side of the narrow roads that snake through the dale. One may not see much brisk striding as the villagers set out each morning. Muffled against the northern chill, they often seem to hesitate on their way, and some seldom manage more than an amble, as though themselves doubting they will ever reach their destination. The impression is misleading, for when they do get there serious work is done.

The atmosphere is companionable in the bakery, where villagers put on white coats and hats to knead the dough and shape the different loaves and buns at a great rectangular table. The woodwork shop makes simple but safe and strong toys for younger children. The trains, the animals and a brightly coloured, moving Millie-pede are handsome to look at and smooth to touch. A good deal of the work in the food-processing centre involves cleaning out jars and bottles, a job for Freddie with his liking for washing-up and his strict attention to standards (once he has accepted them). The candleshop opens in winter when there is less work in the gardens and on the farms. Like much of the work in the village candle-making is an occupation that satisfies the senses, with the smell of the hot wax and the smoothness and colour of the finished candles. The village's five farms practise traditional mixed farming of a kind rarely seen any more in Yorkshire. They use organic methods and have introduced a natural system of waste water purification based on plants. Steiner, perhaps surprisingly, was not a vegetarian and the farms provide Botton with all the meat it needs.

As anywhere else in Britain work stops throughout the village for tea and coffee breaks. Some villagers are strict about observing this time-off, and sip their drink with a concentration others might reserve for good port or old claret. You cannot say the atmosphere is industrious in a conventional way. Villagers have their peculiarities and they do not leave them at the door when they enter a workshop or go out onto the fields, but there is no doubting the usefulness of what they, in a manner suited to them, eventually produce. The village has a central sales department, staffed by villagers and co-workers, that markets the craft products made in all the

Camphill communities in Britain. Botton's share of this, together with sales of its bread, cheese and farm produce to local shops and restaurants provides funds for the village's building programme while its daily needs, greatly reduced by the absence of salaries, are covered by the government grants to which the villagers are entitled. At Botton they would say making money was a necessary but secondary consideration. Visitors being shown round the bakery are as likely to be told now as when Freddie went there that the villager-bakers do their work with pleasure because people need bread, not because they, the bakers, want money.

The village had no pub; there was no cinema nor television; and it was too isolated for villagers to wander off on their own in search of such amusements. The entertainments the village did offer were wholesome when they were not high-minded. There was folk dancing, music recitals, amateur dramatics, lectures. There was a coffee shop, too, near Botton Hall where Freddie lived. People could drop in there at any free moment during the day or after work in the evening. Olivia left money with Gerda so Freddie could go there whenever he wanted. He did not know how to use coins or pound notes but whoever was running the coffee shop would take what was needed from the purse he carried with him. It was a secure world, and a neat one too. Rain clouds might build over the moors where the dead sheep lay by the roadside, but there was always tidiness and order in the dale below.

The orderliness reflected a spiritual purpose for, as at the school in Scotland, Botton's life was guided by a religious perception of the world. Though this remained obscure to Freddie and to others like him who could not even master language, scarcely anyone who watched him during a religious service doubted that candles, music and measured ritual could – though by no means always did – put him into a reflective mood. The services and ceremonies that were a fundamental part of life at Camphill school were all repeated at Botton; that the village's life was linked through its farms and gardens to nature and the seasons made the meaning of the great festivals of the Christian year even more incisive.

Olivia loved Botton from the start. She sometimes laughed at what seemed to her its eccentric ways, but she was captivated by the sight of handicapped people so much at ease with themselves and with others. The disabilities of those she had known as children in Scotland were more pronounced now they were adults, but the tic or strange posture, the ungainly walk or tilt of the head, coexisted with a person who was neither helpless nor ashamed. She loved it most because she saw it as the continuation of Camphill school, a place where Freddie, whatever might be said about him having to lead an adult life, would still be looked after as though he were a child. If Olivia could not care for Freddie herself there was no one she would rather trust him to than Gerda; and that Gerda was once again his house mother she took as a sign there would be no change in his life.

Olivia did not grasp, and perhaps did not want to grasp, that Gerda and the co-workers were supposed to treat the villagers as adults, and equal adults at that. The fact that she had looked after Freddie in Scotland was not supposed to mean this relationship would continue in the village. Arguably the Botton approach was contrived. Wherever you went in the dale, whether to the dairy, the printing press or the fields, there was always a co-worker, usually a young man or woman, making sure the work was properly and safely done.

The relationship was not supposed to be one of nurses and patients, but calling the carers 'co-workers' and the cared-for 'villagers' did not automatically change the balance of power between them. Co-workers had to take charge of many aspects of villagers' lives. A good many did need some measure of looking after: there were regular bath times so their personal cleanliness could be checked (Freddie was able to have a bath on his own but Gerda had to cut his toe nails for him, something he never liked even though they made a game of it). Even the daily meals together might call for a watchful eye and ear on the part of the house parents, and the latter were the natural leaders of conversation at the table. Villagers could take part in village meetings where Botton's plans and problems were discussed, but did that mean they were really taking part in decision-making?

For those who embraced the Camphill attitude this ambiguity did not matter. Co-workers committed themselves to respect the villager as a unique person, regardless of his or her handicap: at Botton this was called recognising the being behind the mask of disability. And though the villagers might depend on co-workers for some things, the latter were in turn supposed to learn from their handicapped colleagues. Gerda thought co-workers with their intellectual habits could benefit from observing the different way in which handicapped people acquired knowledge and skills. The warmth and uncomplicated nature of so many of the villagers was thought helpful in breaking down the co-workers' pride and sense of superiority. And did not König's founding impulse still make itself felt? The little band of émigrés from Hitler's Europe, doubly hated by the Nazis for their Jewish origins and belief in the teachings of Rudolf Steiner, found the meaning of their life

in caring for damaged and confused children who were, like
them, candidates for Nazi extermination. It was hard to
believe this conjuncture of personal and historical fates did not
still mould the life of the inhabitants of Danby dale.

There was, though, another reason why Botton managed to
break the traditional relationship of the powerful carer and the
all but powerless cared-for. It was the handicapped who made
possible the communal life that König and those who came
after him put such store by. Co-workers admitted they might
not be capable of the discipline and sacrifice needed to live in
Botton or any other Camphill community without the
presence of these troubled children and villagers, for they took
the sting out of such a life and gave it a sweet intensity of
purpose. Even admirers of Rudolf Steiner have been known to
say that those who live and work in communities like Botton
are running ahead of history. They call them 'sixth epoch
people living in the fifth epoch', a reference to Steiner's theory
that we are now in the world's fifth (and far from pleasant)
epoch which is to be followed by a greatly superior sixth
where humankind will learn to live according to community
virtues. Thomas Weihs was expressing the idealism of
König's followers when he wrote that 'Like Lazarus who rose
out of the grave, handicapped children have stepped forward
into our midst. Perhaps they too can lead us to a new life.' It
was one of the ironies of Camphill's jumping over epochs that
not all the handicapped who benefited from its villages wanted
to spend their lives there. Every now and then one of the more
mildly handicapped men or women felt sufficiently self-
confident to leave Botton to live an independent life in the
world outside. Such people, it seemed, had remained in
Steiner's 'fifth epoch' and were still wedded to the rush and

noise of modern society in spite of having had the rare experience – if Camphill was right – of living in a better future.

Freddie was unlikely to have such an opportunity and Olivia began searching for ways to bolster his position as a hopefully permanent resident of the village. She made friends with Joyce and Peter Hogg, an elderly couple who on retirement built a small house in Botton so they could be close to their villager son Michael. Visitors to Botton could stay at the Hoggs' house which was next door to the village centre and Botton Hall where Freddie lived (he soon discovered them and made particular friends with Joyce). The Hoggs seemed to have assured permanence for their son, and Olivia tried to do the same for Freddie in a different way. In early 1968 she set up a trust fund worth £7,000 whose beneficiaries were to be Freddie and the Camphill Village Trust, the charity that embraced all the Camphill communities in Britain. During Freddie's lifetime the income was to be shared between him and Camphill. On his death the capital would pass to the Camphill Village Trust.

Olivia hoped this would strengthen Freddie's claim to permanency, but while she was putting the lawyers to work Gerda was struggling to coax the child she had loved into accepting the responsibilities of adult life. Freddie's position was precarious, for if Gerda had not offered to take him in her house he might never have got to Yorkshire, since no one else seemed anxious, or confident enough, to take him on. Gerda was running the village dollshop, a short walk away from Hall North across a footpath running through fields, and she took Freddie to work with her there, a sign of how much supervision she felt he needed. Even under her eye he developed little taste for work, and although he was familiar from his schooldays with the rhythm of his new home she found him moody and difficult.

As a child he used to look at her provokingly, as though challenging her to watch his next bit of mischief. He still gave her provoking looks, but he was different now, robbed of the child's lightness, and for the first time she found him hard to cope with. Although he still hated getting his hands dirty – he would no more play snowballs than he would dip his fingers in potter's clay – he began to take less care of himself and did not wash himself properly without being told to. Gerda thought of him as 'a person of intelligence living in a prison', but he was also an immature young man, she thought, because he did not want to come into too close contact with life, and she began to doubt he would ever learn to work properly. When he did deign to do some task it still was, as Nora Bock had warned, little more than a game for him, and he hurried through it so he could get back to his preferred state of detachment. Gerda remembered it as a time when 'his ego wanted to take hold but could not. He was so out of himself.'

He became unpredictable, especially when he felt unwell – he seemed often to have headaches – and of course was unable to tell anyone about it, though Gerda, like Olivia, could often guess when he was in pain. He began to be fascinated by women, and when he saw their bare arms in summer he liked to squeeze them. It was a passion that never seemed to go any further and Gerda was sure it did not have the makings of a real sexual assault, which she judged would be quite foreign to him for she was sure he was 'a very innocent person'. Far more worrying were the 'sudden attacks' he became liable to. 'They seem to start,' Olivia wrote to Thomas Weihs in Scotland, 'with feeling unwell & then he becomes very restless & often very thirsty & drinks lots of water. He then gets more & more worked up & if anyone annoys him bangs his head incessantly & tears at his clothes & yells & screams & sort of growls like an animal. He pours with sweat & it is dreadful to watch. He does not attack other people & even at times clings to the hand of Gerda . . . as if imploring for help.'

These attacks sometimes lasted twenty-four hours and when one occurred while Gerda was away – her absence perhaps unsettled Freddie – Botton, in alarm, sent him to the local mental hospital at Middlesbrough. It was his first of several visits there for observation and setting of his drug doses. The doctors suspected brain damage to be the cause both of his inability to speak and of the epileptic fits he had while in hospital. They prescribed very large doses (up to 1,200 milligrams a day) of the major tranquilliser Largactil as well as sleeping pills and anti-convulsants. Before long Botton came to suspect the drugs were making Freddie worse; the doctors disagreed, and communications between the two groups of carers deteriorated. Between attacks Gerda found Freddie 'nicer & far more in contact' than he had ever been before, but one day in early 1968 while he was with Gerda in the dollshop something went wrong with the sewing machine he was working on. He lost his temper and, jumping towards her, grabbed her neck with both his hands. The Bloks had just begun to have a family and the incident made Gerda, who was pregnant again, accept she could no longer manage him. Keeping the balance in a Botton house was a delicate matter. No one person could demand an immoderate amount of the house parents' time, let alone when the parents were raising a family of their own. There was no place in the village for someone who could not do a measure of regular work and who needed watching lest he threaten others, even though usually he turned his anger on himself.

The news horrified my parents. Gerda had told Olivia about Freddie's troubling behaviour but, perhaps because it scared her so much, she did not seem to take in everything that was said to her. In her own accounts of Freddie's departure from Botton she did not mention his attack on Gerda. The shock of her son's expulsion from Eden was quickly followed by disbelief as he began to tumble through the health service like a ball left to bounce down steps into oblivion. The hospital at Middlesbrough now said it was the wrong zone for him, and transferred him to York. The York hospital said he was not their responsibility because his parents lived in London. It demanded he be sent south. Thomas Weihs had mentioned Freddie's case to a clinic for the mentally ill in London that professed a particular interest in autism. Intrigued by what Weihs told them they admitted Freddie as a private patient, and undertook to cut back his drugs. Olivia's hope that he would now receive proper attention lasted twelve days. She left a description of what happened. '*Disaster.* [In the clinic] he had a room to himself which he likes but could never go out and was crazy about a lift at the end of the passage wanting to be in it all the time. They thought he was trying to escape but I knew it was just that he loved the lift & wanted to have a look round.'

Shut up in his room Freddie 'rocked & laughed & barked like a dog & clapped his hands till they got blisters on them'. The clinic quickly forgot about reducing his drugs. They claimed he was disturbing the other patients, had bit one nurse and tried to strangle another; and without giving Olivia time to find somewhere else they packed him off by ambulance to

Bexley, a large National Health hospital in London's Surrey suburbs. It was suitable for Freddie, they told Olivia, because 'it had padded rooms which Freddie might need if they took him off drugs'. Her version of what happened was rather different. She told Thomas Weihs that Freddie 'never lost his temper with [the nurses] which I thought remarkable' until they told him he was going to Bexley when he 'pinched them a bit'. Who was telling the truth? The clinic complained to Weihs that Olivia got the wrong end of things, and misled people to get her own way. That Olivia was ready to be manipulative to help Freddie was certainly true; but it also seems probable that the clinic accepted Freddie without understanding the extent of his problems, and got rid of him like the plague when they realised what they had taken on.

'Freddie was such a prince,' Gerda would say many years later. 'There had to come a time when he would be forced to learn, and it was bound to be very hard for him.'

8

Limbo

When Freddie was admitted to Bexley in the spring of 1968 he was twenty-two years old and the hospital seventy-one. Built at the end of the last century to hold two thousand of London's 'lunatics' in discreet seclusion it was typical of the huge mental hospitals that are so despised today and, if all goes to plan, Bexley will be closed by the middle of this decade. But even Freddie's short life had revealed that fashions are as pronounced in medicine as in any other human activity. A remedy that seems enlightened to one generation may look like stupidity bordering on the criminal to the next, but that does not mean those who first used it did not believe they were doing good.

Bexley was one of a number of large asylums built by the late Victorians just outside London. Although its purpose was to banish the mentally sick from the capital, it offered them superior accommodation by the standards of the time. The wards were positioned in a semi-circle, men on one side, women on the other, sixty in each, and they were linked by a visitors' corridor in the shape of a half ring. Administration buildings ran down the centre between the wards, and included a great hall where in the early years dances were held at weekends in which nurses (all of whom lived in) usually outnumbered patients. The hospital had its own farm that provided food as well as work for the inmates, and a fine park planted by the property's original owner Hiram Maxim, the inventor of the machine gun who used the extensive grounds for early experiments in powered flight.

For poor people from crowded central London the new hospital was hygienic and spacious, and its grounds a luxury. But it was built, unashamedly, as an institution with as rational a purpose as factory or railway station, and there was nothing homely about it.

For some patients it turned out to be little better than a prison in which the sentences had no end. Some stayed in Bexley for years, ignored by their families and forgotten by society at large, and it was not unknown for a young woman admitted to the hospital for nothing more grave than post-natal depression to die there sixty years later. After several years in such a huge institution many patients became scared to leave. So used were they to the secure and trouble-free life in the Bexley 'village' that, if they were released, they would put on a show of going berserk in order to get sent back.

For many years doctors had only physical means by which to restrain the disturbed and violent. There was the strait-jacket, the padded cell, the cosh and a chair in which patients were strapped and a front cover closed over them leaving only the hands and face visible. Later methods were scarcely more subtle: lobotomy, a crude incision in the frontal lobe of the brain that could turn the patient into a zombie; and ECT, electroconvulsion therapy or shock treatment that brought on powerful convulsions and was administered without an anaesthetic. Both were considered to be advances in their time, and so was Largactil, the drug Freddie was introduced to by the hospitals in Yorkshire, and which Bexley staff called the 'liquid cosh'.

One of the major tranquillisers or antipsychotic drugs that reached Britain from America in the 1950s, the phenothiazine Largactil became Bexley's key sedative. Used to calm potentially aggressive and dangerous patients, it allowed the hospital to do away with straitjackets and the more primitive cosh. By the time Freddie reached Bexley the unpleasant and even dangerous side effects of such drugs were becoming plain. It turned out he was allergic to Largactil – there was a suspicion it helped trigger his epilepsy – and he was switched to other major tranquillisers. The clinic that despatched Freddie to Bexley repeatedly told Olivia the drug doses prescribed by the Yorkshire hospitals were too high, and that it was impossible to know whether he could be helped until they had been cut back. To sweeten the news of Freddie's expulsion Olivia was assured Bexley had agreed to reduce his drugs, but this did not diminish her horror at what had happened and she telephoned everyone she could think of to protest, and was weeping by the time she talked to Mary Austen, the healer who had Freddie 'on the box'. At Bexley the doctors said no such request to cut back Freddie's drugs had been made, and if it had they could not have agreed because they were under-staffed. It was not much different, perhaps, from what their predecessors might have said if asked to abandon the straitjacket and the padded cell. The implication, at once spotted by an apprehensive Olivia, was that the hospital could only function if potentially troublesome patients – and there was no doubting that was how Freddie would be seen – were kept permanently dozy by drugs.

After a short time under observation Freddie was put in an open ward where as many as fifty male patients might be looked after by three, and sometimes only two, nurses. He was switched to different tranquillisers, haloperidol and chlorpromazine, but the doses remained high. He was also given courses of ECT under anaesthetic which had the effect of temporarily quieting him – 'stunning' him, Olivia said – when he was restless and rowdy, but had no lasting result. He was sent for an electroencephalogram which, like an earlier one made when he was in hospital in Yorkshire, failed to reveal any brain damage. Freddie obviously benefited from an anti-convulsant that diminished the frequency and intensity of his seizures, but neither the powerful tranquillisers nor the shock therapy were of any use for his core condition of autism and aphasia, and the doctors eventually admitted they were doing him no good. It was no dishonour to Bexley that it was helpless, but the result was that Freddie and patients like him were condemned to be controlled by drugs while more positive treatment was given to less difficult cases.

After Freddie's blow-up in Botton and Olivia's experience of other hospitals' reluctance to handle him she tried to see the positive side of his new home. She worried, though, that he was not getting enough fresh air because he was not allowed to roam Bexley's grounds on his own for fear he might get out. The management had decided the hospital gates, which were designed to be kept shut, should be permanently open to avoid giving the hospital a prison-like appearance. This was not so much to please the inmates – there were others like Freddie who suffered from not being able to enjoy the spacious grounds – but to reassure a well-meaning public that was becoming uneasy about locking away the mentally troubled.

A similar motive lay behind the closure, not long before Freddie arrived, of the hospital's farm: Bexley feared that making use of inmates to work its land might open it to charges of exploiting them as slave-labour. One can imagine Karl König grinding his teeth over decisions taken to alleviate the guilt of 'normal' society about the care of its mentally disabled members rather than out of concern for the patients' own needs.

Freddie was at least able to wander around the tunnel-like hospital corridor to visit other wards. Thanks to his Camphill background he was a recognisable personality in spite of his handicaps and several of the nurses took to him and were soon offering him cups of sweet tea when he came visiting. The doctors were elusive: in Freddie's first eight months at Bexley Olivia saw the head doctor and the ward doctor just once each, and then only briefly. But she felt the nurses in Freddie's ward were fond of him, and so they became her regular point of contact with the hospital authorities. She also knew Freddie's comfort and state of mind depended on these nurses more than anyone else, for busy doctors had no reason to spend time on a patient they could not help. When Olivia did talk to the doctors they were likely to feel harassed by her questions and admonitions, while she went away depressed by their inability to do anything for her son apart from prescribing drugs. 'They just don't care, Thomas,' she wrote in an outburst to Weihs, though in calmer moments she admitted the problem was that they were more helpless than uncaring.

After observing Freddie for several months the hospital concluded he was 'perfectly manageable' most of the time, though only if the high drug levels were maintained. But there were also times, 'not all that infrequent', when he 'lashes out and butts people and is very noisy'. He was given a small room off the main ward where the door, which had no handle on the inside, could be closed on him when he became rowdy and unsettled. Once when he was locked in like this he rammed the door so hard with his back that he forced it from its frame, after which the hospital put in a metal frame to stop him doing it again. His old habits of self-aggression such as banging his head and biting his wrists grew worse, and sometimes Olivia arrived to find him with scratches on his face or an eyebrow that had been stitched up.

Bill Walter, a Bexley nurse who knew Freddie well, thought the chief cause of these tantrums was frustration at his inability to communicate, and was not surprised that locking Freddie in his little room sometimes made matters worse. Frustration, or so the nurses told Olivia, also explained the incident in which Freddie pushed over an old man. The man, a fellow patient, had badgered Freddie to talk and the more he insisted the angrier Freddie got. As a result Freddie was sent for a brief spell to the hospital's locked ward until a sympathetic young Indian doctor, supported by the nurses, got him out. Walter's suspicion that frustration was a large part of the problem was confirmed by a London child psychiatrist whom Thomas Weihs persuaded to examine Freddie at Bexley. The specialist had no doubt about Freddie's infantile autism or that, as happened in a minority of cases, his condition had deteriorated in adolescence. But he identified Freddie's chief difficulty as 'intense frustration reactions' because he could not speak. His tests confirmed what was already suspected: that Freddie could only understand simple instructions and make primitive gestures of his own. Demanding more of him risked provoking his anger. The specialist nevertheless thought it might be possible to teach Freddie some two hundred words, 'certainly not normal conversational speech but perhaps enough to circumvent his present difficulties in making his needs known'. If there was progress, Freddie might even be able to work in sheltered conditions, but it was unlikely he would ever leave hospital. Bexley told Olivia nothing of this – one of her frequent cries was 'if only Drs would *tell* one more one would I think worry less' – and it was only thanks to the ever-helpful Weihs that she learnt about this opinion. She thought it too optimistic, partly because she guessed, correctly, that Bexley would not be able to provide a psychologist for such intensive therapy, but also because she was by then resigned to Freddie never breaking out of his silence.

For all its faults Bexley had one advantage in Olivia's eyes, its closeness to London. She could visit her son every week if she wanted to. Often she took a friend with her, and my father would go when he was not away on work, but one thing never changed when she set off in her Mini for the drive to Bexley through the tangle of south London. She approached each meeting with all the excitement and careful preparation she must have shown when going to see Sam Bucknill in wartime Britain; and when she caught her first glance of her son she was illuminated with happiness. Her first task was always to track down the ward nurses to find out if he needed anything or if he seemed troubled by some pain he could not tell them about. Then she took him for a drive. She put Freddie in the back of the car where she would talk to him while he looked through the picture magazines she brought him or just sat rocking gently, and on good days he could seem as happy in his way as she in hers. They kept up the habits of his childhood, stopping at little shops to buy sweets and ice creams – he particularly liked ice lollies, perhaps because of their neon colours – and in cafes to have cups of tea. There were alarms whenever they saw a dog, for he had acquired a terror of them and would scream and try to run away as soon as he saw one. Olivia accepted this as another quirk to be lived with, and she learned to laugh as she manoeuvred him away before he could spot an approaching animal. As outings go they were not much; and they were as shadowed by apprehension as the times she spent with Sam before he sailed to Africa and death.

When she could not be with Freddie she kept up her spirits by telephone calls to the ward. If a nurse gave Freddie the receiver he would put it to his ear and make one of his sounds at her. Sometimes he would take a nurse by the hand and point to the telephone to indicate he wanted them to telephone Olivia, but this was a delicate business for if the nurse called and she was not in, Freddie became upset. She bolstered herself with the hope that the isolation imposed by his autism was now an advantage. Freddie, always disdainful of things and people he was not interested in, might be oblivious, she thought, to the wretchedness of the people he lived among and the dreariness of his surroundings. Perhaps he did not see what she saw when their ramblings through the hospital took them to one of the geriatric wards where old men and women waited to die without even knowing that that was all there was in store for them. She did not know what was in Freddie's memory, and whether he pined for Botton or Camphill. She could not guess whether he understood the future as some-thing it was possible to look forward to or dread. But *she* pined for him to be back in his Yorkshire life and *she* imagined only too clearly a future in which he stayed year after year in Bexley with nothing but slow siege by drugs in store for him.

Her ever-present anxiety strained her marriage with my father. They had got over the crisis triggered by Freddie's departure to school in Scotland and the selling of the farm where he had hoped to lead his ideal life. He got a job with Pye of Cambridge and, helped by his affability and charm, made a success of it, eventually travelling round the world selling telecommunications equipment to countries that were on the brink of setting up television. Often he spent the working week in Cambridge and Olivia would sometimes write to him there to tell him how she spent her days, and to repeat how fond she was of him. The truth was she never minded being on her own in the flat in London. She had many friends and liked nothing better than pottering around Chelsea, and she used the arthritis that was beginning to trouble her as an excuse not to accompany him on business trips abroad. She would apologise for that: 'Do you mind darling having a wife who is so often not able to do things? Bad health is such a bore.' Yet there was an air of contentment in the letters of that time. 'Our lives are odd but *good*,' she wrote to him several years before Freddie went to Bexley.

The forced move to the hospital, and Olivia's determination to help her son without knowing how, destroyed this balance that they had with difficulty achieved. My father thought she was tormenting herself to no purpose, but when he tried to draw her into other things he risked being accused of not caring about Freddie. He loved his adopted son and pitied him, but he loved Olivia more, and perhaps already felt he was losing her to an obsession that was damaging both of them. Aware of how he felt, Olivia was unable to share *her* feelings with him. She wrote two despairing letters to Weihs whose continuing compassion for Freddie touched her deeply and

who seemed the only confessor she could turn to. It was to
Weihs that she revealed her fear that the 'nightmare obsession'
with Freddie was 'destroying' her. 'Thomas, *how* does one
control one's brain, mine seems to have gone mad . . .' Her
wretchedness, she admitted, went 'beyond the normal worry
for a much-loved handicapped child . . . He is in my thoughts
last thing at night & the moment I wake. "What is he doing, is
he afraid locked into his room, are the other patients cruel to
him?" ' The result was loneliness 'because it is a subject I must
hide from my husband. His worry has always been for me &
not for Freddie & at times this has almost parted us.' She could
even only write these letters when she was alone in the flat, for
when she sat at her desk 'the tears run down my face'.

She hated what she saw almost every week at the hospital,
'the drugs with their varied & awful side effects, & then the fits
& the rages & the door with no handle on the inside & all the
poor tough sordid world of overcrowding & noise'. She felt
guilty that Freddie had to live like this. 'If I took him home &
kept him with me always *could* I cope, could I make him
happy?' It would of course mean parting from Roger, but 'this
mad idea' haunted her. So many people had prayed for Freddie
but he only got worse and 'at times I've very nearly lost my
faith – but thank God never quite. Somehow I know that God
is there & that all will be well in the end.' She wondered if there
was a pill to cure her intolerable obsession and answered her
own question. 'I don't think this is a pill thing, do you, more a
firmer faith in God.'

'Wise & good' Olivia called Weihs, and certainly he never
let her down. His unfailingly prompt answers made up for the
lack of time and compassion of other doctors, and for that
reason sometimes made her weep. He was patient, succinct,

firm, but always tender. He told her not to punish herself with
the thought she could do more for Freddie, and above all not
to think she ought to have him at home. That was unreal, he
said with emphasis, and for the moment the hospital was 'still
the most relatively adequate place' for him. He warned her
never to think her devotion to Freddie was to no purpose.
Though Weihs wrote that he, too, felt 'very helpless and
inadequate' he was 'certain that your love . . . is the most, and
probably the only, real help to him. I am deeply convinced
that such real and strong feelings are what really count and
what really help to make things tolerable.' But what reads like
his chief purpose in sending the letter was a carefully phrased
paragraph about her relationship with my father.

> I also feel that I can only too well understand and also
> appreciate Roger's attitude. He, however, does need you
> and your love just as much as Freddie and for Roger you can
> do something on a level where you cannot really help
> Freddie.

At the best of times it was not an argument likely to appeal
to Olivia. In the worst of times that were about to break over
her it did not stand a chance. Though he had bad periods as
well as good Freddie's first two years at Bexley passed
reasonably smoothly. There was, though, a nasty incident
when he was eating fish and a bone stuck in his throat. Not
understanding what had happened he panicked and seemed to
threaten another patient sitting near him with his fork. From
that moment fish joined dogs as something those looking after
him had to avoid at all costs. Then a change of nurses on his
ward seemed to unsettle him; and shortly afterwards he met

two women he had never seen before in the hospital corridor. Olivia left her version of what happened.

> One day he suddenly made sort of advances to two lady visitors in the passage! The nurses told me one had a huge bosom in a very <u>tight</u> sweater & the other practically none. Freddie went up and flipped the big ones in the air and tried to find the other ones! They were quite naturally annoyed & rushed to the head Dr and said Freddie had sexually assaulted them. He's never done this before or since though has always been amused by ladies bosoms also balloons & jelly. I think its the wobble! Camphill says he's never done more than flip them & so did the nurses. But the sad result was that he was put into the locked ward and on a course of hormone pills.

It was typical that she wrote about him as though he were a child for whom bosoms, jelly and balloons were all much the same, although Gerda had told her often enough of his interest in ladies' bare arms. Perhaps Olivia was being disingenuous, but not seriously so. Freddie's interest in women seemed as partial as his fascination with any object that caught his eye and for a while preoccupied him. Neither then nor later did his sexual adventures go beyond this tentative stage. But the women who complained about him apparently made no allowances for the fact that they were in a mental hospital, and the Bexley management reacted as though it were scared they might lodge a serious complaint if no action was taken.

There were already enough question marks in Freddie's record. The incident after he swallowed the fish bone, his outburst against Gerda Blok and the knocking down of the old man all counted against him. If there was another and more serious one the hospital could be accused of ignoring danger signals. Freddie was a big young man, almost six foot tall and quite strongly built, and he had not yet acquired the slouch and slowness that drugs had induced in some of the hospital's older inmates. Olivia naturally found it hard to accept that others might find him threatening, but people who did not know him, or could not hit it off with him, were sometimes scared by his truculent manner even if it was no more than the grown-up version of the cheekiness Gerda had enjoyed in the child. His transfer to N2, the men's locked ward – this time permanently – may have been misguided but it was not altogether surprising, and it was a fate suffered by many autistic people whose ill-understood isolation had exploded in anger.

It might have been worse. Bill Walter, the ward's experienced charge nurse, understood that Freddie had been put in his care chiefly because other wards did not know how to cope with him, and that if time was taken to try to understand his needs (not always easy in crowded and under-staffed conditions) there would be less anger and acts of self-aggression. Under Walter's sympathetic eye Freddie was often let out of the locked ward to wander on his own round the rest of the hospital. He caused no harm though on one occasion local dignitaries filing into Bexley's great hall for a banquet were surprised to find Freddie rocking gently on his feet beside a table set with a pig's head and other delicacies. But though he was allowed these escapes from the ward its noise and occasionally threatening atmosphere affected him and his behaviour deteriorated.

N2 was at the far end of the hospital's semi-circular corridor where the central heating scarcely reached and the masonry walls seemed prison-like in their thickness, a fitting approach to Freddie's limbo. The inside of the ward lived up to the gloom of the corridor that led to it. A plastic screen covered the windows that ran along one wall to prevent the glass being broken, making the room darker than it would otherwise have been and airless, too, and the ward was permeated by stale cigarette smoke. The only furniture were beds pushed close together, tables, chairs and television sets, all of which the inmates smashed from time to time. There were no lockers where Freddie could keep the few objects he possessed, what Olivia called his 'little treasures'. The ratio of five male nurses to twenty patients was perhaps adequate, but the ward took in highly disturbed people directly from the streets and it was possible for all the nurses to be tied up coping with them, leaving little time for routine matters. The nurses stored the patients' clothes and doled them out when they thought a change was necessary. It was not long before Freddie's clothes were lost and he began wearing underwear and even shirts and trousers that belonged to someone else. The ward was grimy. Patients blew their noses on the linoleum floor. There was little supervision of their cleanliness and Freddie soon stopped brushing his teeth. At mealtimes food was pushed through a hatch and patients could take and eat it how and where they liked. Some went out to work at the hospital's industrial unit but Freddie was not up to this. The only times he breathed fresh air was when a nurse took him for a walk in the grounds and when Olivia made her weekly visit and they went for a drive together.

She was horrified by how he looked after only a few weeks, dirty to the point of smelling and irritable as a result, but she was even more alarmed by his behaviour. Apart from violent rocking and head-banging he could become very angry, and for the first time since puberty started to smash things up, perhaps in imitation of the other inmates, some of whom were very violent (though usually not against each other). The nurses told Olivia Freddie was teased because he could not speak, and that the other patients tried to put the blame on him when furniture got broken. 'With no exercise & nothing to do,' Olivia complained to Weihs, 'he gets more tense & restless & then rocks & claps a lot & runs around & then the other patients get annoyed . . . & shout & bully him & this is what causes his temper tantrums.' Freddie was trapped in limbo's logic: the longer he stayed in this ward the worse he was likely to get, and the less likely ever to be allowed to leave.

Olivia picked up rumours from the nurses that the locked ward might be closed down (Bill Walter himself was lobbying hard for that), allowing its more stable inmates to go back to an open or perhaps even mixed-sex ward. This worried Olivia who imagined Freddie 'flapping up the boosums of any fat ladies . . . [and] now he's grown up people don't appreciate that'. If he could not survive again in an open ward what would his future then be? The nurses, 'who only tell me these things because we have become friends', had said they thought Freddie should never have been put in the locked ward in the first place, but he was now behaving so badly she could imagine an even worse alternative: 'one of those awful huge hospitals for subnormals that one has seen on television. But I must try (not easy) not to think about that.'

N2 quickly understood it had Freddie's mum to contend with as well as Freddie. Although almost seventy Olivia was still striking to look at – it was about this time that a middle-aged stranger in a Chelsea cafe complimented her on her 'moss-green' eyes. She was becoming frailer, but this was still hard to spot in the elegant and determined little figure that almost every week rang the locked ward's bell. She never admitted to being frightened by N2's inmates, and when she took friends with her assured them there was no need to be nervous. Her mind was on other things. I went with her once and like her was so concerned with how we would find Freddie that, after we were through the door, I noticed little except for furniture bolted to the floor and vaguely threatening shapes in the background. Never in her life had she felt that Freddie's well-being depended so much on her alertness to his moods and needs. She cultivated his new nurses, knowing his well-being now depended more than ever on their good will, and the best of them won her over by their handling of him. She admired how they coped with his agitated moods by taking both his hands and talking to him quietly until he eventually looked in their eyes and seemed to understand what they were saying. But she knew the nurses were overworked and that there would be many things that if she did not notice, nobody else would.

Freddie's moods varied. One week he was calm, the next (she wrote in a letter to me) he was 'looking very ill & filthy dirty & rocking a lot & rather crazy'. There were three successive weeks when on each visit she discovered something seriously wrong with him. The first time she noticed he had a bad ear infection and took him to one of the doctors who admitted it must have been extremely painful and at once prescribed antibiotics. The next week Freddie came rushing across the ward to her and taking her by the hand dragged her to his bed in a little L-shaped annexe at the end of the ward. This was where the nurses usually put the most violent men but they had moved Freddie there to give him some peace from the bullying and teasing of the other inmates. He 'pulled down the blankets,' she wrote, '& showed me his blankets were swarming with ants, to begin with I thought "lice" [some of the patients brought lice into the ward with them and Freddie had once caught them] but thank God they were ants though bad enough'. She called the nurses who were not surprised for there had been similar infestations before and they gave Freddie a 'much needed bath as he was scratching like anything'. When she went to the hospital the following week he was again 'very restless & looking very ill & they said he'd been "banging his head a bit"'. I found he had got toothache, he showed me a big hole in his tooth. The ward was bedlam and they'd perhaps not have noticed for days, so now they say he is put down for his dentist. Poor love think of being locked in with ants in your bed and toothache.'

This was surely what Thomas Weihs meant when he told her that her love was now 'the most, and probably the only, real help' to Freddie. Too highly-strung, in Karl König's opinion, to handle the difficult little child, her nervous energy and her constant anxiety had become the best and only means to keep up contact with the grown-up son. It was a battle between her obsessive concern for him on the one hand, and his own isolation from the world and the world's inclination to reject him on the other. These were the years when she thought her feeling for Freddie was 'the only really unselfish love I've ever known. It's for him I cry with pity and love, not for me.'

But even her energy had its limits, and there were moments when she feared he would never leave the locked ward and she could think of only one way for him to escape. In a note she wrote in 1973 seeking the advice of yet another doctor she confessed she was unable to sleep and was haunted by Freddie's face. 'He is capable of great suffering I think & great fear & frustration as well as great joy,' yet she could not help feeling

> I'd rather he was dead than where he is now. I love him so much & he is so affectionate when we take him out in the car – kissing me & holding my hand & I feel in despair for him – I'm 68 now & we are getting old & must think of his future.

Freddie had by then been in the locked ward for almost three years. The only future she could accept for him was that either he should go back to Botton before she died or that he would die before she did. She was not given to melodrama: if she contemplated some extreme action the chances were she would carry it out. 'If you knew how often I've felt I *can't* bear it,' she wrote to my father, '& longed to give our dear son a whole box of sleeping pills, it would be so easy.' Religious scruple prevented her – 'for some strange reason . . . one feels it is wrong' – and she was left contemplating an intolerable future. Contemplating it, what was more, in a state of isolation not far removed from that of her son. Though she liked the nurses and believed them well-disposed to Freddie, she knew they did not have much time to listen to her. She made friends with Frank Martin, the hospital's Anglican chaplain, whom she met in the Bexley chapel, a large neo-classical barn opposite the visitors' entrance where she took Freddie to pray after they had been for their weekly drive. When I visited Bexley not long ago faint writing on the chapel door proclaimed 'I will kill you', but inside all was calm, and it was easy to imagine Olivia and Freddie sitting on one of the plain wooden pews between the white pillars that support the blue barrel-vaulted ceiling, he enjoying the light and space denied him in the locked ward and she content simply to be with him. Martin was the hospital's first fulltime chaplain for many years. The psychiatric staff ignored him to begin with – the new drugs had replaced not only the cosh and the padded cell but God, too – but later came to accept him as a useful member of the hospital's team. Martin loved his work and had a good sense of humour and Olivia took to him. He was always ready to listen to her and she, at least, believed he might be doing good when after they had talked he blessed Freddie and her together as she and Sam had once been blessed in wartime Glasgow.

She talked about Freddie to her friends, too, and indeed to almost anyone she met, however briefly, if they seemed sympathetic. People who knew her accepted it as her hobby horse, and if those who loved her did not mind hearing the same stories repeated many times over, others tried not to sit next to her too often at the lunch or dinner table. Throughout this time of crisis I was working in Asia and she talked to me through a series of long letters, in which she did not hide her feeling that my father did not want to listen to her and that her patience with him was draining away. 'He had a slight go of gout again,' she wrote after he was back in London after a fishing holiday in Scotland, 'and a bad cold so immense drama!' The cold prevented him going down to Bexley with her. 'It seems so odd that he is always quite well when standing fishing all day in icy water or plodding across ploughed fields shooting things.' They were still in the trap she had described to Thomas Weihs a couple of years before, she pressing him always harder to match her anxiety about Freddie, he not knowing how to distract her from her obsession without appearing to be selfish and unfeeling. They had, she wrote, some 'pretty violent rows over it all which makes life even more tiring, even to the extent of me saying "I can quite see that it may be so awful that you can't stand it in which case why don't you *leave* me, I'd never blame you & I'd be allright, why don't you go." Then he gets furious, poor old boy.'

At moments like this she would go back over the past, and end up blaming herself as well as him.

> We sat one night from 8 to 11 at the kitchen table arguing about it and at times I feel we've got somewhere but never really I'm afraid. It is unfair on him I suppose but I didn't choose to adopt a handicapped child & get to love it, & I can't help minding all its suffering so much & if I've got to pretend to him all the time it makes the strain so much worse. I don't want him to do anything . . . like a sort of martyr, but because he cares too. But he is such an escapist & so selfish & I expect he thinks I am too! Now it's blown over for the moment we plod on . . . You see he has an absolute genius for saying the wrong thing at the wrong moment & I can never understand why! I'm sure it all stems from the fact that he knew that I wasn't in love with him when I married him & never have been since though I am in a way fond of him & could have become more so if he'd been more able to really help. I should never have married him I suppose & certainly wouldn't have done so if I'd known Freddie wasn't normal.

She could laugh at their plight. 'Don't worry dearest,' she reassured me, 'I won't throw the old boy out because I do think he'd be unhappy & dreadfully *embarrassed* too don't you?! & then I'd feel so guilty.' She would not, however, change her ways.

> I'm afraid I have <u>no</u> alternative but to do what I try to do to help Freddie . . . As I see it I'm old, 70 next birthday . . . & I've had a very full & varied life which is nearly over. So I feel it doesn't matter a bit to me now I've had so much & it is the life & happiness of a young boy we are playing with. But I can't expect anyone else to feel the same, why should they . . .

She imagined a chill future for my father and herself. 'We'll jog along & be friends at times & fail each other at every turn.'

Olivia sometimes puzzled people who knew how much she grieved for Freddie by her continuing capacity for bursts of gaiety. Even when she was with him she was always ready to laugh if he was in the mood, and in her letter to me paragraphs of despair would be followed by others making light of the problems of the greater world around her. The drama of the locked ward coincided with the years of war in the Middle East, of the oil crisis, and with a mood of menace in the life of Britain. 'There is a sinister sort of atmosphere . . . and nothing seems to work properly any more, even the small things,' she wrote at the start of 1974. People, she reported with amazement, were even talking of the possibility of revolution '& someone said to me "you must carry your diamonds with you always so you will have something left." I said I had no diamonds and they looked horrified!' She said she never lost sleep over things she could do nothing about; and it was 'not like in the war when one rushed into the ambulance driving & that sort of thing. By the way we've had a few little bombs nearby, it quite takes one back.'

Perhaps it is 'Armageddon' how <u>do</u> you spell it? Do you
remember [the Bible] prophesied that the world would end
starting with war in the Middle East? <u>Do</u> come back for it
darling, I'd rather we all went off together & as you know
I'm sure the next world will be utterly marvellous!

In fact the past year had brought the first flicker of hope
that Freddie might be rescued from his limbo. Olivia had got
nowhere with the doctors she consulted during the almost
three years since he went into the locked ward. Nothing had
come of Weihs's attempts to get Freddie out of Bexley and
temporarily into a Camphill community so he could then be
readmitted to a different, hopefully more suitable, hospital.
For a time she even considered a leucotomy, the primitive
brain surgery involving an incision into the brain's frontal
lobe, until psychiatrists explained to her its crudeness and the
wider, irreparable damage it was likely to do to a patient's
personality. She was tempted, though, because she thought
this possibly dangerous procedure might quieten him sufficiently to allow him to be moved into an open ward. Hard to
imagine though it was after watching Freddie and Olivia on
their days out together, he was now regarded as irredeemably
unmanageable although his violence was directed against
objects or himself. There is no evidence he ever hurt anyone
else in N2, though in moments of anger he could look
menacing and would poke at people with his hand.

His behaviour puzzled the doctors. It alternated between the
good, when he scarcely needed drugs and was his old likeable
self, and the very bad when the drugs had no control over him.
Camphill villages had discovered that autistic people often
went through a crisis in their late twenties when the aloneness
that is at the core of their condition seemed to become

intolerable to them. Bexley's psychiatrists thought the spells of violence too severe to be explained only by his inability to speak. If none of them openly admitted the locked ward itself as another likely cause it was perhaps because there was no point. There was nowhere else for him to go.

Since the only forseeable treatment was ever higher doses of drugs the doctors were as anxious as Olivia to find some other way to limit what they called Freddie's 'explosions of aggression'. Bexley's neighbour hospital the Brook General had a prominent neurosurgical unit and doctors there suggested a new sort of brain operation being performed by a surgeon in Edinburgh. Olivia gathered that the operation's purpose was to reduce aggression but that unlike earlier brain surgery it did not leave the patient with a crippled personality. She wrote at once to the surgeon, Edward Hitchcock, at Edinburgh University's Department of Neurological Surgery, and got back a guarded answer. Hitchcock said he could not intervene in Freddie's case without being asked to by Bexley, and from what she had told him her son sounded too violent to be brought up to Scotland for the necessary preliminary examination. He had not reckoned with Olivia in terrier-like mood. She had no difficulty persuading Bexley to agree to let Hitchcock see Freddie in the locked ward, and she offered to pay for him to fly down to London in the morning, be ferried to and from the airport by car, and return home to Edinburgh the same evening. Hitchcock agreed, but reluctantly. It meant sacrificing a whole day in a busy schedule and what he had heard of Freddie did not make him optimistic.

The prospect of Hitchcock's visit increased rather than diminished the tension in my parents' life, Olivia's anxiety being reflected in dreams in which she went to airports to meet the surgeon but was never able to find him. In waking moments she tormented herself with the possibility – quite likely, to judge by the tone of his letter – that he would refuse to operate. The fateful visit was fixed for November and Olivia and my father made elaborate preparations for it. She set off in a hired car to meet the surgeon at Gatwick while my father drove in his car to Bexley. The idea, she explained in a long letter to me, was that the surgeon would be returned to his aeroplane in the hired car while she and my father took Freddie for his usual drive: the nurses had warned her Freddie might 'tear the place apart' if she left the hospital together with the doctor.

Hitchcock was in early middle age, with the handsome looks and self-confidence one expects of a successful surgeon, and Olivia at once took to him. She found him '*so* nice' and talked to him all the way from Gatwick to Bexley. He kept on telling her:

'I may have to say no to the operation when I see him.' Freddie we'd been told was in a very disturbed mood, not <u>quite</u> as bad as that day when we took him out but very restless and tense! Perhaps it was best that he saw him like that. It was <u>very</u> nerve-racking. We met Rog [Roger, my father] on arrival at Bexley & then we & Hitchcock were asked to go up to . . . the head psychiatrist's room, who we <u>never</u> see normally! . . . A lot of talk went on & then they went up to the ward with Hitchcock who said he wanted to 'assess' Freddie first by himself & then with us – He said of course it is very hard to assess someone who can't talk & whose moods vary so much. We waited for about an hour in suspense downstairs. Luckily there was a nice charge nurse on who understands Freddie very well. We gather . . . he was very apprehensive & gave each Dr a small pinch as if to say 'I don't trust you!' They took him into the nurses' little room by himself but he wasn't having that & went out to fetch the nurse he liked & brought him in by the hand. There was a lot of rocking & sweating but amazingly when Hitchcock drew some circles & squares etc on a piece of paper & asked F. to copy them, he did it very fast like a tycoon signing some letters & handed it back with great disdain!

Then we were sent for. Freddie by then had been let go & was at the end of the ward & not expecting us. When a patient shouted 'Your mum's here' he came tearing along as he always does with outstretched arms & took my hand & kissed me & started to take me to the door as if to say 'let's get out of here!' Hitchcock saw all this & then I persuaded Freddie to come into the nurses' room with us looking <u>awful</u> poor love sweating & rocking a lot.

Olivia distracted Freddie with a bag of sweets, persuading him to offer them to everyone in the room. A little later Hitchcock took Olivia aside. The surgeon was not a stranger to mental hospitals but Bexley's locked ward had shaken even him. What he would remember from that day was an enormous room furnished with some chairs that were mostly broken and several television sets all with their screens kicked in, and everywhere violent-looking men ('You don't want to worry about these people, dear,' Olivia told him). He found Freddie in his little space at the end of the ward, not aggressive but a bit scared, and scarcely paying any attention to his unexpected visitors. Hitchcock had been told Freddie's behaviour had been getting worse in the past year in the locked ward and, doubting it could ever improve in this frightening place, he told Olivia he was ready to try the operation. He warned her it might make no difference, but said it might also make him 'less tense & stop the violence', though it was particularly difficult to judge the likely impact on people who were autistic.' He said, Olivia wrote in her letter to me, 'that if the only other alternative is a locked ward he has got nothing to lose & if he was my son I'd try it.'

The day ended with Hitchcock being whisked away by the surgeon from Brook General, 'to pick the great man's brains', Olivia thought. It was dark by the time my parents took Freddie for the drive he had been waiting for. My father drove and Olivia sat in the back with her son. He held her hand, and by the time they got back to the hospital he was calmer.

9

Escape

Although Olivia did not know it, the operation Edward Hitchcock proposed to perform on Freddie was as controversial as it was rare. There is no reason to suppose her decision would have been different had she been better informed about what was involved, for she had shown by the experiment of Freddie's psychoanalysis that she was, when desperate, ready to go through any medical door that opened to her. Hitchcock was the only person in Britain at the time with both the technical skill and the new Japanese-made equipment that the highly sophisticated operation required. Called an amygdalotomy, or amygdalectomy, it aimed to destroy through the implantation of electrodes abnormal brain cells in the amygdala, a nucleus on either side of the brain's temporal lobe. Such a delicate procedure was impossible using the rough techniques of earlier brain surgeons who had operated 'blind', and could only guess that they were inserting their instruments into the right part of the brain.

Brain surgery was revolutionised by the invention in the 1960s of so-called stereotaxic instruments that provided a three-dimensional map of the brain. Combined with an X-ray monitoring screen this allowed the surgeon to visualise the brain as he placed the electrodes in it. The result was far greater accuracy and therefore far less collateral damage: it was estimated that an amygdalotomy damaged only a tenth of the brain tissue that was destroyed by an old-fashioned lobotomy. The amygdala was chosen as a target because it was thought to trigger epilepsy and violence related to it. In Britain between 1970 and 1976 just eight such operations were performed to treat aggression, and only thirty for epilepsy. American research showed later that seven per cent of such amygdalotomies brought excellent results and twenty-five per cent significant improvement, while the rest produced no noteworthy change, either good or bad. Another study claimed the procedure gave relief to half of the patients operated on for epilepsy, and to a third of those with tendencies to aggression: Hitchcock was being frank with Olivia when he told her he might succeed with Freddie, but that he also might achieve nothing at all.

Amygdalotomies made up only a small percentage of the new psychosurgery that was carried out in the 1970s. In Britain by far the greatest number of brain operations were for depression or obsessive behaviour, but it was the amygdalotomy's supposed usefulness as a cure for violence that was to make it notorious. The trouble began in America, which in the first half of the 1970s was turned in on itself by the scandal of Watergate and the tragedy of the Vietnam war. All institutions and professions suspected of being used by authority to manipulate citizens came under attack. Proposals had been made to use psychosurgery on violent convicted prisoners, and what could be more manipulative, in the eyes of American radicals, than doctors using brain operations to 'cure' citizens of violence whose real cause, the radicals insisted, was the sickness of American society? The tide of opinion turned so quickly that in 1974 psychosurgery was nearly banned. Similar criticism was heard in Britain, and in Japan the surgeon who carried out the first amygdalotomy was nearly lynched by his students. In America a commission was appointed to investigate psychosurgery but in spite of its members' original doubts about such operations it concluded that they did have value and should be allowed to continue, albeit with safeguards.

When Hitchcock proposed to operate on Freddie all he needed was the agreement of two psychiatrists and the consent of his parents. Today his case would have to go before a commission, and the process is so time-consuming that very little psychosurgery of any kind is being done. The argument over whether operating on the brain is any different from operating on the stomach seems to have been won by those who think it is. Olivia knew she was taking a risk on her son's behalf: she admitted to me she was 'terrified that [the operation] might, if it went wrong, make him worse & that he might not be the dear Freddie we love any more'. But she was sure she had no other choice. Like a general ready to use any means to save a battle that is on the brink of being lost she regarded Hitchcock and his miracle-working Japanese equipment as her last hope of victory.

Her immediate fear was different: that something might intervene to prevent Hitchcock from operating. His agreement was the 'little ray of hope' she had been praying for, hope 'not for a cure, one never expected that, but that Freddie might be made happier & more at peace'. But the surgeon would not operate until Freddie's drugs had been reduced and it needed several weeks before they could be brought down to a level safe for surgery. He was also unable to give Olivia a firm date for the operation. She feared the suspense might go on for months and though she told herself how much worse it would have been if he had said 'no', there were times (she wrote to me) when she felt 'afraid & very old'. Before Hitchcock's visit to Bexley she had dreamed of going to meet him at an airport and not being able to find him; now she imagined everything that might go wrong in the complicated business of getting Freddie and the nurses who were to accompany him from Kent to Scotland. If they went as soon as she hoped it would still be winter and their car might get trapped by snow, and would they have enough petrol which had just been rationed because of the oil crisis?

As her mind circled round these problems a tentative date was set for January, only to be cancelled when a shortage of nursing staff closed down an entire floor of Hitchcock's hospital. He suggested that instead he might come south to do the operation in the Brook General, which only added to Olivia's misery, for it was obvious he preferred to work in his own hospital and with his own surgical team. The only good news was that Bexley, in preparation for the operation, had succeeded in reducing Freddie's drugs. 'Rather funny really,' she commented, 'it made no difference at all, he was no better but certainly *no* worse, they'd always said they couldn't possibly do it when I asked them!' Otherwise conditions in the locked ward were as gloomy as ever, and almost every visit revealed something new wrong with a by now chronically filthy Freddie. Relief came suddenly in early April when Hitchcock sent a message telling them to come to Edinburgh at once. A Rolls-Royce was hired at a cut rate from an Air Force friend of my father with a car hire business so they could take Freddie and his two nurses from Bexley to King's Cross; and at the station an entire train compartment was reserved for them – 'at vast expense', Olivia could not help commenting. Everything would have gone according to plan if a 'stupid' doctor in Bexley, in preparation for the journey, had not 'drugged Freddie into a sort of Zombie' by giving him that morning two hundred milligrams of the powerful tranquilliser Chlorpromazine. He slept through most of the train journey, but cheered up by the time they got to Edinburgh and the Western General Hospital, and seemed to like the single room he was given.

All the notes made on Freddie during his years at Bexley have apparently been lost or destroyed, but one of the nurses who went with him to Edinburgh made a record that has survived of the operation and its aftermath. Woken up early the following morning to be prepared for surgery he was given a bath but then, 'back to his normal inquisitive self . . . took himself off for a tour of the unit'. The operation began at nine and lasted for four hours. The Bexley nurses told Olivia it was the most complicated surgery they had seen and that they were 'terrified for Freddie', but everything went well apart from slight bleeding from the incision into the left temporal lobe that needed re-dressing. After a wretched day of waiting in their room in the Caledonian Hotel Olivia and my father were allowed to see Freddie in the late afternoon. His head was in bandages and he was dozy but he held her hand and was able to sip a cup of his favourite sweet hospital tea. Hitchcock let him get up the next day and a speech therapist called round to 'help him form words (with very little success!)', the nurse's exclamation mark suggesting he could have told the therapist it was a waste of effort.

On the third post-operative day [the nurse's notes con-
tinued] we observed the first signs of annoyance and
aggression, 'finger-prodding' and tense facial grimaces but
he soon settled down, and caused no problem. He spent
much of his time walking round the ward, examining
everything of interest, and going up & down in the ward
lift. He quickly made friends with all the female staff, and at
this stage became the 'ward pet', receiving frequent attention from most people in the ward!

It was the beginning of a new period of suspense. Hitchcock
told Olivia it would be nine months before they could judge if
the operation was having an effect; as she put it, whether it
would 'make *no* difference at all, or . . . help a bit, or a great
deal, to make him calmer & happier & stop the aggression'. At
least she thought she could already tell that the brain surgery
had not changed his personality. Freddie was 'just the same
only very tired & sleeping a lot, no wonder, the 1st night he
had to have his temperature & his blood pressure & all sorts of
tests every ½ hour'. She, too, was exhausted though 'thankful',
and the rare large glass of whisky she allowed herself when
sitting down to write to me made her 'slightly tight'. Later she
remembered their week in Edinburgh as 'enchanted . . . a
wonderful hospital . . . no suffering or fear and such *sweet*
people'.

After eight days Freddie was moved to Bexley's neighbour
the Brook General because it had the necessary surgical
expertise to continue monitoring his recovery. The nurse
found Freddie 'slightly more anxious, and at times . . . tense
and angry', and recorded that he ate several cigarette packets
and on one occasion a woolly hat. He thought this was because
Olivia and my father were no longer constantly with him as

they had been in Hitchcock's hospital in Edinburgh. But it was encouraging, he went on, that 'up till now there has been no sign of any rocking that was so evident in his pre-operative behaviour. He also seems more relaxed & happy, and on the evidence of his behaviour should cause no real difficulty in an open ward.'

Freddie returned to Bexley where he was put in R1, a mixed open ward, sixteen days after he had set out for Edinburgh. My father went back to work but Olivia settled in a pub near by because she had been told it would help if for a while she continued to see Freddie every day. Although she liked the new ward very much they were difficult days. Since she was on her own it was not thought wise for her to take Freddie for his usual drives, and she had to pretend to him she had not brought her Mini. Freddie refused to believe her 'and rushed me round to look for it & though I hid it he always found it so I had to pretend it wasn't mine but the same type . . . It was dreadfully exhausting & a bad idea.' Instead they 'tore up & down the Bexley passages & round & round the garden & drank tea endlessly in the patients' canteen'. Much of the time she found him at his most loveable, but there were moments when he 'became so jealous & possessive about me that he got furious if anyone spoke to me & flew at them', pinching or pushing them away from her. He showed the same possessiveness towards one of the nurses who had gone with him to Edinburgh. It scared her to see him so 'bossy & cheeky' even though at other times he could be funny and make her laugh. For a while she was 'in despair' that the operation had changed nothing or – a fear she shared with no one – might have made him worse. Hitchcock had told them the period of aftercare was vital, and this made every difficult day she spent with Freddie seem more ominous.

At least she felt she could once more rely on my father. She thought he had been marvellous in Edinburgh – 'so sweet, no rows!' – and she was touched when he wrote her a loving letter on their twenty-seventh wedding anniversary while she was staying at the pub near Bexley. She sent back an affectionate answer. 'You said [these years] had been very happy for you & I pray that is really true. Of course I've had happy times too & I just want to say . . . thank you. Because I know they might have been very difficult ones for you & it is amazing that we are still together.' She thanked him for being '*so* wonderful lately, to see you & Freddie holding hands & being obviously so fond of each other has given me great happiness'. She felt he was at last as interested in Freddie as she was and asked, 'Don't you agree that to be interested makes it easier to bear?'

Freddie's alarming possessiveness diminished when she began to cut back her visits and by the time she was again seeing him just once a week he was much calmer. The nurse who went with him to Edinburgh thought it 'very difficult to assess how much the improvement is environmental', rather than the first results of the operation, meaning that just removing Freddie from the foul atmosphere of the locked ward might alone be enough to alter his behaviour for the better. Like most of the Bexley nurses he seemed to agree with Olivia that Freddie should never have gone to the locked ward, and that he came out of it far worse than he went in. The question now was whether with or without the help of the operation he had the capacity to improve still more in the less stressful surroundings of an open ward. By mid-summer Olivia dared to say she thought he had improved 'quite a lot . . . He is still very much the old Freddie, very much in a hurry but he hardly ever rocks & there has been no head banging.'

He had put on two stone since the operation, and had 'a rather large tummy which he seems to think very funny, & with his sort of crew cut hair [his head had been shaved for surgery] he looks a great tough'. He surprised everyone by deigning to take part in some painting therapy, though he copied other people's pictures rather than making his own. He was invited to the Hindu wedding of an Indian nurse and was reported to have behaved impeccably. One old interest remained. There were female nurses in the ward and 'he now & then kisses the bare arms of the prettier ones but they don't seem to mind that & it has made no major problems'.

In July Bexley's new head doctor told Olivia he thought it worth asking Botton if they would take Freddie back for a trial period. She was overjoyed, but knew she now had to persuade his old friends in Yorkshire to give him another chance. Once more it was 'such dreadful suspense', and she tried to keep up her spirits by telling herself that if Botton still found him unmanageable he could return to the comparatively pleasant open ward at Bexley – 'I'd die if he had to go back to the locked ward.' Olivia went up to Yorkshire and Thomas Weihs, whom she still thought 'quite the nicest & most unspoilt & attractive man I know', examined Freddie in London. The verdict was favourable, but it cannot have been easily reached. Even the warm-hearted Weihs's sympathy for Olivia could not decide the crucial question of who was to be Freddie's new house mother. Olivia hoped Gerda Blok would have him back but she had just had another baby and in spite of her affection for Freddie felt she could not accept responsibility for someone who needed so much supervision, and who, she believed, had in his own way resisted growing up.

In the end a volunteer was found and Freddie returned to

Botton in February the following year, a 'triumph' Olivia
called it, though she admitted it was also an occasion shot
through with unease from beginning to end. For the last time
Olivia and my father drove down to Bexley to collect him, a
drive they had grown to hate almost as much as the walk along
the corridor that grew colder as they approached the bolted
doors of ward N2. Olivia thought Freddie understood what
was happening when they packed his few possessions in a case,
and he seemed delighted when they reached the flat in London
where they were to spend the night before driving to
Yorkshire. Olivia sensed he was not feeling well. His face was
a bad colour and at moments he behaved as though he felt
dizzy. She guessed from his gestures that he had a pain in the
stomach. Afraid it might be his appendix she managed to
persuade a doctor in spite of the late hour to come and see him.
Freddie, who was in bed, was unexpectedly charming and did
not resist the doctor's examination, which only needed to be
brief. It was constipation, he announced, but so acute it had
affected Freddie's liver, which explained his sallow colour and
the spells of dizziness as well as the pain in his stomach. It was
Bexley's last, and characteristic, present to them. The one
thing she feared most during his seven years there was that no
one would notice when something was wrong with him, and
she was furious with the hospital for not keeping an eye on
something so basic, for constipation was an obvious possible
side effect of the drugs he was being given. But the last few
years had chastened her. Instead of picking up the telephone
the next morning to convey her rage she decided to say
nothing, for she knew that if the Botton experiment failed
Freddie would have nowhere to go but back to Bexley, and
she could not afford to make enemies there.

Olivia was longing to administer a dose of laxatives but realised this was unwise when they had a day's drive ahead of them, and they set off the next day with him still solidly constipated. The plan was to ease him back into his old Yorkshire life by the three of them staying together for a couple of days at the Botton guesthouse run by Olivia's friend Joyce Hogg. Freddie seemed to know where he was and to be pleased to be back, but he was so obviously feeling unwell that they dosed him with little pills and herbal tea and put him straight to bed.

Olivia and my father valued Joyce and Peter Hogg as guides to a Camphill world that, however much they admired and were grateful to it, at times puzzled them. Although Olivia went to König's lectures in London and later to those given by Thomas Weihs she was comfortable with her own faith and never felt drawn to anthroposophy; indeed never even, as she admitted, had more than a hazy grasp of what it was about. The people at Camphill and Botton never suggested parents should become followers of Rudolf Steiner, and although the religious life of the schools and villages reflected anthroposophical beliefs there was little in it that could not be accepted as general Christian celebration. But the fact that anthroposophy was the core of community life at Botton made Olivia feel she did not understand everything that went on there, or the reasons behind certain decisions that might affect Freddie and herself. Her friendships at Camphill were not built on shared ideas or ways of thought. Her response to Thomas Weihs was emotional; her great affection for Nora and Friedwart Bock and for Gerda was an echo of their caring love for Freddie.

The Hoggs provided a bridge to this world Olivia loved because it loved her son, but in which she always felt a little strange. She could talk to them as she talked to her friends in London, and they could laugh together about what both couples found amusing in Botton's unconventional ways. Most important, she shared with this typically decent couple the knowledge that only comes from having a disabled child. Their shared vulnerability set them apart from Botton's carers who, for all their devotion to their work, belonged to the great majority who have children who are considered 'normal'. Both as carers and fortunate parents Botton's co-workers belonged to the ranks of the powerful; they did not suffer the powerlessness that mothers like Olivia and Joyce Hogg had been forced to accept and constantly fought to compensate.

The day after they arrived Olivia and my father took Freddie round his old village. They had lunch in the house of Gerda. Freddie apparently recognised her and enjoyed himself, even shaking the hand of Gerda's eighteen-month-old baby. Then they went to Dalehead, the little stone house at the southern end of Danby dale where he was to live with his new house mother, Leonie van der Stok. This was a nerve-racking moment for Olivia because Freddie had not met Leonie before, and he gave her and some of the other people in Dalehead a few small pinches. Olivia showed him the little room with a view down the dale that he was to have for his own. She thought he seemed 'a bit worried & suspicious', though he cheered up when they went to a church service 'because he loved the singing'. The next day 'in the early morning he came into my bedroom & sat on my bed & held my hand & seemed to be trying to say "don't go!" I felt awful as you can imagine but told him it was going to be so lovely for him to stay at dear Botton & that we had to go back & do some work & he must be very good & work too & we'd come & take him out soon.' It was always her way to speak to him as though he understood, just as the black boy Luster in *The Sound and the Fury* talks to his charge Ben, asking him, 'How come you cant behave yourself like folks?' although he knows there will never be an answer. Olivia talked to Freddie because she thought he understood a little of what she said; but she talked to him also, I suspect, because she was lonely. Even though she knew many of the words were no more than sounds to him it was a kind of contact with him, and a comfort in her loneliness.

When they took him back to Dalehead the following day she again went up with him to his room to unpack his bag and put out 'all his little treasures'. His possessiveness towards her after the operation had so shocked Olivia that she and Leonie planned the stages of the farewell with Freddie as carefully as if it were a military campaign. They decided it would be best if Olivia and my father left the guesthouse because, although it was a fifteen-minute walk from Leonie's house, Freddie might go there to look for them. They moved instead to a local hotel and waited a day before returning to the village to see him again.

Leonie at once put Freddie to work in the garden. Olivia was glad because he needed exercise so badly, but it also made her anxious. 'He has been rushing about with a wheelbarrow but they do realise that having not worked for so long it will take time to learn to work again. He had a row with a boy who tried to boss him a bit – one's heart stops when one hears of any anger!' When Olivia and my father came back they took him for a drive as though they were again in the routine of weekly visits that he had got used to in Bexley. He seemed quite settled, but a little sad when they said goodbye in the afternoon. They were not so much sad as exhausted. 'I could

hardly see. One's *brain* so tired trying to remember to tell so
many people all the things he'd like to tell them himself & to
make things easier for them & for him.'

They spent the night in the hotel and set off for London in
the early morning. It was a fine, clear winter's day and seen
from the moor road the long finger of Danby dale must have
glowed with all the promise Olivia believed it held for her son
if only all would go well. At York they ran into fog which
lasted almost all the way to London, and once home in the flat
in Cadogan Square she realised that in spite of at last getting
Freddie back to Botton she had no feeling of achievement.
Partly it was because it was only, so far, a trial visit, and she
hardly dared hope it would work 'after so many things have
gone wrong in the past'. But there was something else that
darkened her mood. Although she knew Botton would 'try
very hard & want to keep him if they can', she felt 'dreadfully
depressed . . . [and] apprehensive'. It was as though the escape
from the locked ward had been no escape at all, either for the
mother or for the son.

10

Olivia and Freddie (2)

Before Olivia took Freddie back to Botton she tried to remember and write down all the things she wanted Leonie van der Stok to know about him. The jottings cover ten pages of a small, cheap notebook and they begin with his fears.

Dogs. Has always been terrified of them screams & runs away. No better since operation. Fish to eat because he once swallowed a huge bone & it got stuck & he was very afraid – now makes a fuss if fish comes in at a meal until he is sure people know he can't eat it & say he can have something else.

She surveys his quirks and his problems. He may be difficult about eating after years of hospital food, all 'starch & no veg or salads' and so unlike what he was used to at Botton. He can shave himself with an electric razor – 'can he use one with you?' – and will cut his finger nails, but must be persuaded to attend to his toes: 'he is afraid of having them cut because has a deformed one because one [nail] got pulled off.' He has sore places on his feet 'because shoes hurt & he doesn't tell anyone

– same as toothache if he gets cross its worth asking him. Has had several teeth out in locked ward.'

He has to be reminded to put on clean clothes, and has been gaining so much weight after the operation that he has problems getting on his trousers, though he thinks his new stomach 'funny & beats it like a drum'. He 'loves music & singing but doesn't sing when others do . . . but does tunes in a strange clicking noise with his tongue'. He can be noisy, likes to 'clap his hands & looks v. cheeky – I think it's to get attention for himself. I think the best thing then is to send him off on an errand.' She explains how she arranged an account with the hospital canteen so he could buy cups of tea and snacks, and that he learned to collect cigarettes for the nurses and take them back to the ward. Sending him on errands is also a good way to give him the exercise he needs, and at the same time accustoms him to being out of doors again because the years spent in over-heated hospital wards have made him sensitive to cold. He might miss television, which was on all the time in the hospital and was 'so bad for him I think'.

His drugs (she had brought the list of prescriptions from Bexley) should be cut down, but only very slowly. The only time the hospital tried this it did it too quickly and he got 'very rowdy'. She explains his fascination with women's bare arms, though recently it 'hasn't caused much trouble'. He 'hates people to get angry & shout at him', and when that happens he too 'gets angry & in a panic'.

I love him so much & shall miss not being able to see him so often as Botton's so much further away. But if he can settle & be happy & good I <u>know</u> it is so much better for him . . . [I'm] 70 now & not v. well so can't go on for ever. I do hope

he won't miss me too much but don't think if he is busy &
happy he has much idea of time.

I do not know if she managed to say all this to Leonie, but
she would have been given a patient hearing. Freddie's new
house mother was in her fifties when he returned to Botton for
the second time, and even by Camphill's standards she was a
striking combination of self-confidence and calm. Not much
taller than Olivia though a little more thick set, she was the
daughter of a German mother and an Englishman who had
taken German citizenship on finishing his studies there at the
end of the First World War, and there was a north German
matter-of-factness both in Leonie's manner and in her
appearance. Her father became general manager of the Opel
car company and after selling it to America's General Motors
under the noses of the Nazis he was stripped of his German
nationality and forced to leave the country.

A schoolgirl at the time, Leonie had her own battle with
Nazism. When boys in her class began to join the Hitler Youth
she noticed that 'suddenly their eyes changed, they went quite
cold. And then you knew they were gone.' One day the class
made wooden spoons in carpentry and someone scribbled
swastikas all over her's. She banged the desk with it,
demanded that whoever had drawn the 'ugly marks' rub them
off, and walked out of the classroom. The teacher had to lock
the door after her so she could get away, and Leonie was sent
to England soon afterwards. She first met König when he was
on a visit to Britain in 1938 and at once fell under his spell: 'I
felt whatever he's going to do it is going to be wonderful.' She
joined Camphill soon after its opening and later married a
Dutch co-worker. She had known but not looked after

Freddie when he was at school in Scotland, and by the time he passed into her care in 1975 she was well known for her readiness to take on difficult cases, which no one doubted was the category Freddie belonged in.

Experienced in dealing with parents, Leonie seems quickly to have understood Olivia's strengths and weaknesses as a mother. She sensed a 'very deep connection' between the mother and the son and admired her for having done 'impossible things' to help him survive the terrible years in the locked ward. At the same time she recognised in Olivia the tendency common to parents of the handicapped to treat them as children regardless of their age. For Leonie it was 'degrading' to call a twenty-nine-year-old like Freddie a child because even if handicapped adults 'do things like a child, they do them out of a grown-up need, and not because they are children. And in fact they stop doing childish things the moment they are taken fully at their worth.' Mental age for her was an abstraction, not a description of a real person: an adult was an adult whatever he could or could not do and did or did not understand. 'A person's mental age is what he is. He is a human being, and to be treated like a little child is terrible.'

Leonie was following the logic of the Camphill philosophy of education that had moved Freddie up each year with the rest of his class even though he can have taken in little of the history, science and art that the teachers talked to him about. Leonie saw that because Olivia could not help treating Freddie like a child, he 'played up' to her as though he were a child: it was, she said, what any handicapped person in that situation would do. Gerda had noticed, regretfully, what she called Freddie's reluctance to grow up; Leonie would not excuse him for failing to behave, within his limits, like the grown-up man he was. She would make allowances, of course, for his quirks but she would be demanding too.

The years in Bexley had accustomed Olivia to seeing Freddie heavily tranquillised, but Leonie was shocked by how deeply drugged he was. She found him 'very watery, very slowed up', and sometimes so sleepy that he dozed off in the middle of meals. She began the slow process of cutting back on the doses, and the first time she saw him paying full attention to anything was when she was talking to her house about going swimming and he began to make swimming gestures. Reducing the drugs was tricky enough in itself but the local GP by mistake sent a supply of Largactil, the tranquilliser Freddie was allergic to, and he began to have regular and 'terrible' fits. Leonie remembered him 'just falling like a tree. You couldn't lift him or anything. You just had to wait until it was over and then take him to his room if he could walk.' The doctor, it turned out, had either misunderstood or failed to read Bexley's letter which warned against prescribing Largactil. No one had thought it necessary to warn Leonie about the allergy since everything was spelt out in the hospital notes.

Freddie had to learn all over again how to live in a Botton family house. He reacquired his old table manners that had been displaced by the crude eating habits of the locked ward, though Leonie had to be careful not to seat him next to someone who excited him. He began to help with the chores of daily living that are the ground-note of most people's lives, and whose absence in a hospital defines the irresponsibility of an existence there. Under Leonie's guidance Freddie began to weave again. He mastered the complicated business of setting up a loom, and soon was working on his own for up to two

hours at a stretch. Dalehead was next door to the weavery and
when Leonie went to watch him through the window he
would look up and laugh at her and then go back to his
weaving. He made nice things. Leonie sent Olivia a length of
his tweed which she took delight in having made up into a
long evening skirt.

He became a familiar figure round the village, and a
frequent visitor in the guesthouse kitchen where Joyce Hogg
was always pleased to see him, and allowed him to make tea
for them both. He went to church services, and seemed to
enjoy them, and one hot summer day, noticing sweat on the
forehead of Peter Roth who was officiating, took out his
handkerchief and wiped it away. Leonie was sure Freddie
'suffered with other people' and that he had been moved by
Roth's discomfort. His capacity for compassion was put to the
test by the arrival of a blind girl for a trial stay at Dalehead.
Olivia met the girl on one of her visits and was in two minds
about the experiment.

> She has turned Dalehead in fact everywhere she goes into
> chaos. She has been blind since birth & is very beautiful &
> very clever, can play the piano & guitar quite beautifully &
> shouts & sings all day, sad to say mostly prefers pop music!
> If asked to be quiet she refuses & produces a volley of
> swearwords a navvy would be proud of . . . All the other
> co-workers thought she should not stay because she upsets
> the others so much but Leonie decided to keep her on &
> thinks she will win [the] battle with her.

Olivia would have preferred Freddie's life not to be
complicated by this wild girl, even though he did not seem to
mind her and let her sit in his rocking chair, a prize possession

given him by Olivia (she gave him three in all, which he broke one after the other by his rocking). When the girl got too noisy Freddie 'goes up to his little room & rather grandly lies on the bed & looks at books'. But Olivia was beginning to appreciate what a 'very strong character' Leonie was, and to understand that the disapproval of others would not deter her from doing what she thought right. Olivia appreciated that if Leonie had been different she might not have taken on Freddie either, and it was not long before she felt no one had understood him so well as his latest house mother.

Leonie managed Freddie with a mixture of resolution and affection, guiding him by the tone of her voice, at turns encouraging, firm or reproachful, but never by raising it. Sometimes she would let him come to her room and they listened to classical music together. It was difficult to do anything with him when he was agitated, but when he was calm Leonie had 'really deep conversations' with him, though they could only last for a very short time. She was sure she could 'see him reacting', and that 'he felt quite different when he walked out of my room after that'. He kept his fascination for women's arms, indeed for touching anyone he liked. One summer when there were always visitors to the village Leonie spotted him outside Botton Hall when a party of women arrived in a bus. Freddie stroked the arm of each as they went inside the house until Leonie called his name and he looked at her and went away. No one complained, perhaps because it was hard to be in Botton without being affected by the village's atmosphere of tolerance and understanding.

Olivia continued to make her twice yearly journeys to see him. After the day's outing she took him back to Dalehead for the last meal, the six o'clock tea, and she enjoyed sitting at the

big round table with Leonie and her family of villagers, and
sharing a little in the homeliness of Freddie's Yorkshire life.
But the main pleasure of these trips was elsewhere. She usually
stayed in a hotel that had been built by a rich nineteenth-
century businessman as his ancestral house, and its would-be
grand rooms became for a few days a home she could share
with her son. She often took him back for lunch in the hotel
dining room, where the staff knew Freddie and did not mind
his occasional eccentricity, though nothing he did matched his
boyhood trick of putting Brussels sprouts in the pocket of the
Aberdeen businessman. I went north with her a couple of
times, and it seemed that what she enjoyed most was the hour
after lunch when she took him to her room, supposedly so
they both could rest, but I doubt that much resting was done.
She would talk to him and play with him and by treating him
as a child – misguidedly, perhaps, but that was her way – she
could make the intervening years disappear and Freddie again
became the small boy she and Sam's friends had hoped would
replace her dead husband. They were sweet moments but I
wonder whether they were not as wearing for her as the time
she worried on her son's behalf, for Freddie in good form
made what might have been seem so close.

To 'see his smiling face makes all the strain & horror of the
past worthwhile', she wrote to me after one visit, but even
when everything went well worry never abandoned her. In
summer when she took him for picnics on the moors, or to
walk near Robin Hood's Bay she had always to be on the
lookout for dogs. The moment she spotted one they would
make an elaborate detour in the hope that Freddie would not
catch sight of it too. She kept a postcard of the church in
Danby village, writing on the back of it that this was 'where

we took Freddie & he was so good one Sunday morning'. She encouraged herself by recording such occasions, for his behaviour still sometimes scared her. 'He was sweet to me,' she reported after another visit to Botton,

> sort of looking after me & sheltering his old mum but what was a bit difficult was that he did not much like it if someone, usually someone who he didn't know well, came up & talked to me & [he] got a bit rough at times which as you can imagine made my hair stand on end.

She put it down to his old problem of being jealous and possessive and added Leonie had told her not to worry. The truth was that as time went by Leonie did not talk to Olivia about everything that Freddie did. When she scribbled down her notes on what to tell his new house mother Olivia had written 'may ring him up once a week & send him a little parcel now & then which you can say comes from Mummy'. She probably rang up more often than that. Leonie thought Olivia treated Freddie 'as if he were a raw egg'.

> [She] was in a state of nerves all the time. She didn't trust anybody where Freddie was concerned, even when she brought him back to Botton. She would ring me up and say 'Oh I'm so pleased he's with you', and the next day she'd telephone Joyce Hogg to ask if she had seen Freddie and was everything really all right.

Leonie found it hard to reconcile the constantly tense woman who made these enquiries with the generous and easy-going person she sometimes stayed with in the flat in Cadogan Square. Olivia could slip in a moment out of one character and into the other, and she was equally true to herself as either. But the older she got, and the longer the history of her adventures with Freddie, the more wary she became. 'It will take a long time,' she wrote to me when Freddie had been several months with Leonie, 'to feel quite secure about him. With a handicapped person one loves one's fear for them never *quite* goes.' She was quite aware she was torturing herself almost beyond the limit. '*How* I wish I could stop worrying about him,' she wrote after he had returned to Yorkshire, 'about his fits & bleeding gums, I don't want him to lose his teeth, & the headaches they say he gets. Its just that I can't bear *him* to suffer though I know most people do, its worse for him don't you think?'

Friends did their best to bolster her morale and tell her all would be well. My father, always at the price of complicating his own life with her, tried to persuade her to take a more cheerful view of the future. Over the years I too wrote letters arguing that the calmer she stayed, the better she would be able to help Freddie. Though I was partly thinking of my father when I wrote that, it was also what I really believed. I failed to see that her love for Freddie could only express itself in this tenacious anxiety on his behalf; that this anxiety had helped save him while it damaged her; and that it was also a more accurate indication of what lay in store for both of them than all our words of reassurance.

One day Freddie stopped weaving. Leonie remembers that he 'cut into the threads of his loom and that was the end of it. You couldn't show him the loom again.' It did not surprise her – 'things always come to a sudden end with the psychotic' – and she simply tried to interest him in other sorts of work. He did half days at the Camphill printing press, where he stapled printed sheets or put envelopes into packs. He was not an easy worker – he broke several of the press's chairs by his rocking – but he was easily the fastest. The co-worker in charge of the press thought he worked so quickly because he was lazy. 'He did everything at high speed so he could enjoy doing nothing when he had finished.' It was the same whatever he did, chopping logs for firewood, breaking stones for a new car park, or working in the candleshop where he improved some of the techniques. He might not want to work for long but when he did, Leonie observed, he was a perfectionist as well as being quick.

Freddie's erratic approach to work complicated his life in Botton, but given Leonie's determination to succeed with him it did not threaten his chances of staying there. Far more serious was the return of his outbursts of potentially violent anger. Olivia witnessed one during a visit. She was walking with him in the village when a girl who had the habit of pointing with a stabbing movement towards people's eyes came up to them and made her usual gesture at Olivia. Freddie almost went for her. It was typical, Leonie thought, because his aggression often came when he felt anxious on someone else's behalf. She remained convinced that he never liked the idea of hurting someone and that if hurt was done 'he felt dreadfully sorry'. Even Leonie found him hard to control when he was agitated, though usually all she had to do was call out (but not shout) his name and he would stop. But a person had to have a proper relationship with Freddie to achieve that measure of control, and there were occasions when he was dangerous for the people around him and could have done damage.

Leonie did not tell Olivia about all these incidents. 'One could not tell her the truth. She got so upset.' But Olivia felt something was wrong. 'For a long time now,' she confessed in a letter written at this time, 'I've suffered from an almost permanent feeling . . . of fear . . . about nothing special & I'd love to be able to cure it.' Her anxiety increased when she learned that Leonie was involved in a project to open a new community in Devon that was to be associated with Camphill. Leonie was keen on the idea, and she softened the blow to Olivia and my father by promising to take Freddie and her other difficult charges like the blind girl with her. It is unlikely Botton would have kept him without Leonie. No one else was keen to be his house parent; indeed Leonie's partner in the Devon venture was not enthusiastic about having him, and gave the impression he only agreed because Leonie insisted. Olivia got a shock when she went to Botton just after Leonie had left to prepare the new house in Devon. Freddie's temporary house parents seemed ill at ease with him and Freddie himself was 'tense and keyed up'. The visit brought home to her just how much his stability depended on his relationship with Leonie, and how even in the special world of Botton Freddie could not count on infinite sympathy.

She worried, too, about getting old. 'The most frightening thing I think of nowadays for old people is the feeling that they might, if God doesn't remove them soon enough, become the most fantastic bores.' In 1980, when Freddie was still waiting to join Leonie in Devon, she had a major stomach operation to remove an ulcer, and though it was a success she never regained her old form. Led astray by her old fascination with doctors and the surgeon's knife she had a second operation, also involving a general anaesthetic, to remove a swelling on her cheekbone, although she had had it for years; it was not painful; and in no way spoiled her looks. She persuaded a doctor to prescribe a powerful painkiller called DF 118 for her arthritis, insisting it was the only thing that helped, but, like the operations, the drug contributed to the confusion in her mind. She promised herself she would go to Devon as soon as she felt better, but she went out less and less even in London and gave up driving her car altogether. Her days became a caricature of her old good-humoured Chelsea life. She would walk across the square to Mr Green, the local chemist, to discuss her prescriptions or down Sloane Street to Partridge's food store where she became angry if she did not get instant attention. She went to the Harley Street specialist who gave her painful (and expensive) injections in the knees that were supposed to ease the arthritis. She terrorised the local dentists by demanding each in turn to repair the irreparable damage done her mouth by the slick surgeon who had persuaded her to have her teeth extracted.

It was the collapse of a personality, in the course of which some partly hidden traits were left in relief while familiar and loved ones disappeared. The obsessiveness she had harnessed in Freddie's cause was hijacked by pain and wretchedness, and there were days she could talk of little except how she hurt and ached. At the same time the testiness that had been so pronounced in her old father re-emerged in her. And although her limbs ached and her mind was fuzzy she kept something of her old energy. Like a clockwork toy that was running down she moved uncertainly around the flat in Cadogan Square repeating the same question, losing, finding and losing again the same object or piece of paper on which she had scribbled a name or telephone number (sometimes her own) that she feared she might otherwise forget. There was a time when she went almost every week to Mary Austen's clinic, often just to sit in the waiting room and have a cup of tea and talk to the nurse about Freddie or Sam ('We heard about Sam until we were sick of him'). Later, as she became more confused, she telephoned Austen's clinic almost every day, and sometimes several times a day, to ask the nurse which of her pills she should take and when. Almost two years after the stomach operation she wrote a pitiful letter to the surgeon wondering why she was not feeling better. She dreaded the nights, she told him, even when she took sleeping pills.

> Wake up in <u>so</u> much pain in legs & feet & bones on hips. The nights are full of fear too & apprehension . . . that I will never get better & wonder if I can stand it. Have cup of early morning tea and 2 DF 118 which seems to clear it & nothing else I've tried helps at all.

She told him she worried about Freddie because she could not go to see him any more; that my father was being 'wonderful' to her and added a P.S.

> Can't concentrate or read for long or remember things & people's names . . . It's hard to tell [doctors] how I feel. Its all such a muddle . . . & I don't like to show how very depressed I am. Must be more brave.

She had long kept two or three doctors going at the same time, balancing a well-known homeopathic specialist with more conventional Knightsbridge GPs, and when one of the latter refused to prescribe more DF 118 for her she found another who would. She had joked about her mother's warning that she would one day pay for her misspent youth, and accepted it as part of the bargain she had made with life, but she never reckoned the price would be as steep as this. Although my father was not left alone to look after her the greatest burden fell on him, and terse notes in his pocket diary record the declining quality of their days and nights together. He came to dread her temper. In order to recuperate himself he needed every now and then to put her for a week in a nursing home, but she could be so beastly to the staff that she risked being thrown out. A typical message from her while in one of these homes would report that the garden was nice but the food 'discussting', and as to the nurses 'there are masses of different ones who so far I don't like much'.

My father knew the balance of power between them was changing and that she now depended on him as she never had before. In the past he had had to compete with Freddie and the memory of Sam Bucknill for his share of her, but only a sad parody of the person he loved was now returning to him. He was a man who liked the sunshine. When he added an exclamation mark in his Truslove and Hanson diary to an account of the day's fine weather it reflected a desire to enjoy life, as well as a slightly guilty determination to avert his eyes from its less pleasant sights. Olivia had often quarrelled with him over this – 'he is such an escapist!' – but it helped both of them now. He got out of the flat whenever he could, to play golf at the club where he was secretary, to have lunch at White's, to watch cricket at Lord's. The pleasure he got from these outings gave him the determination to go on looking after her, and to avoid turning bitter towards her. When he managed to go away for a night the notes he left to guide her were as expressively inexpressive as any of the tongue-tied letters of courtship he had written before their marriage.

As your memory is going a bit
don't forget
1) to take your pills
2) go to the loo before it is too late
3) go to bed early
4) sleep well
5) I see you tomorrow <u>and</u> I love you.

In the summer of 1984 I came back for a holiday from
Moscow and as usual rang up Cadogan Square that evening.
My father answered. He was in bed, stricken by a mysterious
illness which he called 'the screws'. It was extremely painful,
and had almost paralysed his arms and shoulders. Nurses had
been called in to look after Olivia. Horrified to find DF 118s
stuffed like sweets in her pockets and handbags they tried to
take them away, only to be beaten off by Olivia's stick. Not
surprisingly nurses did not care to stay for long; my father's
complaint was obviously in part the result of stress; and that
August Olivia was taken to a small private nursing home in
Ealing. The following year she went to a much larger home in
Sussex run by Roman Catholic nuns who were able to provide
the considerable care she now needed.

She began living through something like Freddie's experiences at the worst moments of his life. Like him she had to
struggle to make sense of what was happening to her. If she
had felt lonely since Sam's death she now experienced a
loneliness that was more intense and from which her weakness
of mind and body allowed no escape. She scrawled some
entries in her diary while she was at Ealing, and they were
bleak.

18th November. Again alone all day & no one came, rather sad.

19th November. Still here, & some people nice, but most old & dotty.

25th November (Sunday). Walked to church. Couldn't hear. Cold day. Everyone bad-tempered.

28th November. Never hear from anyone. Sad.

If a place where dazed old women wait to die can be pleasant, the Sussex nursing home was pleasant. There was a fine garden and Olivia's room was pretty, with a view over a lawn-covered court, but she did not make friends with the other residents. She took a brief liking to a ninety-year-old midwife who seemed lucid and humorous until she began repeating word for word what she had said five minutes earlier. Olivia wrote her off as 'absolutely gaga'. I once saw the two of them pass in the corridor. They stopped and peered at each other, like ships in fog that strain to make out another's lights, and then they went their way, as though they had seen nothing. The nuns were nurse-like in white headdresses and white uniforms and, the young novices apart, she did not take easily to them. For all the trouble she caused them the older ones admired the embers of her spirit. Clement Mary, the sister in charge, almost seemed to approve when this daughter of an Anglican parson saw nothing wrong in taking communion from a Roman Catholic priest: 'she had no time for rules and regulations and she was right.'

Olivia kept a photograph of Sam on her dressing table, and in a drawer pictures of Freddie, and she told Clement Mary the story of her life. 'I can't tell you,' she once said to her, 'how awful I think it must be in Freddie's mind.' But to my father, myself and the family she never spoke of Freddie again, and she did not send even a note of thanks when Leonie sent her photographs of him. When we were with her it was as though all memories and worries about him had been displaced by her last obsession: to be taken back to the flat in Cadogan Square. Just as she fought to get Freddie out of the locked ward she now battled for her own release. When we were with her she sounded like the wilful little girl she once had been, for she turned the nuns into 'teachers' and the nursing home into 'school'. She said she hated the teachers and she made up terrible stories about them, that they pinched her and sometimes force fed her (she did not tell us she had used her stick against them when she was angry, and that as a result they had taken it away from her). She sent letters to my father imploring him to come and fetch her. 'I really *hate* it here and so do most of the other people though the teachers make themselves seem *very* nice to strangers . . . I do wish we were allowed to telephone. I'm not, but the teachers can.' Naturally he dreaded going to see her, and the family protected him, explaining he was still too ill to make the drive down. When he did go he had tea with her in a room of reproduction French furniture that was reserved for visitors and she ate chocolate cake for which she had developed a passion. She held his hand, told him that she loved him, and asked again and again when she could come home.

I would go and see her when I was on leave from Russia. Unable to tell her the one thing she wanted to hear I was careful to take smoked salmon, another of her passions, and she would hurry off to give it to one of the nuns so she could be sure of having it for supper that evening. If it was a fine day we sat in the garden which she might gruffly admit she liked, but no other concessions to this school she was determined to leave were made. Sitting in the visitors' room for tea she sometimes touched the hairs on my forearm but for the most part she was far away. At first I expected her to say something about Freddie, whose guardian she had long before asked me to be. When I realised she would never speak to me about him again I hoped it was because everything was decided in her mind, and that she considered that part, at least, of the responsibility had already passed to me.

There are photographs of her in Sussex. A frail old woman stares emptily at the camera. Some of her beauty remains but at last she carries the scars of life she had managed to avoid showing for so long, just as Freddie's face in pictures taken at this time is beginning to show something of what he had suffered. The story of the glamorous woman who adopted a beautiful child was at an end. In the early spring of 1987 she became very weak. The family went to see her every day and when we said goodbye one afternoon she lay back against her pillows and put both hands to her mouth to mime a kiss. It was the gesture of a woman whom many people had loved, but who had been chastened by her own great loves almost beyond the point of bearing. She died early the next morning.

11

Freddie and Mark

On Olivia's death I was given the letter she had written to me at the beginning of 1980, before her first operation and the start of her decline. It reminded me I was to be Freddie's joint guardian with my father and explained a little about the small trust fund she had set up for him and how she sent him pocket money every month. She mentioned Thomas Weihs and Peter Roth, his other guardians, and Joyce Hogg at the Botton guesthouse who was 'so wonderful' to Freddie. She reminded me, too, about Mary Austen who treated him with her 'box' and asked me to consult her – 'she's very nice & I think helps him.' The letter was not the least mawkish, and it ended with a characteristic mixture of affection, humour and exclamation marks.

> Take care of Fred for me & your dear self. I could not love you more than if you were my own dear son & I do feel sure (even though you may not agree!) that I will see you again in the next world!

It was a touching letter, but as inadequate as a plan for the future can possibly be. By the time she died Thomas Weihs and Joyce Hogg were also dead, and an ageing Peter Roth was soon to retire from Botton. As for Freddie, unknown to Olivia he had set out on a new chapter of adventures. He had moved to Leonie van der Stok in Devon in October 1981, but not before a disconcerting correspondence had taken place between the management of the Camphill Devon Community and Olivia's solicitors on the matter of Freddie's trust. There was a real, if small, problem – the amount of Freddie's state support depended on how much income he had of his own – but someone seemed to be making heavy weather of it. In April the following year, when Freddie had been with Leonie for just six months, the Devon management sent Olivia's solicitors a demand for £145.34, adding, 'You will appreciate that we cannot continue to retain Freddie here if our account is not paid.'

As a threat it was not to be taken seriously. The amount of money was tiny and there was never any doubt it would be paid. What upset my father was the letter's tone, so unlike anything in his previous dealings with Camphill. One reason seemed to be that the Devon project, though belonging to the broad Camphill Movement, was unlike Botton not part of the Camphill Village Trust. My father told Olivia nothing about this, and he calmed down when he went to visit Freddie and thought he was flourishing under Leonie's care. Four years later, in February 1986, he got a letter from the assistant administrator of Langdon Hospital in Dawlish.

re: Frederick Bucknill

I am writing to inform you that due to outbursts of aggression towards female staff it has been necessary for Frederick to be placed under Section 2 of the Mental Health Act 1983.

I enclose a copy of leaflet No. 6, which explains his rights under the Act; a copy has also been given to Frederick.

The leaflet explained that Section 2 provided for compulsory hospitalisation lasting up to four weeks 'so that doctors can find out what is wrong and how they can help you'. It gave the address of a tribunal Freddie could appeal to and ended, 'If there is anything . . . you do not understand, the doctor or a nurse or social worker will help you.'

I have sometimes wondered whether Freddie was really handed this piece of paper and, if so, what he did with it (in the old days he might at least have eaten it). My father was at scarcely less of a loss. On his recent visits to Devon Leonie had told him Freddie was troubled by headaches; that he had been in hospital for observation and reassessment of his drugs; and that there had been outbursts of anger. He either had not understood the seriousness of what she told him, or had not wanted to understand, preferring to ignore these signals that something might again be going wrong. The trigger of the crisis was Leonie's retirement at the end of 1985. In a moment of irritation, and perhaps blaming the woman co-worker who had replaced Leonie for her absence, Freddie thrust his hands at her neck. The woman wrote to my father to say how sorry she was. She said no one had put her 'in the picture of Freddie's past' and that she was 'quite unprepared for what happened'. Leonie wrote to him, too, in an attempt to help him face up to the problem he had inherited.

Again and again throughout the years that I have lived with Freddie he has had spells of being violent with himself, with things around him and if anyone got in his way, they had a rough time. Whilst being with me he had twice a long period in hospital for reassessment. Many times I was able to control him, he did listen to me but I could not always be there. Although Freddie is very much loved, when he is wild he is feared.

She thought something organically wrong might be causing his 'storms', but his inability to speak made investigation very hard.

Freddie has had many years of Camphill life which he appreciates and loves. But now for his own safety and the safety of others he must be where there are enough staff to care [for him]. Freddie would never like to hurt anyone and he must be prevented from that for his own sake . . . You know that I love Freddie, that he is very dear to me. We must just hope that he can be helped.

My father was in no condition to start a new campaign on Freddie's behalf. He had largely recovered from his painful 'screws' and was again playing golf and dreaming about autumn fishing in Scotland, but he was seventy-six and the last years of looking after Olivia had left their mark on him. Even in better times he was ill-equipped for the badgering of authorities on Freddie's behalf that Olivia had excelled in, and it was plain he needed help. It was not so plain that I could give it. Olivia had talked to me so much about Freddie that I scarcely knew him except through her eyes which were so focused by love. I kept a few memories of the difficult child who lived at Doiley Hill farm. Over a period of thirty years I had gone with her half a dozen times to visit him in Scotland, Yorkshire and Bexley, and even then my purpose was to support her rather than play an active part in guiding Freddie's life. While she was alive and vigorous it was the only role

anyone else was allowed to play. The only quarrel I ever had
with her was when we were on holiday with Freddie in the
cottage in Suffolk and I suggested something she violently
disagreed with. From that moment I listened to her and
encouraged her, but understood she would not accept more
than that.

Ill-prepared and apprehensive, my father and I set off to visit
Freddie in his new hospital and to see what could be done. He
thought it a stroke of genius that I brought a pile of old
Observer colour magazines to amuse Freddie when we took
him for a drive, though I was only doing what I had often seen
Olivia doing. He was also impressed when before reaching the
hospital I stopped the car at a sweetshop to buy Smarties and
packets of crisps though that, too, had been Olivia's habit for
years. Freddie seemed neither surprised nor particularly
pleased to see us, but he came willingly to the car and climbed
in slowly to sit in the back seat with my father. When I
reversed I felt a nip on my arm and turned to see him leaning
towards me, his face screwed up in agitation, well-known
signals that something had taken him by surprise. He calmed
down when we moved forward and set off through a Dawlish
not yet invaded by summer tourists and along the road that
runs beside the Teign estuary.

I gave Freddie some crisps and he ate them quickly, folding
the empty bag into an immaculate, uncreased cellophane
square which he handed back to me. My father showed him
one of the magazines and, seeing a photograph of a pig, made a
grunting noise as Bobbie had done when trying to teach
Freddie to read. Freddie grunted back, more out of politeness,
I thought, than enthusiasm. Neither my father nor I was used
to the silence that being Freddie's companion imposes and,

encouraged by the pig grunts, I asked, as Bobbie also used to, what the cows said. 'Moo,' he answered, though again without great enthusiasm. My father grunted and moo-ed with Freddie for a while and was so delighted by this limited communication that he seemed not the least self-conscious. But there was a limit to how long an elderly Englishman could keep up such behaviour and I knew he was relieved when I suggested we turn back.

As a visit to Freddie it left, by Olivia's standards, much to be desired. We did not take him out to a meal. We did not examine his clothes to make sure they fitted, or question him as she would have done as best she could to see if anything was wrong with him or hurting him. And in spite of the animal noises, the crisps and the sweets we had not engaged him in the sort of loving play that she enjoyed with him. We failed, too, in the task she would have set about at once: getting Freddie out of hospital and home to the Devon Community. We drove there later that day and it was made plain to us they would not have him back. My father was indignant that so little regret was expressed at Freddie's expulsion, and hurt, too, when he discovered in the weeks ahead that no one else in the Camphill Movement was ready to take him on.

The redeeming feature in the new landscape of Freddie's life was Langdon Hospital itself. In her letter Leonie had reminded my father that 'hospitals are not as bad as they were even ten years ago', and Langdon seemed to bear that out. Though the low white buildings set on a grassy rise just outside Dawlish had the bareness of a military barracks, the wards were smaller and friendlier than at Bexley. We returned to London thinking that if there were no alternatives, Langdon was perhaps a tolerable place for Freddie to live.

What we had not reckoned with was that Langdon itself might not be an alternative. Freddie arrived there at the moment when mental hospitals throughout the country were starting to be run down and replaced by care in the community. It was not long before letters were going back and forward between the Torbay Health Authority and Riverside, the London authority within whose borders Olivia and my father lived. Torbay wanted to get rid of Freddie to Riverside but Riverside, while not refusing responsibility, protested it had nowhere suitable to put him. My father's and my contributions were repeated pleas for Freddie to stay in Devon. We argued that its country calm was more suitable for him than London, a point that no one seriously challenged but seemed irrelevant in a battle between bureaucracies anxious to shift expenditure elsewhere. We were also puzzled by what community care would mean for someone like Freddie. Stories were appearing of patients from mental hospitals being abandoned in bed and breakfast hotels and bed-sitters. We told ourselves surely no one could think this was a solution for Freddie, but what else might they offer him? In the face of this uncertainty the green expanse and fresh sea air of Langdon seemed infinitely desirable.

The hospital began to close down around him, and like stragglers from a defeated army Freddie and other hard-to-place patients retreated from ward to ward. My father died quickly and unexpectedly at the beginning of 1989 and his ashes were buried next to Olivia's in the crypt of St Paul's, the church where she had prayed for Sam Bucknill during the war and after it for her son, and where she and my father went regularly to Sunday service. Freddie was already in his fifth ward when I went to see him that April, for the first time on my own. The ward had itself been moved from its original building to a large, single-storey hut at the back of the hospital grounds. A cheerful nurse saw me coming and took me into a large room where all the ward's inmates except Freddie seemed to be standing doing nothing much. She extricated me from the grinning, curious faces and as we went towards the staff room we passed Freddie asleep in an armchair in an alcove. He was being heavily sedated by a daily dose of four hundred milligrams of Largactil, Bexley's old liquid cosh (at that time I had not discovered he was allergic to it, and the note to that effect had been lost from his medical records).

The nurse was apologetic about Freddie's state. Most of the patients were bad companions for him, she explained, for though they were of far lower intelligence they had learned how to bait him and make him lose his temper. The hospital was closing down its old therapy sections so there was little for people to do except hang around the wards and make a noise. It was the noise Freddie hated most – he particularly disliked pop music – and all the nurses could do was let him escape into the dormitory, though even there he might find someone who would annoy him.

Freddie came into the staff room holding his arm out stiffly from his side in greeting and leaning slightly backwards. 'Who's that?' the nurse asked. 'Ma,' he answered curtly, as though his mind was on other things. Even when Olivia arrived to see him there had only been a flash of pleasure before his attention returned to whatever mysteries preoccupied him. He followed me unprotesting to the car and climbed into the back with the exaggerated slowness of an old man. I was nervous about taking him for a drive on my own and kept an eye on him in the rear mirror. He was meticulous as ever in the way he ate the crisps I gave him, rocked a little in his seat, made some clicking and popping noises. We talked a bit in pig grunts, but I did not feel his heart was in it. Mine certainly was not. It was raining hard and there was a good deal of traffic and I looked at my watch and decided we had had enough. It was still raining when we got back to Langdon. I gave him an umbrella for the walk to the ward and he held it over his head but not mine. In the other hand he had three empty packets of crisps. He vanished when we got inside and I last saw him sitting alone at a table eating his lunch. I called out goodbye but he did not look up.

The rush to community care was the result of an unlikely alliance that, miraculously, worked to Freddie's benefit. Conservative politicians keen on cutting expenditure by closing down giant mental hospitals found themselves apparently of one mind with mental health activists who wanted to revolutionise the care of, and attitudes to, the handicapped. Freddie and those like him whom no one could imagine leading even a semi-independent life were to be moved into small residential homes. The problem was that hospitals were shutting down before these homes had been set up. The Riverside Health Authority, strapped for cash as it tried to find places for its own difficult patients, had no reason to accept one of Torbay's, especially when it knew the patient's family preferred him to stay in rural Devon. London procrastinated skilfully. And whatever the Torbay Health Authority managers might have felt, Freddie's consultant psychiatrist appreciated the argument my father and I repeatedly made that the capital was a poor place for someone like Freddie to live.

In May 1989 the psychiatrist wrote to tell me Freddie was moving into a community care home for six people soon to open in Totnes. Even at this stage, though, Freddie remained at the mercy of people's perceptions of him. The house proposed for him was not like an old mental hospital that had to accept whoever was dumped at its door. Its manager needed to be sure Freddie would fit in with the other five residents, and also to feel confident of coping with him. He and his staff had a look at Freddie and 'decided they would be unable to accept [him] due to his potential and occasionally actual aggression and particular interest in females'. In other words, he scared them.

There was no point in being indignant. Freddie's problem had long been that some people did not take to him, and were apprehensive about him even when they had never seen him in threatening mood. I was not frightened of him, but I was still unsure of him, and nervous about what he might do in a public place if a dog suddenly appeared or something else happened to alarm him. When Olivia had looked at Freddie she saw the adored child, and this never changed however worrying his behaviour or bedraggled his appearance. Perhaps that was true, too, of those who had looked after him and taught him when he was a boy. I saw only an ungainly, slightly heavy man whose shirt and trousers often did not meet at the back; whose youthfulness of face was contradicted by its sadness in repose and the lines around his eyes. Anyone seeing him for the first time would spot him as a strong character, and not naturally submissive. A doctor once wrote in Freddie's hospital notes that he was 'quite an attractive personality when you get to know him', but most people did not have the time to get to know him.

Getting to know him was made harder by his lack of speech and his self-absorption, and I certainly made only slow progress. When I started to visit him more often I tried to put into practice what Leonie said about controlling him with her voice and I spoke to him firmly but quietly, but I quickly discovered he was capable of taking control of situations himself. When he had grown more used to me he would stand and look at me, one foot in front of the other, and rock backwards and forwards. Sometimes he put his face quite close to mine, and there would be a hint of defiance in his eyes. Perhaps this was a grown-up variant of the 'provocative' looks he had given Gerda Blok at Botton. They were challenging, but not unfriendly.

In these moods he made it plain what he wanted and would say 'Ker! Ker!' as soon as he saw me. He was like that the day I first took him out for a meal. He was on good form during our drive and when I played a tape of Schubert's *Moments Musicaux* he kept time by clicking his tongue. We drove once more along the Teign estuary and when I told him to look at the boats at anchor he looked up, though only briefly, and there was a slight smile on his face. Later when I suggested a walk along the beach at Dawlish he did not object, and even put his arm in mine and pulled me along at a brisk pace. The railway runs between the sea front and the beach and to get to the sands you go under a bridge. Freddie sensed there would be a good echo here and made several explosive popping sounds with his mouth. I caught sight of a man walking a dog ahead of us on the beach. Horrified, I was about to turn back when I noticed Freddie had also seen it but did not seem upset. The dog passed near to us and Freddie moved a little closer to me, but he did not make a sound. Had the fear of dogs been forgotten or had he conquered it? His life threw up questions like this that could not be answered.

I had already spotted a place to eat. When Olivia took him out she chose either restaurants in smart hotels or workmen's cafes for she had discovered they were the most likely to be tolerant of eccentric behaviour. I picked the Signals Buffet in Dawlish station, a small cafe favoured out of the summer season by anorak-ed schoolchildren and quiet elderly men. I asked him what he wanted to drink and he said, 'Ter, ter.' When the tea came he added two spoonfuls of sugar and, shaping his lips into a careful O, blew on it twice and began to drink although it was still very hot. He held the mug in an unusual way, putting his thumb through the handle and steadying it with three straight, slim fingers along the side. We ate fishcakes and chips and he was halfway through when I remembered his fear of fish. It was another question that had no answer. Perhaps he did not associate the round cakes with the creature whose bone had stuck in his throat and scared him in the canteen at Bexley; perhaps he was learning to live with fish as well as dogs.

There was no trace now of the child who had been so difficult about food. He attacked his plate with the method of a Prussian general executing an attack. First he softened up its contents with precise applications of salt, pepper, vinegar and tomato ketchup. Next he cut the fishcake into three large pieces, eating one after the other before moving on to two lettuce leaves and a slice of tomato until finally, in steady mouthfuls, he destroyed the pile of chips. I ordered ice cream and three yellow scoops came in a blue bowl. When only a yellow film was left at the bottom of the bowl he tilted it and scraped from bottom to top with his spoon. He put the bowl down but seemed dissatisfied. He picked it up again and gave more well-mannered scrapes until the blue china shone as though it had just been washed.

He looked across the table at me only when he had finished. It was his steady gaze, neither truly curious nor truly friendly. He seemed, though, to accept me, and to know me well enough by then not to be apprehensive of me. It was how I might look at an object I knew well without understanding its inner workings, a car engine perhaps, or a video recorder. Outside on the pavement he became agitated for the first time that day, jerking his right arm into the air in a sort of reverse fascist salute and saying 'Er! Er!' I only understood what he wanted when he took me by the arm and walked me quickly across the street where he disappeared into Dawlish's main public convenience.

It was not the behaviour of someone who was a perpetual menace. Langdon knew he would do best in a 'quiet, measured environment' and that was exactly what the shrinking hospital could not give him. His ward allowed him neither the peace nor privacy he needed, yet even in these unsuitable surroundings his worst outburst happened when a nurse shouted at him angrily and Freddie put his arm around her throat. The doctors recognised it was the nurse's fault, and though some of his carers remained nervous of him, others felt he would be easy enough to manage if care was taken to anticipate his moods.

The debates on what to do with him continued. When the chance came up to put him in a house run by the Torbay and District Care Trust in Dawlish there were objections that he should not live in a town where in summer so many women holiday-makers would have temptingly naked arms. The objections was overruled, perhaps because by then Freddie was the last patient from Torbay Health Authority left in the shrinking hospital. In early 1991 he moved to a pleasant,

roomy house in a quiet residential street in Dawlish. The
house had a large garden. He could see the sea from his
bedroom window. The seven residents, described as having
'above-average care needs', ate together with the staff on duty
in a warm kitchen. There was a small sun room where Freddie
soon found a favourite chair. He had gone through a period of
acclimatisation to his new home during which he visited there
for lunch and tea and other occasions before moving in, and it
was a sentence in a letter from the new house's manager telling
me about this that made me aware that something unexpected
was happening. 'It must be said that at any stage should Fred
show dislike of the house and those people living within it,
then his choice would be respected.'

Choice was not a word I used, either for myself or Freddie,
when thinking about his future, yet here was someone telling
me that if he did not like the new home that had with such
difficulty been found for him he would not have to live there. I
soon discovered that Dave Coyle, the house's young
manager, did not treat Freddie or anyone else who lived there
as a patient. For him they were people with lives, albeit
unusual ones, to live, and with the right to as many choices as
they were capable of making. Dave belonged to a new
generation who believed the handicapped were often de-
valued, rather than treated as people in their own right, by the
institutions and professionals that were supposed to care for
them. Having started his own career as a nurse in a large
mental hospital Dave had a strong dislike of the traditional
relationship between handicapped and carers in which the
latter had all the power. It was typical, he thought, that nurses
and doctors making notes about people like Freddie would
write 'so-and-so has been no trouble', but seldom 'so-and-so

has been in good form'. This was the carer as sentry, not as advocate of the cared-for's interests.

I sensed in this approach a trace of the idea that there are no mad people, only people society finds it convenient to call mad; a stronger trace of 1960s Western Marxism with its assertion that all institutions are oppressive; and a large measure of the undying radical dream of taking power from the powerful and giving it to the powerless. 'Empowerment' – giving power to the previously helpless inmates of mental hospitals – was the ultimate aim. There was therefore logic in insisting people like Freddie be described as having 'learning disabilities' rather than as being 'handicapped'. The former implied power might be acquired, the latter could easily be understood as something final. The official 'aims, objectives and standards' of Freddie's new house declared that 'all people have the inherent right to be seen as developing human beings with unquestionable potential for growth and increasing independence'.

So much for the theory. In practice, and against all expectation, Freddie was once again living a life in which he could behave in many respects like an ordinary person. As at Botton there were chores he could do and liked doing: putting the milk bottles out, drawing the curtains, bringing in the shopping. And although his new home had a washing machine (which he learned how to use) there was still drying up to be done. If he woke up at night, as he often did, he could go to the kitchen, make himself a cup of tea, go to the lavatory, and then back to bed. It might not sound much to people who lead an ordinary existence but some of the men and women Freddie was now living with had spent their lives in institutions and hospitals where they had never been able to do these everyday things for themselves. When they were in the kitchen together at mealtimes Dave would go round with the tea bags and instant coffee asking which they wanted, a choice till then as unlikely to be offered them, Dave liked to say, as he being asked to pick between a Ferrari and a Fabergé egg. Freddie found himself sharing a room with a man who would not even pour himself a cup of tea until, after watching Freddie many times, he tried it for himself.

Dave took choice seriously. That year it was decided Freddie would have a week's holiday and he showed him a number of travel brochures. Freddie seemed to like the ones of York – at least he took them and put them under his pillow – so to York they went. They explored the Minster where Freddie sat 'in awe' for fifteen minutes. They would have got to the ruins of Rievaulx Abbey if Freddie had not refused to climb over a stile. And they visited the National Railway Museum where he went ahead of the others to climb into the engine cabs.

What this so-called care in the community could not do was make Freddie and his companions part of the community around them. Apart from living in what looked like an ordinary house in an ordinary street he did not have much more contact with the world around him than when he was living in a hospital. He did go to special riding classes and to church. He might be taken the short walk into the centre of Dawlish to go to a cafe or do some shopping. But this was not living in a community as he had known it at Botton, nor could it ever be until most of the people living around him shared at least some of the attitudes towards the handicapped on which a place like Botton based its life.

Some societies may have got closer to this ideal than we.

Old Russia had revered at least some of its mentally afflicted, those men and women (mostly men) who were called Holy Fools and who dressed in rags in spite of the northern cold and were capable of long fasts unless offered food they liked, just two of their characteristics that suggest that they may, like Freddie, have been autistic. The Russian people even took it in their stride when one such man succeeded to the throne after Ivan the Terrible. 'Russians believe Holy Fools are under God's protection,' a historian explained, 'and the presence of such a "fool" on the throne of Russia brought comfort and consolation to the nation deeply stricken by the terror of Ivan's reign . . . God would thus show his mercy to a nation which obeyed its helpless sovereign.' But who was to blame the citizens of Dawlish, who had never been asked if they wanted Freddie living among them, if they failed to greet his appearance in their midst with the same enthusiasm?

Dave's generation of professional carers envied the ability of Camphill communities to give disabled people a life built round meaningful work. The Dawlish house offered little hope of that, and for much of the day its residents had little to do. Perhaps Freddie, given his intermittent interest in work in the past, did not mind but the lack of work hurt him for it reinforced his crippling detachment from the life around him. Dave's objection to Camphill was that it 'did not live in the real world'. Camphill's answer was a rhetorical question: what is so splendid about a world of growing violence, sexual disorder and social disintegration that Freddie, with difficulties enough of his own, should be made to live in it? From the Camphill point of view the new mental health orthodoxy seemed driven by guilt: first society had shut its troubled members away because it did not want the embarrassment of seeing them on the streets; now it was over-reacting by making them live in the thick of things, though it was by no means certain that that was always better for them.

It was Freddie's fate to fall into the care of people with powerful and often irreconcilable convictions, to pass from the hands of one orthodoxy to another. There were the brilliant but limited, and potentially dangerous, treatments by child analysis and, later, psychosurgery. There was drug therapy, grasped at as a way to humanise the treatment of the mentally ill but itself at risk of becoming a new brutality. Freddie had been enveloped in a way of life deduced from the cosmic theories of a Central European sage. Now he had fallen into the hands of warm-hearted revolutionaries bent on giving him power, though like all revolutionaries they sometimes seemed unaware that the people in whose name their revolution was made might not appreciate it, or be capable of living up to it.

Dave and his colleagues had more in common with Camphill than either of them might like to admit. Both were pioneers who moved ahead of their contemporaries. However different the religious belief or social theory they referred back to, when they looked at Freddie they saw a person, not a set of chemical reactions to be controlled, or a faulty mechanism for surgical correction, or a tangle of infantile passions demanding to be straightened out. All these other remedies might be offered with the best intentions, but they were of little use unless Freddie could live in the human surroundings he had known in Yorkshire and that Dave and those who worked with him hoped to provide in Dawlish.

Karl König wrote that 'normal people are all potential epileptics or latent psychopaths; we all conceal autistic or schizophrenic traits that have not yet become apparent.' I have recognised in Freddie a magnified version of my own quirks. As I grow older I become as set in some habits as he is in many more of his. He has his way of doing things and does not like it to be changed. Like me he eats his food too fast for his own good but resists any suggestion that he might do otherwise. Dave has discovered that trying to get him to slow down can be 'like walking on egg shells'. What Dave calls Freddie's 'strong moral sense' makes him fold up empty crisp packets instead of dropping them on the floor of my car. I may not have his obsession with cleanliness but I too am irritated by disorder. As for his self-absorption and inability to share his feelings, they are a gross parody of the isolation we all endure, though we do not make it so plain by our behaviour. Hardest to imagine, let alone share, is the terror caused by the inability of his mind to reduce what he perceives to a tolerable coherence, though perhaps an inkling may be had during depression and fatigue when our thoughts and perceptions resist being corralled into any pattern that makes sense. At such moments a fraction of the fear and the feeling of vulnerability that haunt Freddie may not be far away.

Needing a practical guide for my visits to Freddie I turned to the one I knew best. Flawed though she may have been as his mother and mentor, Olivia held out to me the example not of love – that was her unique gift to him – but of enjoyment. I did not want to go on treating him like a child and I soon stopped buying large bags of sweets whenever I went to see him. But I told myself these visits would become drab duty unless I could take pleasure in them as Olivia had done. Even when she went to see Freddie in the locked ward she went expecting he would make her smile. She shared in his way of doing things and laughed at anyone who gave them disapproving looks. To my surprise Freddie made it easy for me to follow her example. At Camphill they talked of the guardian angel they were sure would intervene to save him at moments when his life became too harsh. I thought the angel's greatest contribution to his survival was his character. Too cocky ever to be taken for granted, there was always a hint he might like to make contact if only the distance separating him from other people was not so great. If he often seemed absent, it was a benevolent absence. When his fingers played with some simple object like an empty tube of Smarties or a piece of plastic there was nothing of the half-wit about him. He was thoughtful, even if his thoughts could not be translated into language.

When we go for walks I talk to him, about Olivia, about his life and the people who have been good to him. The best walk is along a footpath that runs between the estuary of the river Exe and the railway line to London. He gets irritated if the path is wet and is meticulous about rubbing mud off his shoes, but on a bright day he will turn his head to the sky and laugh and he walks quickly even if the wind is so strong that the sailing boats remain at anchor. If I alert him to an approaching train that, too, might make him laugh with pleasure for, a little late in life, he has developed the interest in trains often shown by autistic people. His interest, though, is sporadic. An Intercity express can rush by with a thrilling blast of its siren and he acts as though he hears nothing. I have given him a steam train video, *Trains of the L.N.E.R.*, and his last Christmas present to me was the Dalesman's Railway Calendar. He has pictures of trains, too, in the room he now has to himself but 'his little treasures' that Olivia always worried about were lost long ago and I cannot even remember what they were. He does have a good-looking wardrobe and chest of drawers and a family of small Teddy bears. I have given him a photograph of Olivia and my father. He scarcely looked at it when I handed it to him but apparently he does sometimes pick it up and tap it with his fingers. A Thai box I gave him at the same time was a more obvious success, for he discovered that if he pulls the top off quickly it makes a gratifying pop.

I tested his memory by reintroducing him to Bobbie whom he had last seen with Olivia in Yorkshire over twenty years before. Aged ninety-two, she dressed for the occasion in a green and white check dirndl, a dark green shirt, green stockings and green shoes. Her wig was chestnut flecked with grey and she wore dark glasses. Freddie came down the drive to meet us. He held out an arm in his usual vague greeting but he bent down so Bobbie could kiss him on the cheek and put her arms around his neck. He made no fuss of her after that, and if he did know who she was – he could hardly mistake her for anyone else – it was as though she had never been away. We took him out and when we came back he disappeared to his room as is his habit, so we went upstairs to say goodbye. He was lying on his bed with his shoes on looking at an old magazine. 'Freddie, take your dirty shoes off the bed,' said Bobbie and he did at once in the absent-minded way of a boy who is engrossed in what he is reading.

Unsure of what I could expect of Freddie if I took him on more adventurous trips I spent two days with him during his last year's summer holiday. He was staying in a holiday village in north Cornwall accompanied by two of Dave Coyle's staff, John, Freddie's 'key worker', and Jo, an eighteen-year-old trainee, both prized by Dave because they have never worked in mental hospitals and are therefore uncontaminated by their patronising ways. Young enough to be Fred's children, they treated him with deference – it was his holiday and their job was to guess what he might like doing – and showed affectionate tolerance of his ways. On the first morning we went for a walk along the cliffs, Freddie gripping a yellow plastic comb in one hand and his handkerchief in the other. Sometimes he took John's arm, sometimes mine. He made heavy weather of the stiles we had to climb over and when John asked him if he wanted to go on or turn back he gestured abruptly in the direction of the car. In the afternoon we went for a ride on the Bodmin and Wenford Railway where a little steam engine called Swiftsure pulls some old Great Western coaches for a twenty-minute journey through the Cornish countryside. Freddie inspected the driver's cab, and rocked a little in his seat as Swiftsure pulled off. He seemed to enjoy it, but he showed none of the obvious pleasure of a party of young handicapped men who were also on the train and gave hoots of rapture as we puffed out of Bodmin station. We had tea when we got back to Bodmin. Freddie squeezed the last drop from his tea bag and, noticing there was some milk left in the little carton by my cup, grinned at me and took it for himself.

When the next day we drove to St Ives Freddie went heavily to sleep almost as soon as the car started. He propped his elbow on the arm rest, and would have slumped forward had it not been for the seatbelt. Sometimes when I take him out he slows down by the time we return to the house and one day sat curled up so tightly in the car I thought he would never get out. Perhaps it is surprising he manages to keep his head so often above the tide of drowsiness induced by the drugs he takes. They have been reduced since he left hospital but to control his epilepsy he still has sixteen hundred milligrams a day of carbamazepine and nightly doses of clobazam. While the combination has been effective – he has had only two seizures since he moved into his new home in Dawlish – the side effects can include dizziness as well as a slowing down of thought and movement. He also takes a daily seventy-five milligrams of Neulactil, a powerful tranquilliser that controls aggressive behaviour (his supply of pills for the week's holiday was brought in a plastic container the size of a workman's lunch box).

He livened up when we got to St Ives. He tried to jump the queue to get into the new Tate gallery that has been built there overlooking the sea, and the light from the water reflected on the gallery's white interior walls seemed to excite him. John sat down in the sculpture gallery whose curved glass wall looks onto the shore and Freddie joined him. I had just taken a photograph of them when Freddie leaned towards the middle-aged woman in a smart summer dress sitting next to him and put his hands on her bare right arm. John detached him calmly and explained he meant no harm. The woman made a joke of it. 'How nice of someone to be interested in my old flesh.' It was the first time I had seen him do this and I was terrified. I thought of the angry woman in the T-shirt whose breasts he flicked in Bexley, and the locked ward she had unknowingly condemned him to. John says 'most people understand' when he behaves like this, and perhaps his own and Jo's calmness encourages others to be understanding too, but a grain of anxiety had worked its way into my mind.

Freddie's mood got worse as the day went on. We went into a shop to buy sandwiches to eat on a cliff above the beach and when I tugged his arm to move him out of another shopper's way he turned round and gave me a scowl and three small thumps on the chest. After we had eaten we walked to the harbour and he took my arm and sometimes my hand, making me feel his tiredness at each step. John took him into a shop to buy a pair of shoes for him. Freddie submitted, but if he could have talked he would have been grumbling. I realised I did not know his shoe size or any other of his measurements, and wondered why Olivia had not given me a list of them when she wrote the letter entrusting him to my care.

His feet were leaden as we went back up the hill to the car park and he lent still more heavily on my arm or on John's, and cupped a hand over his nose, a sign of extreme weariness. I sat behind him in the car and as he began to doze his head tilted forward and for a moment I recognised the shape of the young boy's head that I know so well now from looking at the old photographs. If he had turned round then I would have expected to see the child Olivia saw. He went to his room as soon as we got back and when I looked in to see if he was all right he was half asleep on the bed. There was no point in telling him, as Bobbie had done, to take his shoes off the cover, and I knelt down to unlace them. Without thinking I bent forward to smell his socks to see if they needed changing, and knew that this was what Olivia would have done.

EPILOGUE

On my way back to London I stopped at Tintagel, the castle on the fist of slate jutting into the Atlantic that legend says was the birthplace of King Arthur. Friedwart, Freddie's teacher at Camphill, had told me how at the age of thirteen Freddie played the part of a squire in the school's King Arthur Pageant. After watching the knights try in vain to pull the sword Excalibur from the rock Freddie, to everyone's horror, stepped in front of Arthur and put his hands round the hilt, only to leave the sword in place and retire with a smile. How splendid, Friedwart thought, that he acted so perfectly in the spirit of the pageant. When I heard this story I thought it would be satisfying to take Freddie to Tintagel to see if he again reacted to the Arthurian atmosphere, but I quickly discovered what a foolish idea it was.

English Heritage, which looks after the site, is too respectful of archeological evidence not to remind visitors that there is nothing to link the ancient castle with Arthur, if ever such a king existed. More to the point, getting to the castle calls for a tough scramble up steep and slippery steps. Even if the stone-walled enclosure on the grassy headland outside the castle gate was once Camelot's garden, Freddie could never have been induced to make the climb to see it.

It was the last lesson I took back from Cornwall. Our imagination imposes too heavily on people, and there is no limit to how much can be wished onto a silent man like Freddie. Many dreams have been dreamed for him, and some of them have been noble. The wisest of the dreamers, though, have recognised that he is more than an obedient actor in the stories they have devised. In spite of the odds against him he has acquired some power to live his own life and to make his own story. In its course he has brought many fates together into a pattern I find beautiful as well as sad. No one will ever feel for him again as Olivia once did, but since he cannot tell his story to himself, let alone to others, I at least could try to tell it for him.

ACKNOWLEDGEMENTS

My warmest thanks go to those people who helped me gather material for this book: Dr Mary Austin, Dr Cynthia Bainton, Gerda and Peter Blok, Nora and Friedwart Bock, Dr Paul Bridges, David Coyle, Celia and John Durham, Dr Judith Gould, Karen Gretton, Ann Harris, the late Professor Edward Hitchcock, Grace Martin, Christine Nickles, Professor Sir Michael Rutter, Leonie van der Stok, Bill Walter, John Watson, Dr Lorna Wing.

I have been greatly helped by two recent books by Uta Frith, *Autism: Explaining the Enigma* (Basil Blackwell, 1989) and *Autism and the Asperger Syndrome* (Cambridge University Press, 1991). The best account I have come across of what it is like to be autistic written by an autistic person is *Nobody Nowhere* by Donna Williams (Doubleday, 1992).

Anyone who wants advice on autism should contact the National Autistic Society, 276 Willesden Lane, London NW2 5RB (telephone 081 451 1114).

Information about Camphill and publications by Karl König (and Anke Weihs's pamphlet *Fragments from the Story of Camphill*) may be obtained from the Camphill Village Trust, Delrow House, Hillfield Lane, Aldenham, Watford WD2 8DJ (telephone 0923 856006).

I am grateful for permission to quote extracts from:

The Wild Boy of Aveyron by Harlan Lane, Harvard University Press, 1977.

Autism and the Asperger Syndrome edited by Uta Frith, Cambridge University Press, 1991.

Autism by Uta Frith, Basil Blackwell, 1989.

Children in Need of Special Care by Thomas Weihs, Souvenir Press, London, 1971.

A Candle on the Hill: Images of Camphill Life edited by Cornelius Pietzner, Floris Books, Edinburgh 1990.